SANITY CHECK

An Alan Llewellyn Novel

by

Walt Breede

Sanity Check
by Walt Breede

Signalman Publishing
www.signalmanpublishing.com
email: info@signalmanpublishing.com
Kissimmee, Florida

Cover design by Rob Cheney

Author photo by Betty Breede

ISBN: 978-1-935991-92-2 (paperback)
978-1-935991-93-9 (ebook)

Library of Congress Control Number: 2013930135

SIGNALMAN
PUBLISHING

Printed in the United States of America

Dedicated to Barbara and Richard,

two dear family members who left early.

Prologue

Randall's Island, New York City
June, twenty-some years ago
A Saturday

The temperature in the stadium in the morning raced up through the seventies and eighties and was right at ninety—in the shade—at one thirty. God knows what it was down on the track in the blazing sun when the gun went off for the start of the four-by-eight-hundred-meter relay. Mindszenty High's Paul "Fig" Newton led off for the Cardinals and had a comfortable lead when he handed off the baton exactly one minute, fifty-nine seconds after the start. John "Skull" Scully ran a scorching first lap and hung on to run his eight hundred in one minute, fifty-eight, point three seconds, a personal record. The Cardinals' third runner was Jim "Keys" Kehoe, who opened the lead even further with a split time of one fifty-seven, point two, also a personal record. When Alan "Loose" Llewellyn took the baton, the Cardinals' lead over second-place Saint Polycarp was about twenty meters. At the start of the gun lap, Llewellyn could see and hear his teammates screaming from the infield. Halfway through the third turn, he could hear footsteps and he could tell they were a lot closer than twenty meters behind him. He tried to pick up the pace, but the Saint Polycarp anchor passed him midway through the backstretch. Loose cranked up his speed, starting his kick about a hundred meters early and managed to stay within two strides of the leading runner. At the top of the home stretch he stepped outside and tried to accelerate past the leader, but there just wasn't enough gas in the tank. The Saint Polycarp runner opened his lead to about five strides and the Cardinals finished second.

Llewellyn couldn't hide his disappointment but did try to smile bravely when the winning runner shook his hand. As he walked off the track, he saw Father O'Keefe, the Mindzenty coach, and his teammates standing together. They all had huge grins on their faces.

"Sorry guys. You gave me a huge lead and I blew it. I'm sorry," he said, despondently between breaths.

He couldn't understand why they were all grinning. Father O'Keefe held up his stopwatch.

"School record!" he shouted. "All four of you ran under two minutes!"

"But I blew the lead. We should have won!"

"Alan. You just ran a one fifty-eight, point one, eight-hundred meters! All four of you were under two minutes. You broke the school record by almost nine seconds! Seven fifty-two, point six! Congratulations!"

One

Chestertown, Virginia
January 30th – Present Day
Saturday

It was Saturday. No school. And on this particular Saturday, no track meet. On the Weather Channel they were calling for snow for northern Virginia. It was still half dark when I opened the door for the newspapers, and I couldn't see any stars when I looked up. I thought it might be a good idea to get a quality run before the snow started, so I had a piece of toast with strawberry jam and washed it down with black coffee. I tried and succeeded in dressing for a below-freezing run without waking Maria. I didn't wake our daughter Elizabeth on my way out, either. But, as she approaches her entry to the teenage years, she seems to sleep sounder and later whenever she can.

It was all gray and cold in town. I ran toward the railroad tracks, hung a left just before the station, and then took another left and headed upstream, following the gray-black Rappahannock River. I could see a couple of guys in running gear up ahead, leaning against a car and stretching their quads. As I passed them, they started running and caught up with me immediately. Alarmed, I picked up the pace to about a six-fifteen per mile, and they did, too. Having lived in the Middle East for a couple of years, anyone moving into my space was a cause for concern. I jacked the pace up to under six, knowing that I couldn't maintain that for very long.

The one on the right said "Can we *please* slow it down, Mr. Llewellyn? I'm Agent Luke Wallace, U.S. Secret Service. This is Agent Mike Atwater. We'd like to talk with you, but you're *killing* us!"

"I'm killing myself, too," I said and immediately slowed to a jog. "Could I see some ID?"

They both flashed fancy cards hanging from lanyards around their necks. These days, who the hell knows what is bogus and what is real? What I did know was that these guys were opposite twins. Both about six-three with wide shoulders and narrow waists. Plenty of neck muscle. Like NFL defensive backs. With neatly trimmed, close-cropped haircuts. Except that Agent Luke was African-American and Agent Mike was fair and blond.

"Okay, what's going on, guys? Why does the United States Secret Service want to talk to an obscure high school math teacher and track coach?"

"That's what we're here for. To tell you what's going on. President Kehoe needs to talk with you. Let's run just a wee bit faster."

I accelerated into an easy lope, and they came along, apparently without distress at the steadier, saner pace.

Jim Kehoe, my Joszef Cardinal Mindszenty High School classmate from Clancyville, New York, had just finished his first year as President of the United States—POTUS. I, along with all of my fellow Cardinals, were proud and delighted to have one of our own in the White House. I remembered Jim as a solid citizen, a hard worker on the track team, and a guy with a truly charismatic personality. Even though we were on the same thirty-two-hundred-meter relay team, we were never particularly close friends, and we lost touch after graduation. I did remember that we set a school record in the relay that, to the best of my knowledge, was still standing today. Seven minutes, fifty-two-point-six seconds. After graduation, he went to Holy Cross, I entered the Naval Academy, and that was that. I never saw him again and certainly never imagined that he would end up in the White House. Nor did I imagine that he might want to talk to me after he moved into number sixteen hundred Pennsylvania Avenue.

"First of all, when you get home, go to the Blue Pages in your phone book," said Special Agent Luke. "Go to 'United States Secret Service' and call the number in the book. Identify yourself and give them our names. Luke Wallace. Mike Atwater. The person on the phone will tell you that we are in fact Secret Service and are under orders to contact you. Got that?"

"Luke Wallace. Mike Atwater," I said. "Got it."

"Okay. Here's our message. Actually it's President Kehoe's message," Agent Luke began. "And this is classified top secret, code word, 'Shadow.' The president will go for a ten-mile run on the Quantico Marine Base next Saturday morning. You're to meet him at the rifle range entrance on the road that loops around the Marine Basic School and the FBI Academy. At eight seventeen. You'll be wearing this around your neck. And you'll run with the president for a short distance."

He handed me a red lanyard with an ID badge that had my picture on it. I wondered where they got the photo. It looked like they'd taken it in Chestertown. I knew the location where he said to meet the president. It was near the lake where Elizabeth and I fished every once in a while.

"Either I or Agent Atwater will be running out front of the president and will meet you on the side of the road. We'll slow to a jog and let the president catch up. Then you guys can shoot the shit."

"Any idea what he wants to shoot the shit about?" I asked.

"No, sir," he said. "None whatsoever. But he was very emphatic about needing to talk to you. And very emphatic about keeping your chat closely held. The Marines won't let the press on that part of the base Saturday, so your little jog-and-talk will be way out of the public eye."

"Okay," I said. "I guess I'll see you in a week."

We were nearing Einstein Brothers' Bagels on Route One. The toast-and-jam fuel in my system was about burned off.

"Thanks for the message, gentlemen," I said. "I'm stopping here for bagels for my family." I slowed down to a walk and headed into the steamy restaurant. The two Secret Service guys kept running and didn't look back. I took a ten-dollar bill and a one from the pocket of my sweats and bought three bagels—an everything with cream cheese for Maria, a blueberry with cream cheese for Elizabeth, and a pumpernickel with salmon spread for me. Then I jogged home. It started to snow gently just as I turned into our street.

I barely noticed the Asian woman walking past our hundred-year-old Colonial on Prince Henry Street. I say, "barely noticed." But I did notice. Even though she wore a fur-lined, hooded parka, I could tell that she was quite attractive. Somewhere between twenty and thirty. And I knew I'd never seen her before. Here in the neighborhood or anywhere else. But I didn't really give her a second thought. She was walking a fat little Welsh corgi through the softly falling snow.

Two

Chestertown
January 30th
Saturday

I unlocked the front door, let myself in, and heard an upstairs toilet flushing. My Nike runners' watch said eight forty. Early for the Llewellyn women on a Saturday. I bet myself that whoever was up would go back to bed. I lost.

I happen to live with two of the most beautiful women on the planet. Maria came downstairs first. From the look of her, she must have swept a brush through her healthy mop of black hair. She was wearing her Naval Academy b-robe over Black Watch plaid pj's. She spotted the Einstein bagel bag in my hand and flashed her great smile.

"Bagels—Yay!" she said.

I met her at the foot of the stairs and planted a smooch on her perfect lips.

"What's this?" she asked, grabbing my new Secret Service ID, which was hanging by its lanyard from my neck.

"Secret Service ID. Let's have coffee and bagels, and I'll tell you what I know—which isn't a whole helluva lot," I said. "But it *is* interesting."

I put the bagel bag on the table and was pouring us coffee when I heard the sound of not-so-tiny-anymore feet on the stairs. Twelve-year-old Elizabeth has black hair, too, but hers is a bit coarse and wavy like mine would be if I let it grow—which I don't. She has my green eyes as well, but fortunately, the Good Lord blessed her with her mom's fine features. Lately, He'd been endowing her with a number of less-subtle hints of femininity of the sort that fathers stress over. Like boobs and hips and longer legs. Now the whole family was up and about before nine on a Saturday morning, not a normal occurrence in our house.

"I'm going running with the president next week," I said. "He wants to talk to me."

"What-what?" stammered Maria. "The president of what?"

"The good ole USA," I said.

"Dad—are you serious?" asked Elizabeth. "You're not," she added, with a knowing smile.

"Right. You're pulling our legs," Maria said.

I held up my new ID and described my little encounter with Agents Luke and Mike. Wallace and Atwater. I remembered that I needed to make the phone call. I took a bite of my bagel, got up and jotted the two names down on a sticky note by the phone, and took a phone book from a drawer. Maria and Elizabeth were looking at me like I had two heads. I found the Secret Service number in the Blue Pages and dialed it. Truth be told, I had a few misgivings. No doubt, the United States Secret Service had caller ID. If Wallace and Atwater were bogus, I'd probably be put on some sort of Secret Service shit list. I didn't need that. I crossed my fingers as a woman answered.

"United States Secret Service. Chestertown office. Good morning."

"G-good morning," I said. "My name is Alan Llewellyn—"

"I've been expecting your call, Mr. Llewellyn," she said, interrupting. "I take it you met with Luke and Mike."

No last names.

"Um, yes. Yes I did."

"Everything clear?"

"I think so, yes," I said stupidly.

"If there's any change, you'll be notified. In person," the voice said, emphasizing the "in person" part.

"Okay. Sounds good."

"Bye, Mr. Llewellyn. Have a nice day."

"Thanks. You too. Bye."

I hung up the phone.

"I think it's for real," I said.

Three

Chestertown
January 31st
Sunday

Sunday was—Sunday. The day was kind of gray, but not too cold. Yesterday's snow only amounted to a dusting. The Llewellyn family— all three of us—went to nine thirty Mass at Saint Katherine Drexel, as was our custom. After church, I fixed bacon and eggs and toast for all, and we enjoyed each other's company and our cholesterol-laden breakfast. I rationalized the cholesterol by thinking Elizabeth was young and active, Maria went to the gym and worked out five days a week, and the old man tried to run everyday. I treasured these Sundays. It seemed like a good thing to start them with an ancient religious ritual followed by a hearty American breakfast. The second cup of coffee together with the *New York Times* hit the spot in rounding things out.

Maria is a freelance writer and amateur historian. We live in a target-rich environment for her. Chestertown has a Colonial past as well as a Civil War past. The surrounding area has Civil War battlefields of the sort that abound in Northern Virginia. The Wilderness, Fredericksburg, and Chancellorsville—you get the idea. But every once in a while, she jumps off the reservation. The Hundred Years War. The Reformation. The Enlightenment. If it happened, she's interested in it. And she researches it and writes about it. And she does it very well. This morning she was tapping away on her laptop.

By the time I got through the *Times' Arts and Entertainment* section—I'd reserved the *Book Review* and *Travel* sections for just before lunch—I could hear Elizabeth conspiring on the telephone. I felt the need to get off my ass and run off some of the breakfast. I went upstairs and changed. Tights, long-sleeved t-shirt, cotton gardening gloves. No hat. The temperature outside was pushing fifty. Maria was still typing away.

When I got back forty-five minutes later, I was red-faced, runny-nosed, and sweaty. I stepped inside and heard the cackle of young, female voices. No surprise—Elizabeth's best buddies, Tala and Esmé, were with her in the family room. All three girls were sitting on the floor. A cordless phone was on the floor as well, although it appeared to be not in use at the moment.

"Hi, Dad," chirped Elizabeth.

"Hi, Mr. Llewellyn!" chorused her two girlfriends. They giggled. No doubt because of my appearance. Dads in tights with runny noses were no doubt mightily comical in the girls' eyes.

"Hi, ladies," I said with an attempt at aplomb.

Elizabeth's friends always seemed to have me at a disadvantage. They were a true Mutt-and-Jeff pair. Esmé was short but what she lacked in size, she more than made up for in eyeballs. The eyes were large and brown and always bored into my own eyes as if she knew my deepest thoughts. Which I found unsettling. Her friend, Tala, seemed a lot more innocent around the eyes, but she was quite tall and had this very disarming way of looking me straight in the face. Which she couldn't do very well at the moment since she was sitting on the floor. For which I was thankful. It's tough being a father and feeling intimidated by your twelve-year-old daughter's girlfriends.

When I came back downstairs twenty minutes later, the girls were still there. But I had showered and changed into a pair of corduroys and an old Oxford shirt. I felt marginally more in control.

"What have you guys got planned for today?" I asked.

"We're trying to decide between going to a movie and working on a social studies project," Tala volunteered.

"Tough decision," I said, heading for the refrigerator.

The girls giggled.

"Dad—can you drive us to the movies at twelve forty-five?" Elizabeth asked.

"Sure, Sweetie," I said.

Maria looked up from her *New York Times* crossword and rolled her eyes. I felt like an inept dad, but somehow it didn't bother me all that much. I drove the girls to the movies.

Four

Chestertown and Quantico Marine Corps Base
February 1st – 6th
Monday - Saturday

The next week was not one of my better ones as a teacher and a coach. I didn't sleep well, for starters. Which was most unusual for me. The nagging question of what the hell Jim Kehoe wanted to talk to me about held sway over my thought processes and moods. I was edgy with Maria and Elizabeth. I lost my train of thought in class a few times and had to scramble to catch up. I managed to get myself together enough to host a dual track meet with our cross-county rival, Sheffield High School, on Wednesday. Crystal, my co-coach, and my Augustine Washington High School athletes came through—in spite of their bumbling head coach— and both the boys' and girls' teams won convincingly. By Friday, I was going nuts. Fortunately, there was no track meet on Saturday, so I didn't have to worry about that. The district championship meet was next week on Wednesday. Regionals were a week and a half later, and the state championship was the week after that.

As is our family routine, I went out for takeout dinner Friday evening. A gourmet deli in town offered ceviche, *Caprese* pesto *insalata,* and "Italian" chicken wings. That, plus a fresh loaf of ciabatta and a super Tuscan red wine, should have made for a feast, but I don't think I tasted anything. I dutifully asked Maria how she was progressing on a magazine piece on the Battle of Antietam. She gave me an answer, but I don't remember what it was.

I hit the sack at eleven. The last time I remember looking at the digital clock between tosses and turns, it read three thirty. The alarm went off at seven. I really didn't need the coffee—I was way too wired already. What in hell could Jim Kehoe, President of the United States, want to discuss with former naval officer and current math teacher, Alan Llewellyn?

14

Both of the main women in my life got up to wish me luck, and for that I was profoundly grateful. Without their hugs, I probably would have driven my battered Explorer into the river. Security at the Quantico gate appeared to be beefed up. There were five heavily armed Marines spread out around the gate on both sides of the road. A sergeant with an M4 carbine on his shoulder and a holstered 9mm Beretta handgun checked my ID and consulted a clipboard while a corporal with some sort of short shotgun kept an eye on the proceedings.

"Good to go, sir," said the sergeant with a salute.

It took me another eight or nine minutes to get to the rifle range entrance, and I arrived there and parked at two minutes after eight. I jogged up and down a little, stretched some, and jogged some more. At eight fifteen, I caught sight of a slow-moving military police vehicle coming my way, its blue lights flashing. I stood on the shoulder of the road and saw a lone runner behind the MP cruiser. As he approached, I realized it was Mike Atwater, the blond Secret Service twin. I stepped into the road.

"Hey, Alan," he said. "Let's jog. And don't burn up the road. We want the boss man to catch up with us."

I could see a little cluster of runners coming toward us, followed by another MP vehicle with flashing blue lights. I fell in beside Atwater and started jogging.

It was sunny and cold with no wind. Not bad for February in Virginia. After jogging for a couple of minutes, I heard footsteps and felt a hand on my shoulder.

"Hey, Alan."

It was the President of the United States.

"Good morning, sir," I said.

"Forget about the formalities," he said. "Remember, we're high school classmates. And teammates. Out on a run."

I picked up the pace to stay with him. I estimated that we were running at about seven minutes, thirty seconds per mile. I could handle that. For a while.

"Yes sir," I said.

He laughed.

"No 'sirs,' either. Can you still run eight-hundred meters in under two minutes?" he asked.

"You've got to be kidding. I can maybe break three minutes. But not by much."

He laughed again.

"A likely story. We don't have much time," he said. "I wanted to meet you here at Quantico so nobody would see us. No White House gate record of your name. No tourists posting home videos of us on *YouTube*. No record of your name of any kind. For what I have in mind, our relationship *must* be totally clandestine."

"I understand, mister—uh, Jim," I said, even though I didn't.

"I need a sanity check," he said, as we loped across a small bridge. The winter woods of Quantico were stark on both sides of the road.

"*What?*" I said. I was really puzzled now.

"The clowns in the intelligence community are so damned politicized that I have no idea whether what I'm getting is the best analysis that brilliant minds can produce or political flapdoodle. Plus, there's such a huge and unwieldy mechanism producing the so-called intelligence that I have no idea if it's worth a shit. "

"Flapdoodle?" I said.

"You know. Bullshit," said the President of the United States.

"I thought a flapdoodle was some kind of crossbred dog," I said.

That got another laugh.

"Remember that National Intelligence Estimate on the Iranian nuke program? The one where the so-called 'consensus' of the U.S. intelligence community said that the Iranians had quit trying to make a nuclear weapon? That was total horseshit. The Iranians are probably only months away from putting a nuke warhead on one of their missiles. Then it'll be only a matter of weeks before they send it off to Israel. Unless the Israelis take them down first. Which they will."

"So, when it comes to the Iranian nukes, at least, it sounds like you've got things figured out. What do you want me to do?"

"I'm not worried about the Iran-Israel issue. We're on top of that. Or the Israelis are. But the intelligence community has become so huge, so laden with separate offices and contractors that I just don't trust the bastards anymore. They're all competing with each other. For money. For influence. Or power. Whatever. What I need is a 'star chamber' of experts to secretly check on intel community products and give me a judgment call as to their worth. A little off-line nest of spies, if you will. Experts on China. North Korea. Militant Islam. Russia. South America. The whole fucking world. I want you to build it and run it. Quickly and quietly.

"I also need you to keep it small and very close to the vest. Twenty or thirty people max. What I need to know soonest is *your* availability. This is a full-time gig. We'll hide you on a campus somewhere close by, give you a pot of black money, and let you go to work. But it'll be full-time and then some. I know you're a public school teacher and have a family. I want to know if you can break loose from your teaching job for at least a year—preferably two. Without screwing up your future prospects in public education. If that's truly what you want to do for the rest of your life. If not, there's a career for you here as long as there's a Kehoe administration. And very probably thereafter as well."

"Jesus Christ, Mr. President," I said. The enormity of what he was asking me to do was breaking over me like a fifteen-foot wave.

"I know, I know. It's a huge, tough nut to crack. Talk to your wife. See what you think. You'd be doing a vital service to your country. I'm inviting you and Maria to Camp David for an early dinner on Thursday. A Marine chopper will pick you up at five forty-five at the Quantico Marine Air Facility. Dress is casual. I'll spell out the job parameters and answer any and all questions you—and Maria—have. You'll be back home by nine thirty."

"Can we bring our daughter, Elizabeth?" I asked.

"By all means," said the President.

Ahead, I could see two "white top" Marine helicopters landing in an open field that the Marines' Basic School regularly used as a landing zone. They called it LZ Hornet.

"Here's where I finish up," the Leader of the Free World said, slowing down. "Mike will fix you up with a ride to your car. Thanks for coming. And I'll see you Thursday."

He shook my hand and turned off the road and jogged towards the choppers whose rotors were still turning. I stopped and watched as a Marine in pixel-camouflage utilities stepped out of one of the choppers and saluted as the president approached. The president returned the salute and climbed aboard. The Marine followed him into the bird and both helicopters took off with a roar and headed north, gaining altitude quickly.

I glanced at my watch. It was just past eight twenty. My chat with the president had lasted about three minutes.

Agent Mike appeared out of nowhere.

"Hey, Mr. Llewellyn! We'll give you a lift to your truck."

He hooked his thumb toward a black Expedition across the street, parked on the shoulder of the road and aimed back to where I'd parked.

"No thanks, Mike. I haven't even broken a sweat yet. I need to get a workout in. So I'll run the rest of the loop and get back to my truck the long way."

I figured it would be around another eight miles up and down the hills of the Basic School loop to get back to the Explorer.

"Okay, sir," he said, popping a casual salute. "See you Thursday."

Mike was apparently in on the presidential plans.

Five

Lieutenant Colonel Yang Zemin gazed out the window of his office located in an apartment in Richmond's "Fan." The streets in the Fan radiate out toward the northwest at differing angles, like the blades of a handheld fan. Hence the name. The naked, gray limbs of the beech and oak trees were not unlike the Scholar Oaks of Beijing in February. And, like the trees of Beijing, he knew that they would be bursting with green in a few weeks.

There was a light tap on the door.

"Enter!" said the colonel.

A young woman, dressed in a pale green sweater and a gray wool skirt stepped into the room and bowed slightly.

"Good afternoon, Comrade Colonel," she said, her voice barely above a whisper.

Quing Maili was a Jill-of-all-Trades at the clandestine Peoples' Republic of China Intelligence Office based in Richmond, Virginia. Lieutenant Colonel Yang Zemin was the Officer-in-Charge of Intelligence Operations for the United States East Coast. He had arrived a week ago after his predecessor had been diagnosed with lung cancer and, to his dismay, sent back to the Peoples' Republic for treatment. He had hoped to receive treatment for his cancer in the United States.

The "front" for Yang's office was the American-Chinese Cultural Exchange Association or ACCEA for short. The association offered free Mandarin language courses and occasional guest lectures on various phases of Chinese life and culture. They also sponsored cut-rate tours to China.

Colonel Yang was five feet, three inches tall. His face was triangular with a broad forehead and a sharp chin, giving him a somewhat vulpine look. He preferred tweedy, wool clothes, even in the heat of the Richmond summers. He felt they gave him a look of professorial gravitas.

Maili was five feet, eight inches tall and slender. She spoke excellent American English and was fluent in Spanish and Japanese as well. She wore expensive skirt-and-sweater combinations. During the hot months in Richmond, she substituted light-colored, lightweight cotton blouses for the sweaters. She and Yang avoided being on their feet in Yang's office at the same time, feeling that her height advantage made things awkward.

"Good afternoon, Maili," Yang said. "What news do you have for me?"

"The American President has made contact with an obscure teacher of mathematics. Our research has revealed that the teacher is a secondary school classmate of the president. His name is Llewellyn. Alan Llewellyn. He lives in Chestertown, Virginia. Teaches at Augustine Washington High School in Stafford, Virginia. He's married and has a twelve-year-old daughter. We do not know why President Kehoe contacted this Llewellyn, but it appeared the contact was deliberately clandestine."

"Get a surveillance team on this teacher, Llewellyn, immediately."

"It is done, Comrade Colonel. A team is in place and active."

"Excellent. And Kehoe's classmate? What of him? How did he react?"

"After the clandestine meeting with Kehoe on the Marine Corps base at Quantico, he went home. To his wife and daughter. He appears to continue to live his normal life, Comrade Colonel. He sent no extraordinary email. Made no extraordinary phone calls."

"Has a traffic analysis been done on his communications?"

A "traffic analysis" was merely an analysis of what came and went with a target's communications. Telephone and email. It is analogous to one's mail delivery person learning whatever he or she can about someone from the mail one receives and sends out. Without opening it. For example, over the course of a week, if a "target" received mail from the National Wildlife Federation and the Friends of the Earth Society and sent an envelope to one or the other, a traffic analyst might conclude that the target was an environmentalist. A subscriber to *Field and Stream* and *Outdoor Life* was probably a hunter or a fisherman—or both. That's a gross oversimplification, but you get the idea.

"Yes, Comrade Colonel. Nothing out of the ordinary."

"It must be nice to be so stupid and carefree," Yang mumbled.

"Yes, Comrade Colonel."

"I take it that this information is from *Mongoose*?"

"Yes, Comrade Colonel."

"Well and good."

"As you know, Comrade Colonel, *Mongoose* is normally serviced on Tuesdays or Wednesdays. He made an extraordinary emergency drop early this afternoon. Apparently he felt that the information on this contact, clandestine as it was, justified altering his routine. He signaled *emergency drop* with a lunch at the restaurant on F Street and made the dead drop at the agreed-upon site in the National Zoo."

Yang chuckled.

"*Mongoose* is worth every dollar we're paying him. For now, let's just keep an eye on Llewellyn and let our mole do his job."

"Yes, Comrade Colonel."

"'Yes, Comrade Colonel. No, Comrade Colonel.' That's what you always say, Maili. Come over here and sit down beside me."

"Yes, Comrade Colonel."

"See? Why don't you try and discard some of that Party formality and relax a bit? We—you and I—spend a lot of time together. You're an attractive woman. Perhaps the two of us can take advantage of that. And enjoy one another's company somewhat. Would you like a glass of French champagne?"

"That would be nice, Comrade Colonel," the girl said.

The colonel picked up a tiny porcelain bell and shook it once. A young man entered.

"Champagne. The French. For two," the colonel ordered.

"Yes, Comrade Colonel."

"Thank you, Li," Yang responded.

The young man bowed and left the room.

Six

Chestertown
February 6th
Saturday

By the time I had the Explorer off the base, it was nine thirty, and my running clothes and I were clammy and cold from sweat and winter, so I cranked up the heater. Then the windshield fogged up. I dicked around with the defroster and heater and finally got the windshield clear and my body somewhat comfortable. As I headed south on I-95, my mind wasn't at all comfortable with what the president had said.

"Quit your job," he'd said, in effect.

"For one or two years," he'd said.

"Build a nest of spies," he'd said. "A 'star chamber.'"

"For providing 'sanity checks' on stuff the U.S. Intelligence Community is producing for me," he'd said.

"On a campus somewhere nearby," he'd said.

"Secretly," he'd said.

"Don't call me 'sir,'" he'd said.

"Come to Camp David Thursday for dinner and we'll discuss it. Bring Maria and Elizabeth," he'd said.

I felt like I'd fallen through some sort of wormhole into a parallel universe. And now I was tumbling back into the present day.

When I pulled into the driveway in Chestertown, I was chilled again and ready for a long hot shower and a cup of hot coffee. Maria and Elizabeth were dressed. Maria was working the Sudoku in the paper, and Elizabeth was talking on the phone. They both kind of stared at me questioningly as I came into the house.

"I need a hot shower and a hot cup of coffee," I said. "Then I'll give you the scoop. Promise."

They exchanged looks like they were listening to a crazy man. Maybe they were. I poured a mug of coffee and nuked it for thirty-nine seconds. While the microwave whirred, I dropped the little bomb to the women.

"We're invited to Camp David for dinner. Thursday. A Marine Corps chopper is picking us up at Quantico at five forty-five."

The microwave beeped, I grabbed my coffee and headed up the stairs. The hot shower was just what I needed. Hot swigs of coffee helped too. I decided to bag shaving, toweled myself dry, put on cords and a Navy sweatshirt, and went back downstairs.

Maria and Elizabeth chorused the question, "What is *really* going on?"

I told them. As much as I knew. Which wasn't much. Didn't matter. The Thursday date with POTUS at Camp David was enough for them. They started jabbering about what to wear and the meaning of "casual" immediately. It really tightened their jaws when I swore them to secrecy.

"We can tell absolutely no one. No one," I repeated. "Not my rule," I added. "The president's."

Seven

Virginia and Maryland
February 11th
Thursday

It was the second lousy week in a row for me, productivity-wise. Fortunately for my students, I could teach the math stuff without thinking too much because I had taught it all many times before. And I knew it worked—the kids, in fact, learned. We had a neat sort of give-and-take classroom relationship. They were involved and engaged, and I could tell when they were getting it. Or when they weren't. And when they weren't, I'd circle the wagons, go back, and try something else. But I was still all wrapped around my own axle about what the president had said.

With the track team, Crystal bailed me out in telling me what District Championship entries we needed to make. Thanks to her, we got the entries in accurately and on time.

Wednesday night, I went to bed early—nine o'clock. I fell asleep immediately. Trouble was, I awoke at two thirty, and that was it for the night. I switched from my left side to my right and back for more than an hour and then got up at three forty-five. After making coffee, I graded tests till I heard the first newspaper hit the stoop with a thump at a little after five thirty.

By the time I got to school a few minutes past seven, I was wired from the coffee, and my mind was going in a thousand different directions about this evening's dinner at Camp David. I kept telling myself to relax, it was just a casual dinner with Jim Kehoe, and Maria and Elizabeth would be there. I wondered who else would be there. I had no idea.

My zit-faced wonders probably didn't realize it, but they bailed me out too, God bless 'em. The students-plus-math combination swung my thoughts away from my self-absorbed angst to dealing with the problems and theorems at hand, and I got through the day fine, thanks to the kids and the math.

Track practice was Siberia. We had twenty-five knots of wind racing down out of the north and the temperature was hovering just under thirty degrees Fahrenheit. We had an easy workout for the distance runners, but even the shot-putters' noses were running. The pole-vaulters stayed low because of the wind. Crystal and I turned our athletes loose a half-hour early and left at four thirty.

An hour later, a Marine MP was directing me to a VIP parking space at the Marine Corps Air Facility at Quantico. Maria and Elizabeth were twitching around excitedly.

"This way, sir and ma'am," the Marine said. His rank insignia said he was a lance corporal. He looked like he was about sixteen.

We followed him into the front entrance of one building and then out another door that led to the ramp. A VH-60 helicopter was parked about forty meters away, its rotors thumping and its turbines howling.

"Right this way, sir and ma'am," he said again and broke into a little jog towards the chopper.

Another Marine was waiting alongside the door. He offered his hand to Elizabeth and guided her into the passenger compartment. I don't think she had grinned like that since a couple of Christmases ago when Santa gave her a copy of *Harry Potter and the Sorcerer's Stone*. Maria and I followed. The Marine hopped aboard, made sure we were belted in, and the chopper's engines started to roar. Then the door closed, the noise abated, and we were airborne.

The shadows on the thin layer of snow were long and the sun was starting to dip behind a mountaintop when the chopper flared and settled at Camp David.

Jim Kehoe—President Kehoe—was at the side of the LZ, along with his golden retriever. We climbed off the chopper and its turbines whined down to a halt. There was a pleasant odor of wood smoke in the cold, mountain air. The President of the United States and his dog stepped forward.

"Welcome Alan. And Maria and Elizabeth," he said, holding out his hand. "This is Sham—short for 'Champagne.' She's my special buddy."

We humans all shook hands. Sham wagged her whole body as well as her tail.

"Let's go in, have a seat by the fire, and have a cocktail," he said, gesturing towards the house.

I still didn't know what to say. Sham led the way to the door. Mike was standing on the porch. He wore a leather jacket and blue jeans. He nodded and smiled as we approached the door.

"'Evening, Mr. and Mrs. Llewellyn. Elizabeth," he said.

"Hi, Mike," I said and we went inside.

Maria took up the conversational slack.

"This place is beautiful," she said, looking around. "So peaceful. You probably hear that a lot."

"I do, but I certainly don't mind hearing it again. And again. It confirms what I felt the first time I came up here. If I could, I'd work here all the time and fly back to Sixteen Hundred Pennsylvania Avenue one day a week to sign papers. But the U.S. Government doesn't work that way, unfortunately."

Then Elizabeth chimed in.

"Mr. President, are there bears here in the woods?" she asked.

"They tell me there are bears, but I've never seen one," the Leader of the Free World said. "There are tons of deer and I see them almost every morning that I'm here."

We turned down a hall, and I saw Luke, the African-American Secret Service twin, look up from a desk. He grinned and waved.

When we got to the fireplace, Sham flopped on the floor with a contented little sigh and started gnawing at the little ice balls between her hairy toes. A Navy steward was waiting to take our drink orders. He seemed to know what the president wanted. Maria asked for a glass of chardonnay, Elizabeth asked for a Sprite, and I requested a scotch on the rocks. He was back with the drinks in less than a minute. Mine was quite brown and pretty deep and I made a mental note to go slow and easy. The president raised his glass that could have been a gin-and-tonic or soda water with a lime wedge.

"Cheers and welcome to the cabin in the woods, Llewellyns," he said.

"Cheers, Mr. President," I said.

"Hey. Keep it informal. We're kind of like family. Remember you and I go back a long way."

He turned to Maria.

"Did Alan tell you about the job I've offered him?" he asked.

"Yes sir, Mr. President," Maria answered. "But his description was pretty vague. Setting up some sort of secret office to double check the stuff you get from the U.S. Intelligence Community. On a campus someplace. That's about it."

"A couple of dozen bodies and what you described as a 'pot of black money,'" I added.

"You must have questions," he said.

"Oh yes, sir—uh, Jim," I said. "The big one is: why me? I don't really have the background for something like this."

"Fair enough," he said. "Actually, your lack of 'background' is one of your most important qualifications. Let me tell you a little about our nation's capital and how things work, from my standpoint.

"First of all, there's the 'bubble.' Every president has one. Every president has a staff. And that staff, with the best of intentions, erects a bubble for the boss. Just like the docs did for that kid on that crazy Seinfeld episode. So, I end up hearing only what they think I want to hear. I try and get past that by having the *New York Times*, *Washington Post*, and *USA Today* on my desk first thing every morning. And I kind of cycle through the TV cable and network news a few times a day. But, you know, what I get from the papers and the networks is, in large part, the party line from the Washington insiders with a few morsels thrown in from their buddies in New York, Chicago, and Los Angeles. And they're all members of the same club. The correspondents who cover politics are politicians in their own right. They just don't have to campaign and worry about vote counts. Look at Bob Woodward. Do you think he would be able to write what he does without being part of the very establishment he writes about?

"Then there's a large subset of this political establishment—the Intelligence Community. CIA. NSA. DIA. FBI. More than two dozen agencies or activities or what have you. Not to mention the drones on the House and Senate committee staffs. It didn't take me very long to figure out that the folks who *do* have the 'background' for your job are all current or former members of the Intelligence Community. One would hope and expect that they'd be apolitical. Above politics. Unh-uh. No way. Nobody in Washington is above politics. You've lived and worked separate from that rat pack, so you're not loaded down with their political baggage. Also, I had my personal staff run a low-profile background check on you. Your Navy record shows that you're someone who can make things happen. Your teaching and coaching backgrounds reflect the same thing. Plus, I know you from the good old days. You're the guy I need. Our country needs you. I think I'm capable of making that call."

"You mentioned your personal staff doing a background check," I said. "Are they in on this little project?"

He shook his head.

"No. Your name was in the middle of a list of names of 'possible candidates for sensitive positions.' Syd knows. He's in on everything. For obvious reasons."

"Syd" had to be Sydney Girtler, the vice president.

"The only other staff members that know that I'm even thinking of implementing this 'sanity check' project is Walt Whitehead and the two Secret Service agents you've already met. Besides the three of you."

I'd read or heard somewhere in the news media that Walt Whitehead was the White House Chief of Staff. And that he'd been a state assemblyman in New York. I assume he and the president were political cronies of some sort.

"Here's another question for you," I said. "To whom will the sanity checkers report?"

He hadn't yet made that clear. Now he did.

"To me, personally. And the reporter will be you, personally. Or your number two guy. As I said, Walt will be read in on the program. If I'm out of the country and something important is breaking, you'll get it to him. He will get whatever you tell him to Syd Girtler. And to me, of course."

A little *bong* sounded from somewhere in the house.

"The chime means that they're ready to serve us dinner," announced the president. "I promised I'd have you home by nine thirty. I know teachers work hard and get up early."

We sat down at a linen-covered, candle-lit table, and the president led us in grace before meals. *"Bless us oh Lord and these Thy gifts..."* Just like at home. It was just the four of us. And Sham. Her manners were excellent. She flopped in the shadows, her chin resting on her paws. No begging. But I bet that the stewards didn't have to sweep up crumblets from underneath the table after dinner.

The president turned to Maria.

"You mentioned something important, Maria," he said. "'Secret' is the operative word for this project. Whether Alan takes the job or not. The issue of an independent entity checking Intelligence Community products for the President of the United States is extremely sensitive. Hell, it's explosive. And has got to be extremely close-held."

"I understand, Mr. President," Maria said.

"We all do," I added.

The steward brought steaming bowls of lentil soup to the table. He then poured white wine from a napkin-wrapped bottle into the adults' glasses and something pale from a cut-glass pitcher into Elizabeth's wine glass.

"Apple juice, Miss Elizabeth," he said.

"Do you have any more specifics, Mr. President?" Maria asked.

"You bet. It'll be a one-year, renewable contract, starting whenever Alan can start. Which I hope is ASAP. Annual salary one-hundred-forty K. Plus a car. Your office will be on the Martha Washington University campus right there in Chestertown. Your cover and that of the others in the group will be U.S. Government researchers specializing in international affairs. You and some of the professionals on your staff will have to give an occasional guest lecture or seminar at the university to maintain your cover. You can walk to work and go home for lunch. The car is for meetings at Quantico, here at Camp David, Washington, or wherever."

I was excited at the prospects and challenges of a White House appointment. Even a secret one. Plus, it paid considerably more than my teacher's salary. Being able to walk home for lunch was over the top. But I needed some time to absorb it all and kick it around with Maria.

"Do we have to give you an answer this evening Mr. President—uh, Jim?" I asked.

"No. Of course not. You need to talk it over with your family. How about if I send Luke and Mike by your house at five thirty, Monday evening for your decision? That way you guys could discuss it together over the weekend. And we can stay off the air."

The steward glided in and removed our empty soup bowls. He returned with plates of what appeared to be nut-encrusted fish, beets, and potatoes *au gratin*.

"These are fresh brook trout," said the Leader of the Free World. "A couple of the off-duty Marines caught them this morning right here on the Camp David compound."

I thought it would be bad form for me to ask about how well stocked the Camp David waters were, so I didn't. But I bet the Marines didn't have to work too hard to catch the trout.

Elizabeth wasn't shy.

"Did they catch them on flies, Mr. President?" she asked.

"I'm pretty sure they did, but I don't know what size or pattern. Are you a fly fisherman, Elizabeth?"

"Yes, sir. At least I try to be."

"Actually, she's pretty darn good," I added.

"Well, we'll just have to get you back here for some fishing. The Marines can show you the ropes."

Elizabeth's grin lit up the room.

We made small talk through dessert—vanilla ice cream with raspberries and a drizzling of a yummy sauce that I couldn't identify—and coffee. At one point, the president excused himself and returned a couple of minutes later, pocketing a cell phone. As I took a last sip of coffee, I could hear a helicopter's engines starting outside.

"I promised you I'd get you home by nine thirty," the president said, folding his napkin.

I folded mine and stood, and the girls followed suit.

"Thank you for a delightful dinner, Mr. President," Maria said.

"Thanks, Jim," I said. "I'll have an answer for you on Monday."

"I'm glad you came and glad I was able to meet your family," the president said. "I hope you can work it out and say yes. I don't have a backup plan—I'll really have to scramble if you turn me down."

"Yikes," said Maria as we walked through the cold to the chopper. "*That's* what I call arm-twisting."

"These guys play by a whole different set of rules," I said.

"He is really nice," Elizabeth said.

We boarded the chopper. The flight lasted less than the half-hour drive from Quantico to home. It was nine twenty-five when we rolled into the driveway.

"Whaddaya you know," I mused to the women. "A politician who keeps his word."

Eight

Lexington and Chestertown, Virginia
February 12th – 13th
Friday – Saturday

Our Regional Track and Field Championship Meet was the next day at the Virginia Military Institute field house on the campus in Lexington. We left the Augustine Washington campus at six fifteen in the dark. It was a good day for our athletes and our school. The boys' team came in second in the region and qualified thirteen kids for the State Meet. Our very young girls' team finished third and qualified ten athletes—two of them in two events.

We arrived back at school at nine forty-five p.m. All the parents were there, waiting for their kids when we pulled into the school parking lot. Thank the Lord for cell phones. All the kids were gone within two or three minutes. Crystal and I took less than five minutes to sign off the bus paperwork and stow the team's gear and lock it up.

"I'll lock the gate after you leave," I said, ever the gentleman.

"Thanks, Alan," she said. "I'll see you Monday."

She hopped into her little Scion, and I watched her taillights disappear around the bend in the road. Then, as I slipped the padlock through the chain link on the gate, headlights lighted me up. I wondered if Crystal had turned around to come back for something.

But it was a male voice that called out "Hi, Alan!"

"Luke?" I asked.

"Right the first time," he said, climbing out of his black SUV, which was now eyeball-to-eyeball with my Explorer. "Sorry for meeting you like this, but the boss man has some additional words for you. And he doesn't want to screw around with email or phones for obvious reasons."

"Do you want to come by the house for a drink or a cup of coffee?" I asked.

"No, thanks," he said. "Mike and I will stop by at seventeen thirty on Monday as planned. We want to minimize the exposure of any possible connection between you and POTUS. And this'll only take a few seconds."

"Fair enough," I said. "What's up?"

"He wants to make sure that your relationship with him is totally clear to you," Luke said. "For starters, he wanted to emphasize that you report only to him. He, in turn will share it only with Chipmunk and Chanticleer."

"Chipmunk and Chanticleer?" I asked.

"The vice," he said. "Syd Girtler is Chipmunk. Chanticleer is Whitehead, the chief of staff."

"Secret Service code names for the vice and the chief of staff," I mumbled more or less to myself. "What's the boss man's code name?"

"Cheetah," he said. "The first lady is 'Chatelaine.' Anyhow, just so you know, neither he nor the other two guys will be sharing whatever you tell him with *anybody*."

"Um, suppose CIA gives him a paper that says '*a* equals *b*,' and I give him a paper on the same subject that says '*a* does *not* equal *b*, but rather *a* equals *c*.' What happens then?"

"Up to him. My guess is that he'll consider all inputs and then decide what he thinks is most credible and best for the country. But your stuff will not see the light of day. Unless it's camouflaged. Like 'coming from allied sources' or something like that. There will be absolutely nothing that ties your products to you and the White House. The fact of your *appointment* coming from the White House can be known. The fact of your direct support to the boss man or the White House must remain a secret and tightly compartmentalized. That's what he wanted you to know."

"That's it?"

"That's it," he said. "See you Monday evening. Enjoy the weekend."

He popped that little salute of his, climbed into the Expedition, executed a three-point turn, and I watched his taillights disappear around the bend. I stood there alone, still holding the chain and padlock. I was starting to get those wormhole-parallel universe feelings again. I shivered, snapped the padlock, and climbed into my truck.

When I got home, Maria and Elizabeth were in their pajamas and yawning. I gave them a quick summary of the regional track meet results before phoning them in to the local rags' sports desks. By the time I finished talking to the duty sports reporters, my girls had both plopped silent kisses somewhere near my mouth and disappeared up the stairs.

I poured myself a light scotch, glanced at a pile of uninteresting mail, and turned on the eleven o'clock news, which I watched through sports and weather. The gel-headed weather weasel was predicting spring-like conditions for tomorrow. I turned off the TV and drained the scotch, wondering whether I'd dreamed about Luke bringing me the message from Kehoe. *President* Kehoe. Keys.

To hell with it, I thought. I put my glass in the dishwasher, checked the locks, and turned off the lights. I was too damned tired to think. That would come tomorrow. I went to bed and was asleep by the time my head hit the pillow.

Next morning, I was the first Llewellyn household member out of the rack at six thirty, which was normal. I put the coffee together quietly, and the machine started croaking and dripping. I retrieved the newspapers and checked the sports pages for the track and field results. There was a respectable headline: *Patriot Boys Run to Second, Girls Third in Regional Track*. The story that followed was fair and accurate. Couldn't ask for more than that.

I turned on one of the cable news channels and half-watched as I skimmed the newspapers. It was hard to tell whose idiocy was most egregious—the TV talking heads or the printed pundits. Finishing my coffee, I realized that I was hungry. I went into the kitchen and broke out the large cast-iron skillet. The clock said six forty-five. I decided to wait until seven o'clock before starting the bacon. I knew that the smell of frying bacon wafting through the house would bring hungry women downstairs, so I sat down at the kitchen table and did the crossword puzzle to kill a little time and give the girls another quarter hour of sleep. At seven sharp, I put the bacon in the skillet and turned on the gas.

Elizabeth was in the kitchen by the time I turned over the first strip of bacon in the pan. Maria was there by the time I turned over the last. I took orders for eggs and toast and set the table around them as they shared the papers. They were almost half finished when I sat down with my two over-mediums stacked on top of four slices of bacon.

"Luke—one of the Secret Service guys—came to see me at school last night," I said, cutting a piece of bacon with my fork.

"Last night?" Maria asked. "Good grief! You didn't get home until ten fifteen. What was that about?"

"The president just clarified what he already told me. Or told us, at dinner," I said. "The only other guys in the loop for what I tell him are Girtler and Whitehead. And my little gang does not exist as an intel provider."

"Well, well," she said. "What do you think?"

"I'm not sure what I think," I said. "Last night I was too tired to think. This morning, I've been trying to avoid thinking about it. Luke confirmed last night that he and Atwater are still coming on Monday at five thirty. So I guess I've got to think about it between now and then."

"Can I tell Esmé and Tala that you have a 'White House assignment' and not go into details?" Elizabeth asked.

"No, Sweetheart," I said. "Not yet. I haven't decided to accept the job. So sit tight. I have until Monday to make up my mind."

She grinned as she used her fork to cut a bite-sized piece of bacon on her plate.

"Daddy," she said. "I think you made up your mind before we got on the helicopter at Camp David."

I didn't say anything. The little vixen. Except she wasn't so little anymore.

The TV weather genius got the forecast right for a change. By ten o'clock, the mercury was nuzzling sixty degrees. I went out to root around in the yard and clean up the flowerbeds where crocuses were poking up little green points. By eleven forty-five, I was sweating. I checked the thermometer outside the mudroom. Sixty-nine. It felt good.

Out of a corner of my eye, I saw the mail-person's little truck pull away, so I went back out front to retrieve the mail. As I approached the mailbox, I noticed the fat corgi waddling by on the sidewalk. But this time his walker wasn't a beautiful young Asian woman. This time it was an Asian woman who might have been beautiful once upon a time. Actually, I corrected myself and thought that, although she was a long way from young, she did have a certain imperial beauty. A Ming Dynasty Empress. I wondered idly if she was the other corgi-walker's mother and if perhaps a new Asian family had moved into the neighborhood.

Nine

Chestertown
February 13th – 15th
Saturday - Monday

I left my work boots in the mudroom and padded into the kitchen in my socks, glancing at junk mail and bills. Putting the mail on its usual place on the counter, I poured myself a glass of water and sucked it down, savoring the coldness. I could hear the stereo playing jazz in the family room and footsteps upstairs. Maria was working on her laptop; the upstairs footsteps must have been Elizabeth's.

"So what are you thinking now?" Maria asked.

"Is there a new Chinese family in the neighborhood?" I asked.

Maria rolled her eyes. She reminded me of Elizabeth when she did that.

"Not that I know of," she said, flicking a lock of hair off her forehead. "What's that got to do with what you're thinking about the president's job offer?"

"Nothing," I said. "It's just that I've seen these two different Chinese women walking the same dog in front of our house. Hell, they may not even be Chinese. I suppose they could be Korean."

"Your mind works in strange ways," she said.

"Sorry," I said, laughing. "I still don't know what I'm thinking about the job. Actually, my thoughts are all jumbled up. I'm going to take a shower."

I put my water glass in the kitchen sink and went upstairs.

As I was stripping off my sweaty clothes, I thought I heard our heavy front door thudding shut. I adjusted the water, stepped under it, and slid the glass door closed. I was rinsing shampoo out of my hair with my eyes shut when I heard the bathroom door open and close. I finished rinsing and opened my eyes. Even though the shower was steamed up, I could tell Maria was naked.

"Can I come in?"

"Where's Elizabeth?" I whispered.

She giggled.

"On the way to the mall with Esmé and Tala," she said. "She just left. Toni is taking them."

Toni is Esmé's mom.

I slid the shower door open.

"Welcome," I croaked.

I sensed something in Maria—desperation? Anxiety? Whatever it was, it was something that wasn't always there. But it didn't quell her passion. Or mine, for that matter.

About forty-five minutes later, we were both pulling on our jeans.

"I made us a couple of chicken salad sandwiches," she said. "There's a bottle of *prosecco* in the fridge and some apple pie left over from last night's supper, which you missed."

"I saw the pie after you and Elizabeth hit the rack," I said. "But I was too tired to eat it."

We went downstairs. I opened the *prosecco* and put on a CD of Boccherini's guitar quintets. We toasted. The bubbly wine had a clean taste with a hint of apple and maybe a dash of citrus with the finish.

"Have you started thinking, yet?" she asked.

"I started thinking in the shower. Then you came and distracted me."

"Well, *I've* been thinking," Maria said. "Actually, maybe it hasn't been 'thinking.' Reacting, I guess. At a much lower level of rationality than thinking. Gut-think rather than brain-think."

"And?"

"Oh, I don't know. Actually, I *do* know. I have a feeling of uneasiness about this whole business. At the same time, I think you should take the job. How many times do people get offered White House appointments? Especially, one as critical as this one. It may be secret, but it's still a lot more substantive than just shuffling papers and doing seating diagrams."

"I know," I said. "But I've always put a lot of faith in your gut-think. Your instincts are incredibly good."

"But in spite of them, I just said that I think you should take the job. Don't you?"

"Yeah," I said. "But your instincts give me pause, as they say. Still, I like it that you're in favor of my taking it. And I *can* walk home for lunch. Who knows what might happen then?"

"Who knows indeed? I think, between the two of us, we've arrived at what you're going to tell Luke and Mike Monday evening," she said.

"What about Elizabeth?"

"I think she feels the same way I do," she said. "Inexplicably uneasy but hopeful that you'll do it. Keeping her dad's White House work a secret will be frustrating for her, but I've no doubt that she will.

"What about vacation?" she asked, changing the subject. "Will you get any?"

"I don't know. I'll have to talk to the boss man about that. I'm sure there'll be some. Hell, presidents go off on vacation all the time. Presumably, their flunkies can get time off as well."

When Agents Atwater and Wallace showed up Monday evening, I offered them a drink. They both asked for coffee. I had a scotch and gave them my answer to take to President Kehoe. It was "yes."

Both agents stood up and grinned. We bumped fists and shook hands.

"Congratulations!" they said, almost in unison.

Luke took a letter-sized envelope from an inside pocket and handed it to me. I could see it was White House stationery.

"Here's a letter from POTUS," he said. "It could be helpful in smoothing out your departure from your present position."

The letter was short.

THE WHITE HOUSE

Washington

February 15

To Whom It May Concern:

Alan Llewellyn has graciously accepted my request to serve in a special and extremely sensitive assignment in the Government of the United States. His talent and experience are crucial factors in his service to his country. It is my hope that he will begin his service no later than March first of this year. Please extend him every courtesy and consideration.

Sincerely,

Jim Kehoe

James M. Kehoe
President of the United States of America

I thought to myself that Kehoe may indeed turn out to be a great president, but he doesn't know anything about teaching high school kids. The letter might help with my principal and the schools' human resources guy. But it wouldn't help much with the ones who really count—the students and the athletes. To kids that age, relationships are really important. To any teacher or coach worth his or her salt, those relationships really count as well. To walk away from them in the middle of the year was going to be a disaster. Regardless of who was offering me the new job.

Luke had just said something that I didn't catch, woolgathering as I was.

"Sorry, Luke," I said. "I was thinking ahead, I guess."

"So was I. He's going to want to know when you can start."

"Two weeks from today," I said. "March first. Like he said in the letter."

"Good to go," said Mike. They both shook hands with Maria and me again.

"Have a great evening, Llewellyns," Luke said.

"Congratulations again," Mike said.

"Stay on top of your email," Luke added. "If the subject line contains the phrase 'fly-fishing,' open it. It's from the boss man or his staff."

He handed me a card. It had what looked like a phone number, complete with area code and that was all. Luke held up his cell phone.

"Rings right here. For emergencies," he said. "Oh, and there's one little detail. You need to add one to the first three digits before dialing, two to the second three digits, and three to the last four. And please don't write that down. Just remember—one, two, and three. Add. Ten is zero, eleven is one and so on."

"Jesus Christ," I said after closing the door. "What have we got ourselves into?"

Maria gave me a big hug. Elizabeth came down the stairs.

"I was wondering the same thing," she said. "I'm also wondering when he's gonna invite me fishing."

Ten

Washington, D. C.
February 16th
Tuesday

Congressman Erik DiRienzo from New York changed out of his gray pinstriped, suit and into shorts and a long-sleeved t-shirt. He covered the shorts and t-shirt with a red and silver all-weather *GORE-TEX* running suit. It was cloudy outside. The weather channel said it was thirty-six, but the wind made it feel like twenty-five. Rick, as his many friends knew him, pulled on a pair of black gloves, a pair of L.L. Bean sunglasses, and a black Navy watch cap. He doubted if anyone would recognize him once he got outside the Rayburn Building. He was wrong.

He started running right away as a feeble defense against the cold wind. A man who appeared to be a bicycle courier said two words into a cell phone.

"He's out."

Three quarters of a mile away, a man in a minivan said the Mandarin version of "Roger."

DiRienzo ran down Capital Hill on Constitution Avenue, headed onto the mall on Third Street and then headed west on Madison Drive. Despite the cold and gloomy day, there were knots of sightseers everywhere. Lunch-hour runners like him also abounded. He ran directly at the Washington Monument three-quarters of a mile away, as he passed the National Gallery of Art. No one seemed to notice the second-term congressman from New York.

No one, that is, except the man lying in the back of a silver-gray Honda Odyssey. The man was almost completely covered with empty cardboard boxes. He hit the bolt of the Stevens Model 200 Long Action rifle gently with the heel of his hand, making sure the bolt was home. Pushing the rear door of the minivan a little more open, he clutched the pistol grip

42

of the rifle stock and pulled the butt more tightly into his shoulder. He could see the target clearly now. The red-and-silver tracksuit made it easy. Aligning the cross hairs of the scope with the man's midsection, he took a deep breath and let it partially out. He took up the slack in the trigger and squeezed gently.

Congressman Erik DiRienzo looked like he'd hit the elastic limit of an invisible bungee cord. The .30/06 Swift Scirocco II bullet was traveling over twenty-five hundred feet per second when it slammed into his chest, knocking him back three feet before he fell, a gaping exit wound between his shoulder blades. Blood spread out from beneath his torso. His sightless eyes stared up at the gray skies and people started screaming and dialing nine-one-one on their cell phones.

The driver of the Odyssey put it in gear and started forward. The man lying in the back pulled the door shut and covered himself and his rifle with empty cardboard cartons. Minutes later, the vehicle turned off the George Washington Parkway and into the southbound lanes of I-95.

Eleven

Chestertown
February 16th
Tuesday

I thought my life was on fast-forward all the time, but things really took off on me after the visit from Luke and Mike. I checked my email at six the next morning. There were five messages with "fly-fishing" in the subject line. "Fly-fishing in Alaska" was the first one. I opened it.

Mr. Llewellyn: Please contact Marge O'Connor at (907) 794-5555 for info re your fishing trip.

I replied with an, "Okay. Will do. Thanks," and jotted down the name and number on a post-it note. Then I shut down the computer and finished getting ready for school. I'd try to call during my planning period. I had to talk to my principal as well. And human resources. It was going to be a busy day.

I checked the 907 in the phone book. It was indeed the area code for Alaska. I waited till lunchtime and called on my cell.

"Angling Headquarters," announced a female voice after the third ring. "This is Marge."

"Good morning. This is Alan Llewellyn."

"Ah, yes. Mr. Llewellyn. I've just mailed you some forms you need to fill out for your trip. Please fill them out and pop them in the mail back to us in the envelope provided as soon as it's convenient."

"Will do," I said. "And thanks." I figured, "...as soon as it's convenient" meant ASAP when it came from the White House, even if it came via Alaska.

"Thank you, Mr. Llewellyn. 'Bye."

The rest of the day flew by in a jerky haze. I'd talked to Lisa Walters, my principal, and showed her the letter from the president. She was

44

impressed but not happy. I think she was a Democrat and that might have added some salt to the wound of a teacher jumping ship in the middle of the year. I called Dr. Sam at HR right after faxing him a copy of the Kehoe letter. He retrieved the fax and whistled when he came back on the line.

"Have you told Lisa?" he asked.

"Yes. Just a few minutes ago. It wasn't the highlight of my day."

"Probably not hers, either. How about the kids?" he asked. He meant my students.

"Not yet. I'm inclined to sit on it pending further guidance from on high. Also, I don't want to prolong that particular agony any more than necessary."

"I guess that means you don't want me doing a press release saying, 'Augustine Washington Math Teacher Accepts—"

"Sam!" I interrupted.

"Suspicion confirmed," he said, chuckling. "We *do* have to hire someone, so I can't exactly keep your departure a secret. Not to mention the fact that when you tell your students, it'll be all over the county within hours."

"I know," I said. "But just don't put anything in lights in the sky—at least till I get further instructions."

"Fair enough," he said. "And congratulations."

Crystal and I pulled the plug early after a real polar bear practice with the wind out of the north—again—and occasional snowflakes whipping through. The only kids at practice were those heading to the state meet on Friday and Saturday. When I got home, I was surprised to hear Channel Four News voices coming from the living room. Maria and Elizabeth occasionally watch Oprah at four. But I was the one who usually tuned in the news. I wondered what was up.

Twelve

Chestertown
February 16th
Tuesday

When I walked into the living room, both Maria and Elizabeth stared at me. No smiles, no hellos. I felt a sudden chill in my gut that wasn't related to the cold outside.

"What's going on?"

"Somebody shot a congressman. On the Mall. Killed him. While he was jogging during his lunch hour," Maria said.

"Which congressman?" I asked.

"Rick DiRienzo of New York," she said.

Two sharp taps on the glass of the back door sounded over the voice of the Channel Four anchor. Both Maria and Elizabeth jumped.

"Jesus Christ!" I whispered.

Wishing I had a weapon, I raced to the door and pulled the curtain aside. It was Mike Atwater, the Secret Service guy. Not knowing what to think, I pulled the door open.

"Mike! C'mon in. What the fuck's going on?"

"We need to talk. Let's walk around the block. Tell Maria you'll be back in ten minutes. Oh, hi, Maria."

Maria doesn't spook easily, but one look at her told me that she didn't like any of this at all.

"Back in ten, Sweetie," I said and stepped outside. I still had my jacket and gloves on from track practice.

"Been watching the news?" Mike asked.

"Yeah. Just now. I got home from practice a couple of minutes ago. Maria told me about the congressman."

"Okay. Let me fill you in. It was an assassination, pure and simple. Pros. And DiRienzo is—or was—an old buddy of POTUS. They go way back. Kind of like you. Except they were in college together, not high school."

"What's that got to do with me?" I asked, afraid I wasn't going to like the answer to my question. The idea of some asshole shooting Kehoe's old friends wasn't exactly appealing to this old Kehoe friend. But Mike's response was even worse than I had imagined.

"I'm getting to that. The boss man wants you to take a look at this thing and give him your take on it."

"*What? My* take? That's crazy!"

"Hold your voice down!"

I lowered my voice, but I was no less adamant.

"That's fucking insane! For a bazillion reasons. Primary one being that I'm not qualified. I'm sure there are a half-dozen or more police organizations that are up to their asses in this thing."

"More," he said.

"Hell, you guys are probably involved."

"Yup. Big time," he said.

"So it doesn't make any fucking sense for a math teacher from Chestertown, Virginia, to start screwing around with an ongoing investigation into a congressional assassination. I'd probably draw attention to myself—which isn't what the boss man wants—and piss off a lot of people in the bargain."

We reached the corner and turned right.

"You're right about the boss man not wanting any undue attention on you. Listen to what he told me to tell you."

He started reciting. Like a schoolboy with a photographic memory. Who had memorized the president's exact words.

"'Tell Alan that'"—he made air quotes with his gloved fingers— "'... this is another case where I need a different pair of eyeballs looking at it. Just like the sanity check thing. Except this one's early and he has no staff. Ask him if he can give me eight hours. I understand that he's still got his teaching job. And coaching. Maybe he can carve out eight hours over the weekend. No interfering with the cops, FBI, you guys, or whoever. He's to stay off the skyline. Just go through whatever he can find. News media stuff he can get from the Internet. And anything else that he can get his hands on without tipping off anybody in the official investigation. I know that he doesn't have the resources to track license plates and car rentals, so emphasize that he doesn't need to get down in those technical weeds. Hell, he should *not* get involved in any of the details. Rather, he should take a quick look at the big picture and tell me what he thinks.' That may not be verbatim, but it's close," he said.

We turned the next corner. I could feel the air turning colder. There was a hint of wood smoke.

"How—when and where—do I tell him what I think?"

"Be at the Quantico Marina on the Potomac River at seventeen hundred on Sunday. Have five or six sentences summarizing what you think listed on a three-by-five card. A fifty-six-foot cabin cruiser will pull in at exactly five. It's his boat that he dragged down from Mamaroneck. He'll be aboard. You'll have a quick visit, summarize what you think, give him the index card, and then both you guys are outta there."

"Shit," I said. "I'm betting that there will be only one sentence on the three-by-five."

"What's that?"

"Professional hit. And that's because you told me it was."

We turned the next corner.

"Don't sell yourself short," Mike responded. "Like he said, he's hiring you as an alternate set of eyeballs."

"Okay. I accept that. But just where do *you* come in? If I were you, and I learned that the president was hiring some Chestertown dipstick to second guess the cops—*and* the Secret Service—in an important investigation, I'd haul ass to my boss and tell him all about it," I said.

"Alan, old buddy," he answered. "My boss is your boss. Jim Kehoe. President of the United States. There are no other loyalties for me."

"Okay. I'll be at the docks at Quantico at seventeen hundred, Sunday."

I turned the last corner. Mike went straight.

"See you Sunday," he said, over his shoulder.

"Jesus Christ," I muttered. It was as much a prayer as it was an oath.

Thirteen

Chestertown and Fairfax
February 16th – 20th
Tuesday - Saturday

"How can you say there's no connection between this new job of yours and the assassination of the congressman?" Maria asked.

I had changed clothes, lit a fire, and poured a glass of sherry for Maria and a scotch for myself. Elizabeth had gone upstairs.

"I mean, he gets whacked at one o'clock and there's a Secret Service agent sneaking around our back door four hours later! How much more of a connection do you need?"

She was pretty worked up.

"All I'm saying, Sweetheart, is that just because DiRienzo is—or was—a friend of Kehoe's doesn't mean that whoever murdered him is going after Kehoe."

"*He* must think that's a possibility," she said. "Otherwise, why on earth is he asking you to take a look at it?"

"Just personal interest, I guess. After all, he and DiRienzo were good friends."

That sounded lame to me even as I said it.

"Exactly," Maria said. "I don't know what all the connections are. But there *are* connections. Remember when I told you my 'gut-think' on this whole job thing was a little bad? Well, it just got a lot worse. And, unfortunately, the train has left the station. We can't stop it now."

I hugged her. It didn't really work.

Thursday afternoon, as I was finishing up my sixth period geometry class, Lisa, my principal, showed up with a young woman in tow. They didn't come in, but stopped outside the open door. I assumed she had just interviewed an applicant for my position and was showing her around the school—a pretty good sign that she was hired.

"Who's that?" piped up Connie Braxton suspiciously when the two women had gone. Connie was one of the students with very few inhibitions when it came to saying—or asking—what was on her mind.

"Dr. Walters and some other woman," I said.

"I can *see* that," Connie snorted. "Who's the other woman?"

"I have no idea," I said, lying through my teeth. Half-lying. I did have an idea, but I didn't know the young woman from Adam. Or Eve.

Next day was Friday, the first day of the two-day Virginia State Track and Field Championship Meet at George Mason University in Fairfax. Crystal and I drove up together in the Explorer after school. Stephanie Stoneham, our high jumper, rode with us. She was the only Augustine Washington athlete competing on Friday evening. Tomorrow, Saturday, we'd have over twenty athletes and would travel by school bus. Today Steph jumped five feet, nine inches—a personal record—that was good enough for a silver medal. On Saturday, both thirty-two-hundred-meter relay teams also got second-place medals, and Bill Parker got a bronze medal for finishing third in the thousand-meter run. We were finished by three thirty, but by the time the school bus got us back to school, it was four forty-five, and I walked in the door of fifteen-oh-six Prince Henry Street at five fifteen. I decided that I'd try and comply with President Kehoe's impossible tasking tomorrow. He'd asked for eight hours, and I'd give him at least that. Tomorrow. Meantime, I planned to spend a few Saturday evening hours enjoying my little family. Cocktails by the fire, grilled New York Strip steaks, maybe a movie at home.

Fourteen

Washington, D. C.
February 21st
Sunday

I set the alarm for six on Sunday morning and went to seven o'clock Mass by myself. One of the deacons preached—make that read, past tense—the homily. It was dreadful. I figured I'd gotten an early start on my term in Purgatory by sitting through it. After Mass, I hit the road for a quick trip up to the National Mall. I got there at eight forty and found a parking space on Constitution Avenue. The Mall was not crowded. Skies were cloudy and a thin coating of frost lay on the dormant brown grass. I walked to where I thought the congressman went down. The National Park Service had apparently cleaned up the blood. There were a few flowers strewn about at one section of the road. Dead roses and carnations, withering in the cold. I looked around. I was about halfway between the Capitol and the Washington Monument. Up ahead of me, towards the Capitol, I saw a photographer. At least I thought he—or she—was a photographer. There was a tripod with some sort of gizmo on it—I assumed it was a camera. The person alongside it wore jeans and a bulky, hooded parka. Hence my ambivalence about gender. I started walking towards him or her. I had no idea what I was looking for.

"Good morning," I said.

"Hi," she said. She looked very young. Twenty-ish.

"Professional?" I asked.

"Not yet," she said with a grin. "Student. Corcoran."

She lifted the camera—a Canon digital SLR—and the tripod and moved the rig about eight feet to her left. I followed. She glanced at the viewfinder and then moved them about another four feet.

"Class project?" I asked.

"Yup," she said. "I was starting Tuesday. When somebody shot that congressman."

"You were *here*?"

"Right around here. I'm trying to find the exact spot. I had just set up my camera right on the location I needed when he went down over there and all hell broke loose."

"You saw the congressman get shot?" I asked, incredulous.

"Not actually," she said. "I was getting ready to take some pictures of the Capitol and the reflecting pool when I heard the shot and then saw someone in a red sweatsuit lying on the sidewalk."

"Did you talk to the cops?"

"No. I folded up my tripod and got the hell out of here," she said. "I didn't know it was that congressman that got shot until I heard it later on the news."

"But you actually heard the shot?"

"Oh, yeah. At least I'm pretty sure. I heard this loud bang—I thought it was a car backfiring. Then I saw the guy in the red sweats down on the sidewalk. And people started screaming. So I hauled ass."

"Did you notice anything else?"

"Are you a cop?"

"No," I said. I debated with myself about whether I should flash my Secret Service ID badge at her. My guardian angel dissuaded me from doing that.

"Just curious," I said.

"The only thing I noticed was a gray soccer-mom minivan that left right after the shot was fired. I almost walked into it as it pulled away. But I did snap a picture of it."

"No way! You actually got a shot of the van?"

"Yeah, I did. I'm sure I still have it."

She fiddled with buttons on the camera and then held it up for me to see. It was a side view of the passenger side of a silver-gray van. No license plates visible. Reflections on the windows made it difficult to make out much from the driver's silhouette. But who knew what the pros could do with it?

"You really should talk to the cops," I said. "They'd probably pay you for that photo."

"No way. I do that and the hassle will be unbelievable."

"Why do you say that?" I asked.

"It's always a hassle when you get mixed up with the cops. Plus, it might be an international incident. My life's complicated enough. My boyfriend is a nut case. My roommate is an alcoholic. I come here early on a quiet Sunday morning looking for peace and quiet to take some pictures and now some stranger is asking me a bunch of questions."

"Sorry," I said. "I was just trying to make conversation. I take a lot of pictures myself. But I'm just an amateur."

She moved the camera and tripod again.

"What made you say talking to the cops would cause an 'international incident'?" I asked.

"I think the driver of the minivan was Japanese."

"Japanese? What made you think that?"

"His looks. Japanese or Chinese. You know. Asian-looking."

She put her forefingers at the outer corners of her eyes and pushed up an eighth of an inch or so.

"Plus the van was a Honda," she added.

As if only Asians drove Hondas. Thank the Lord that this creature was studying photography and not medicine or engineering.

"You didn't see the license number by any chance?" I asked.

"No. By the time I thought to look, the car was too far away. I'm pretty sure it was a Virginia plate, but I'm not even positive about that."

"I really think you should talk to the cops. I don't think they know much. And shooting a U.S. congressman here on the Mall is pretty serious stuff."

"Maybe I will," she said. She gave me a look that told me she had no intention of talking to the cops and was sorry that she'd said so much to me.

"Good luck with the photography," I said.

I walked away and glanced at my watch. Two minutes after nine. Eight hours till my rendezvous with the presidential yacht. I couldn't believe my luck at running into a witness. I wondered if the girl was bullshitting me. I realized I'd never know. But she did have a picture of a gray minivan. Which she said was a Honda.

Fifteen

Chestertown
February 21st
Sunday

It was ten after ten when I pulled into the driveway at fifteen-oh-six Prince Henry Street. Maria's Jetta was gone. I was sure she and Elizabeth were at nine-thirty Mass. I let myself in and started to try and wrap my arms around the assassination of Congressman Erik DiRienzo. I figured I had less than six hours before I had to leave for Quantico and the president's yacht.

With the digital image from the girl's camera still fresh in my mind, I went to several Honda web pages and concentrated on minivans. I concluded that the girl was right; the van was probably a Honda. It looked like an Odyssey.

Then I started thinking about the van's driver—the one the ditzy girl photographer said was "Japanese" or "Chinese." DiRienzo's New York congressional district was upstate and probably didn't have many Asian-American residents. I surfed around and learned that the number was even lower than I had guessed. So low that the probability of the driver of the van—and by extension, the shooter—being ethnic Asians and DiRienzo constituents was virtually nil.

What about other U.S. residents? I asked myself. I Googled "DiRienzo," and there was a ton of stuff. All of it very uncontroversial. He was pretty conservative, especially for a New Yorker. Pro-life. Anti-gun control. Anti-big taxes. Pro-military. Anti-big government. Probably enough there to make a lot of New York lefties screech in outrage. But not likely, I felt, to attract the attention of an Asian-American assassin.

So, I turned my attention overseas. Once again Congressman DiRienzo came across as a moderate, non-controversial Republican. He was a Vietnam vet, but non-controversial there as well. No inflammatory comments or speeches on hot-button issues involving East Asia.

The only "special" thing about him becoming a target was his connection to Jim Kehoe, President of the United States.

So, I started reading stuff on China and Japan. News items, blogs. Foreign. Domestic. In my mind's eye, I saw phalanxes of FBI/CIA/NSA geeks doing the same thing that I was doing and doing it better and more effectively. But I slogged on.

The Japanese seemed to be pretty wrapped up in their own economic woes. The U.S. and Japan had negotiated the relocation of a number of U.S. military units from Japanese territory, but from what I could see, the talks were conducted without rancor. DiRienzo had made no public comment on the issue. There were some weirdo Japanese political and religious factions, but it didn't make sense for them to put a hit on a fairly obscure U.S. congressman.

The Chinese were a different kettle of fish. I read several articles about their ongoing military buildup, particularly their naval modernization. Most of the foreign affairs gurus who were quoted seemed to agree that China wanted to keep their best customer—the good ole USA—buying their stuff. There were a few wild blogs that were howling that the Chinese were trying to destroy us by poisoning our food supplies—and those of our pets! These were difficult to take seriously. There were other blogs that were loaded with innuendo to the effect that, while the Chinese wanted the United States to keep buying their stuff, the guys at the top also wanted to increase their influence—if not outright control—over American policy making. I didn't know whether I should take that line of reasoning seriously or not.

One thing that did get my attention was the almost stridently negative tone of reports of PRC Government statements about the Kehoe administration and Kehoe himself. I couldn't really find a reason for the venom. I'm no Sinologist, but I have observed that, when it comes to the actions by the PRC, it's sometimes tough to figure out whether ideology or pragmatism has the upper hand. The only thing I could find in the media was the U.S. Government's somewhat tepid support for Taiwan's continued existence as a separate political entity from the PRC. And, to my untutored eye at least, that didn't represent any real change since the days of the Nixon administration.

I heard Maria and Elizabeth come in from church, but other than saying "hi," they left me alone. At a little after noon, I took a break, had a peanut butter and jelly sandwich and a cup of coffee.

"How's it going?" Maria asked.

I told her about my witness on the mall.

"Did you get her name?"

"No. According to Mike, Kehoe wants me to avoid getting involved in the 'details' of the investigation."

"But still. It appears that the cops don't know anything about that girl," she said.

"They don't know that I'm trying to give the prez an 'alternate' view of the hit on DiRienzo, either. And that's the way he wants it. Besides, I advised her to go to the cops."

"Do you think she will?"

"No."

"And how is your 'alternate view' coming along?" she asked.

"Right now, it's a mish-mash. I'm up to my ass in a ton of downloads and notes that I can't really make sense out of."

I glanced at my watch.

"And I've got to get all that boiled down to a three-by-five card in three and a half hours."

Sixteen

Quantico and the Potomac River
February 21ˢᵗ
Sunday

To get to the Quantico Marina, one must go through the military part
of the base, cross the Amtrak rail lines, and then go through the tiny
civilian town of Quantico. I parked in front of a Greek restaurant in the
town. There were lights on in the restaurant. It was open. I had read
somewhere that Greek immigrant fishing families had settled the town
of Quantico. A glance at the town's phone directory would support that
contention. It was eighteen minutes before five as I started to climb out
of the Explorer. I dialed home on my cell. Elizabeth answered on the first
ring. I pictured her pouncing on the phone.

"Hi, Sweetie. Ask your mother if she'd like Greek food for dinner,"
I said.

I heard her ask and could hear Maria's enthusiastic assent in the
background.

"Tell her I'll have it with me when I get back home in about an hour
and a half," I said.

Then I went into the restaurant, ordered a Greek salad, some stuffed
grape leaves, and three *souvlaki* sandwiches to go. I paid and told them I'd
be back to pick them up in forty-five minutes or an hour and started to walk
to the docks a couple of blocks away. It was five till five when I got to the
river. I saw a small, white craft powered by a tiny outboard approaching
the marina. It sure as hell wasn't a fifty-six foot yacht. The guy who was
driving waved and I waved back. As he got closer, I realized it was Mike.
As he approached the dock, he put the motor into neutral and tossed me a
line, which I caught and wrapped around a cleat on the quay wall.

"Hop in," he said.

"I was expecting the President of the United States in a fifty-six-foot
yacht," I said. "Nothing personal, but this is kind of a letdown."

58

He grinned.

"Hop in," he repeated. "The yacht's downstream, probably turning around even as we speak. The boss man's aboard and you will be too—inside of five minutes—if you get your ass into the boat."

I sat down on the dock and lowered myself into the boat. Then I retrieved the line from the cleat and pushed us off. Mike put the little outboard in gear and we putt-putted out of the marina and into the river. The Potomac was surprisingly choppy due, no doubt, to a stiff, cold wind blowing out of the north. I looked downstream where Mike headed the skiff.

"*Eliza Dee*," he said. "Mamaroneck, New York. Thar she blows!"

"I think you mean, 'Sail Ho!'" I said.

"Whatever," he said. "The boss's boat."

The yacht slowed and Mike tucked the dinghy neatly alongside. A couple of sailors dressed in blues tossed lines into the boat. Mike made one fast to a cleat and I made the other one fast to another cleat forward. One of the sailors gave me a hand and I was aboard.

"This way, sir," she said. She led the way aft. A Marine opened and held a door for us.

"Welcome aboard," announced the president. "Drink?"

Jim Kehoe stood in a cabin that looked comfortable but not sumptuous. He wore a tan pullover and olive-green corduroy pants. Tan Topsiders rounded out the yachtsman image. He had eyeglasses pushed to the top of his head. There was a desk in one corner of the cabin with some papers and folders that looked as if they had recently been worked on. Luke got up from a starboard leather bench seat, holding a copy of *Sports Illustrated*. Mike had followed me into the cabin.

"Hi, Alan," Luke said. "You're dry, meaning Mike didn't dump you in the river getting out here."

"My loyal Secret Service troops—or your loyal Secret Service agents—are just learning the finer points of small-boat seamanship," Kehoe said with a grin. "I detect a little bit of friendly rivalry."

There were two portholes on either side of the cabin. A glance through one of them suggested that we were going in a big, slow circle. A forward bulkhead held a neoimpressionist rendering of the tidal basin at cherry blossom time. A steward stood behind a small bar. Leather chairs and a sofa surrounded a square coffee table. Unseen speakers carried the skilled plucking of Christopher Parkening rendering Segovia.

"I could use some coffee if you have some made, sir."

He held up two fingers and the steward nodded.

"Coming right up," the president said. "And a reminder. It's Jim."

Fourteen years of wearing the blue suit didn't make this informality come easy to me.

We shook hands, and I took the three-by-five card out of my shirt pocket.

"Are you ready for this?" I asked.

He gestured for us to sit and we did so. Luke and Mike huddled in an aft corner of the cabin and conferred in whispers.

"Number one," I said. "Congressman DiRienzo was murdered by professionals. I estimate the probability of that at point nine-five. Courtesy of the Secret Service."

Out of the corner of my eye, I saw Mike give a "thumbs-up" in our direction, even as he continued his muffled chat with Luke in the corner. Multitasking all the way.

The steward returned with a silver coffee pot, two mugs, cream, and sugar.

"Still take it black?" the president asked.

"What a memory," I said.

He poured, we sipped.

"Number two," I continued. "Fatal shot was fired from a gray minivan parked on the Mall. Probably a Honda Odyssey with Virginia tags. Van departed the Mall immediately after the shooting. I estimate the probability of the foregoing being true at point two. Twenty percent."

The president raised his eyebrows.

"Number three. Driver of the van was Chinese. Probability point zero five. Five percent."

We both took another sip of coffee.

"Number four. Chinese government was behind the hit. Probability point zero-zero-one. One-tenth of one percent.

"Number five. PRC Government is sending a personal message to you by whacking DiRienzo. Probability greater than zero, but still finite."

I put the index card on the coffee table and slid it over to him. I half-expected the president to have a couple of Marines throw me over the side into the Potomac. Instead, he leaned his head back and appeared to stare at the cabin's overhead. Then he looked down again and smiled.

"I just love it when someone confirms my own suspicions. Independently. At least with numbers three, four, and five."

"But remember, Jim. My probabilities on those guesses are extremely low. Bordering on the infinitesimal."

He tapped the three-by-five card with his forefinger.

"Duly noted," he said. "If I told you I'd spoken with Rick DiRienzo a little over a week ago about being appointed vice president, would that change your probabilities? Syd Girtler has a heart condition and is thinking of resigning at the end of the year and spending more time with his grandchildren."

I didn't say anything. Just sat there and looked stupid. The president stood up and I did too.

"I didn't say that. You didn't hear it," he said.

"Hear what?"

"You've got the idea. Now I've got to get this tub headed upstream. You're welcome to come along and join Franny and me for dinner at the White House."

"Thanks, Jim. If I accepted, there are two women in Chestertown— whom you now know—who are expecting Greek takeout and would be highly pissed if I failed to show up with it."

"Fair enough. I'll have Mike run you ashore. And thanks, Alan. This is exactly the kind of thing I'm hiring you for."

"You're very welcome, Mr. President. Sorry about the low probabilities. And you shouldn't forget that they *are* very low. Long odds, to say the least."

"That's what I never get from the Intelligence Community. The long-odds stuff. And that's the kind of stuff that jumps up and bites us in the ass every once in a while. So thanks again."

We shook hands.

"Say 'hi' to Maria and Elizabeth for me," he said, with a grin. "And enjoy the Greek food."

Five minutes later, I was climbing out of the dinghy onto the quay wall in the marina. Forty minutes after that, I pulled into our driveway on Prince Henry Street. The Explorer smelled like a *taverna* minus the *ouzo*.

And I hadn't said anything to the president about the mole. But there had to be one. *Had* to be. There was no way the Chinese were getting that kind of inside scoop—especially about Kehoe's chat with DiRienzo—from satellites.

Seventeen

Chestertown
February 26th - March 2nd
Friday - Tuesday

Friday at school, I broke the news to the kids that it was my last day. I told them I had a classified assignment given me by the President of the United States, and I had no choice. Their reactions varied. Most of them seemed to feel that I'd totally betrayed them.

"You're our *teacher!*" they said. "You *can't* leave us!" Several of the ninth grade girls actually cried. Needless to say, not a hell of a lot of learning went on in Mr. Llewellyn's math classes that day. I made the mistake of telling my first period Algebra One class at the beginning of the period and the ensuing brouhaha prevented us from ever getting to *any* algebra. The other classes already knew about my impending departure by the time they came through the door.

It was even tougher sledding with the track team. The season was over. I was finished and so were they. So I had to call a meeting after seventh period. I put the announcement in and crossed my fingers, hoping that nobody would show up. Fat chance. They all showed up. I was packing personal classroom stuff into cardboard boxes. I told them what I'd told my math students. Most of them seemed to know already. Once again, a number of the younger girls cried. I felt like a total turd.

On March first, the mercury made it up to seventy-one degrees Fahrenheit. The crocuses had come and gone and a few daffodils were blooming in front of our house, which faced south. March first was a Monday and also my first day on my new job.

I'd already reacted to a bunch of "fly-fishing" emails. Everything you'd imagine—fingerprinting, drug tests, a physical, but surprisingly little paper. My new office spaces at Martha Washington University were being painted and furnished, so I'd be working from home for a few days. Luke and Mike had delivered a new high-end laptop and two new cell phones, all Government Issue. One phone was strictly for POTUS inner-circle traffic, the other for the world at large, but mainly government. Luke reminded me of the emergency number and the codes that went with it.

"Don't forget it," he said.

I spent most of March first fooling around with a table of organization on a legal pad, keeping in mind the president's guidance to hold the numbers to thirty or fewer. After toying with it for a couple of hours, I figured I could do what the president wanted with a total of sixteen bodies, including myself. I figured wrong.

At five o'clock, I went for a run. It was still warm and it felt great not to have to bundle up against the cold. It was pretty humid, but that felt good, too.

As I finished and slowed to a walk in front of our house shortly before six, huge, warm drops of rain began pelting down. By the time I reached our mudroom in back, the rain had turned into a downpour of tropical proportions. At ten o'clock, when I went up to bed, I could still hear liquid dripping from the eaves, so I was surprised when I glanced out the window before turning in and saw snow falling.

By six a.m. on the second, the temperature was twenty-one and about six inches of snow were on the ground. There were some pretty sporty icicles hanging from our roof. Flakes the size of nickels were still falling. I clicked on a local TV news show, ascertained that All Saints Academy was closed and taped a note to that effect on the mirror of the bathroom Elizabeth used.

I got the coffee started, retrieved the papers, and surfed through bits and pieces of various morning news shows. When the coffee was done, I poured myself a mug and rooted around in the freezer till I found a package of breakfast sausages. I put some water in a small skillet, dropped the frozen sausages in, put a lid on the skillet and turned on the gas. Then I rooted around some more and turned up pancake flour and a half-pint of blueberries. Since I was working from home, I really couldn't goof off all day like I used to when I was a teacher and a snow day came along. But at least I could have a yummy breakfast with Maria and Elizabeth. By the time the sausages were thawed, I'd mixed up the pancake batter and decided to wait for the ladies.

It's not possible for me to start playing with an organizational structure without thinking about at least some specific bodies to fill some of the key slots. I knew that I needed a secretary or office manager—and soon. But

I didn't think having one start working for me while I was working from home was such a hot idea. Our house is roomy—but not *that* roomy. So, I'd wait till I opened up shop on campus.

The next job I needed to fill was what I'd probably call "vice chairman" or "deputy director." In reality, it would be an alter ego, someone with whom to brainstorm. The first name that popped into my mind had an Annapolis connection. Darpley Roentgen Taylor. I'm pretty sure "Darps," as he was known, was the smartest guy I'd ever known. He had finished number one in our class at the Naval Academy, then had gone into the Navy Nuclear Power Program. Somewhere along the way, I'd learned that he had got out of the Navy, picked up a Ph.D., and was running his own consulting business. It didn't take long for me to find *Savants, Inc.* in the online yellow pages. I went to the firm's website. "Consultants to Governments," it read. "Solvers of Real-World Problems—National and International." It listed Darpley R. Taylor as "Scholar-in-Chief." It had links to studies: www. InterpretingLawoftheSeaTreaty, www.MakingSenseofKyoto, www. BangsforBuxGlobalWarmingorDisease, to name a few. And there was a phone number with a two-zero-two area code. The nation's capital. I looked at my watch. Five till seven. I dialed the Savants' number, thinking I'd leave a message, but wasn't all that surprised when I heard "Savants. Taylor."

"Darps!" I said. "You're up early."

"Wait a minute," he said. There was a brief pause. "Alan? Shipmate?"

"Damn! You're good!" I said.

"I know," he said. "I also have Caller ID. And why, pray tell, are you calling me at seven o'clock on a snowy morning?"

"Because I just thought of you and figured that, if anybody in D.C. would answer the phone, you would."

"Well, you've got me there," he said. "But there has to be more."

"Oh yes. Much more. Can I buy you lunch?"

"When and where?"

"Globe and Laurel. Route One in Stafford. Two or three miles south of the main gate of the Quantico Marine Base. Noon tomorrow?"

"Make it twelve thirty and I'll be there," he said. "If the roads are still a problem, I'll call."

"They should be fine by tomorrow."

We rang off and I jotted the time and date in my planner.

It was a good thing we had made the lunch date for tomorrow. At two minutes past nine, Luke called.

"Coffee at Imperium in twenty minutes?" he asked.

"Roger that. See you in twenty," I answered.

The snow had stopped, and Luke already had his *cappuccino* when I walked into the coffee shop at nine twenty. He looked a little frayed around the edges.

I ordered a *due-doppio espresso*, ladled sugar into it, and sat down.

"What's up, amigo?" I asked.

"Whitehead. The White House Chief of Staff. And I don't really know what's up. Just that he seems to have a wild hair up his ass and wants to meet you for lunch. Today."

I took a slurp of coffee.

"What makes you think he has a wild hair up his ass?"

"Just a feeling I got. I was looking at the boss's schedule yesterday, and he and the chief are scheduled to meet with you next week at Quantico. Then, Whitehead called me a minute or so before I called you this morning and said he wanted to meet you for lunch. Today. He was matter-of-fact, but I think I sensed a little testiness there."

"Where are we having lunch?"

"*Buzkashi.* An Afghan place in Alexandria. Whitehead spent a couple of tours in Afghanistan. You're scheduled to meet him at noon. Reservations under Whitehead's name. I gather he's a regular there. And if you don't mind, I'll drive. I won't go into the restaurant with you, but I think it might be useful if I'm there when you come out."

Eighteen

Alexandria and Chestertown
March 2nd
Tuesday

Luke drove my new black Expedition. Also government issue. I wondered about the federal government's fixation with black SUVs. He dropped me a half block from the restaurant in Alexandria. The temperature had climbed above freezing and the street and sidewalk were slushy. It was five before noon when I went through the door.

"My name is Llewellyn. I'm meeting Mr. Whitehead here for lunch. I'm told he has a reservation."

"Right this way, sir," a dark-skinned man in an expensive suit said. He led me to a table and handed me a large and tasteful menu. "Would you care for a drink?"

He flashed me a dazzling smile.

"Yes, please. I'd like a Bloody Mary."

The drink arrived quickly, and Whitehead came in about five minutes later.

"Alan," he said with a big, mouth-only smile. "Sorry I'm late."

Walt Whitehead was aptly named. His hair was all white and cut very short. It made a pronounced widow's peak in the middle of his high forehead. His eyebrows were as white as his hair. His face was tanned and, for the most part, unlined. His mouth resembled a coin slot in a self-service newspaper rack. He could have been anywhere from thirty-five to fifty. He wasn't wearing glasses and his eyes were the same color gray as the slush in the Alexandria gutters.

"Good," he said. "You've got a drink. I'll have a *Tsingtao*, please," he said to the host.

A waiter returned immediately with the Chinese beer and poured about two-thirds of a glass. Whitehead picked it up.

"Did you know that German settlers started brewing *Tsingtao* beer in China early in 1903?" he asked.

"No sir. I had no idea."

"Cheers!" he said, flashing the grin and lifting the glass. "Glad to finally meet you. And welcome to the team."

"Thank you sir," I said. "And cheers."

I'd only had a sip of the Bloody Mary before he'd arrived. It was delicious. After our little toast, I took another sip. Still delicious. I could taste Old Bay, horseradish, and a generous dose of *Stolichnaya*.

Whitehead put his glass down. He looked down at the tablecloth for a second and then looked up at me. His gaze changed from friendly grin to pure malevolence.

"What the fuck did you think you were doing when you implicated the Chinese in the DiRienzo assassination?" he hissed.

I waited for a second or two, swallowed and said: "Excuse me, sir. Would you run that by me again?"

He leaned over and poked the table with a forefinger.

"I said, what the fuck did you think you were doing when you were pointing fingers at the Chinese? You've got zero evidence that they were involved in offing DiRienzo. The secretary of state is all pissed off at you. The whole State Department is pissed off at you. So are the CIA and the NSA. You're not exactly off to a promising start."

I leaned back and thought for a few seconds. I chose my words carefully.

"If I didn't respect the Office of the President and the incumbent so much, I'd throw this goddamn Bloody Mary in your face, Whitehead. You can take this lunch and stick it up your ass."

He held up his hand.

"Now just a—"

"I'm not finished! Our boss—yours and mine—told me to give him my take on the DiRienzo whack job and that's exactly what I did. And if I understand him correctly, he doesn't want you or the State Department or CIA or NSA spinning what I'm telling him. If he's changed his mind on that score, I'll strike my colors and go right back to teaching high school math. But I'll get that word to him myself. I'm sure as hell not going to depend on you for that. Meantime, you can go fuck yourself!"

I stood up, dropped my napkin on the chair and left. If I tried to tell you that my pulse rate was normal, it would be a huge lie.

Well, that does it, I thought as I was walking out the door. *Telling the White House Chief of Staff to go fuck himself. I'll probably be lucky to get a job teaching pre-algebra to death row inmates in Mississippi.*

Outside, Luke pulled even with me in the Expedition and I climbed in.

"Fast lunch," he said.

"I just told the White House Chief of Staff to go fuck himself," I said.

Luke let loose a rip of laughter.

"Goddamn. I'm sorry I missed that!" he said and laughed some more.

I sat in silence till we cleared town and headed south on the George Washington Parkway.

"I can't believe it," I said. "The snotty bastard started giving me a ration of shit about the report I gave the boss about DiRienzo's murder. He seemed especially pissed about me mentioning the Chinese. Said the secretary of state, CIA, and NSA are all pissed off. How the fuck do they even *know* about my little three-by-five card?"

"They probably don't," Luke said. "Whitehead probably was blowing smoke up your ass."

"But why?"

"All politicians are pricks. And Whitehead is a politician. Ergo. He's a prick as well. He wants total control over *everything* that reaches POTUS. That includes your stuff. My guess is that he just used the Chinese angle to browbeat you into lining up with the rest of the jerkoffs that toady up to the boss. And to him."

"Well, then. What now? I just walked out on the asshole after telling him to go fuck himself. I don't see how I can proceed with business as usual."

"That's *exactly* what you do need to do. Keep building your organization. Move into your new office spaces on campus. Have your meeting with the boss and the chief and re-verify the ground rules as you understand them."

"The only problem with that," I said, "is that I could be just digging myself into a deeper hole. Suppose Kehoe decides to change the ground rules? Has me reporting to Whitehead all the time. I'm hosed. The President of the United States is buying more useless drivel. And that prick Whitehead is in the catbird seat."

"I don't think that will happen. I think the boss will jerk Whitehead's leash a little and tell him in no uncertain terms that it's a straight pipe from you to him. No playing the stuff back to anybody. If he doesn't, you should just threaten to quit. You could probably negotiate a princely severance package. Holy shit—imagine the book you could write!"

"But, goddamn it, Luke. I don't play those kinds of games. I'd never even *think* of writing one of those Washington insider books about this stuff."

"You know that. And I know that. But nobody else knows that. Everybody else thinks otherwise. Anyone else in your shoes would write that book in a heartbeat. This is Washington. That's what people do. Stab somebody in the back, grab the money, and run."

I rode the rest of the way in silence. The gray of the sky and the melting snow and the naked beeches and oaks complemented my thoughts and mood perfectly.

When Luke pulled the Expedition into my driveway, he turned to me as he put the truck in park and turned off the ignition.

"So what are you going to do?" he asked.

"Just what you suggested," I said. "Business as usual. And I'll put all the cards on the table next week when I meet with the boss and Whitehead."

"I'll talk to you before then about 'all the cards on the table.' You may want to hold a few cards back in reserve. Meantime, I'll use Secret Service channels to leak a little of Whitehead's toxic interference back to the boss. See if I can get a reaction. From the boss. Or Whitehead. Or both."

He handed me the keys and opened the driver's side door.

"Whatever happens," he said with a grin. "I think it's great that you told Whitehead to go fuck himself!"

He closed the door, went down the driveway to the sidewalk and turned left. Toward the river. Apparently Walt Whitehead wasn't "Mr. Congeniality" with the Secret Service.

Nineteen

Chestertown
March 2nd
Tuesday

Maria glanced at her watch when I walked in. She was working at her laptop, surrounded by what looked like library books and opened magazines.

"Couldn't have been much of a lunch," she said. "Is Walt Whitehead a fast eater?"

"I don't know. I walked out. Right after I told him to go fuck himself."

She gasped.

"You didn't! The White House Chief of Staff!"

"Yes I did. The bastard started to chew my ass for the briefing I gave Kehoe on the DiRienzo hit. Said the State Department, the CIA, and NSA are all pissed off. About the Chinese connection I made. Like he's been broadcasting it all over town. That's when I told him what I told him and walked out."

"Have you been fired?"

"I don't think so. As far as I know, Kehoe is the only one who can fire me. I'm starving—I think I'll fix a sandwich. Have you eaten yet?"

"Yes. But there's some tuna salad left in the fridge. What happens now?"

"Luke suggested that I continue the march. Business as usual. He said he thinks Whitehead is bullshitting. As part of a power play. That he doesn't want me or anyone else to have direct access to the boss. Apparently, I have a meeting scheduled with Kehoe and Whitehead next week. I'll go over the ground rules with both of them. Meantime, Luke is trying to get word of Whitehead's little tirade to Kehoe through Secret Service channels."

I retrieved a Tupperware bowl of tuna salad, a jar of dill pickles, some lettuce and mayo from the fridge and started building a sandwich.

"I'll never understand the ways of Washington," Maria said.

"Me, either. Luke says that if Kehoe allows Whitehead to filter our stuff, I should threaten to quit. Kehoe would be so scared of the book that I'd be sure to write about this whole fiasco that he'd agree to whatever I want."

"That doesn't sound like you," she said.

"It's not," I said, pouring a glass of pinot grigio.

Maria turned back toward her laptop and I headed for the kitchen table with my lunch and the latest issue of *Field and Stream*.

She stopped typing and looked up.

"Oh yeah," she said. "Remember you asked me if a Chinese family had moved into the neighborhood?"

"Yup."

"Well, I saw an Asian woman pushing a stroller across the street yesterday. She could have been Chinese."

"Hmm," I said, taking a bite of my sandwich. "I guess we must have some new neighbors."

After lunch, I went through my email. Nothing there about being fired. Luke's advice seemed to be okay. There was one "fly-fishing" message. It appeared to be an ad. I opened it. *Sign up now for fly-fishing course for Bay rockfish and bluefish. Deadline is 3 p.m., March 10. Course location is Lake Lunga Recreation Area, Quantico.* That meant meeting at three on March tenth on the base near where I had my little jog with the president. With the boss. And, if Luke was right, Whitehead as well. *We shall see,* I thought.

I went back to my draft organization chart. Darps was still on for lunch tomorrow—at least as far as I knew. Another crucial staff member would be the office manager. Thinking of my lunch with Darps at the Globe and Laurel brought to mind Judy Palladino. Judy was a neighbor who had been a consulting client of mine. Our first meeting was at the old Globe and Laurel. I'd been able to help her recover a family heirloom that a shadowy Italian religious group had stolen from her. At the time, she'd held a fairly high position in the Marine Corps computer systems acquisition bureaucracy. She seemed to be a real go-getter, cool under fire, and we got along well. I wondered if she'd be interested in going to work for the White House. Right here in Chestertown. I also wondered if there were creative human relations tactics available to get her a pay raise and keep her government bennies. I made a note to ask about hooking up with some government HR gurus.

The front door slammed. I glanced at the clock icon on the laptop. Three-ten. Elizabeth was home. Time for a break.

"Hi, Daughter," I said as Elizabeth walked in.

"Hi, Dad."

She was sorting through the mail that she must have retrieved from the mailbox on her way in. I studied her for a second. An amazing combination of coltish kid and pretty young woman. Wavy, black hair, a little mussed by the wind. Maria's delicate facial features. Which I considered absolutely beautiful. Now standing about five-four, Elizabeth had grown almost three inches in the past year. She wore a navy pea coat over her All Saints uniform, the lower half consisting of a blue plaid kilt and navy blue knee socks. She was still wearing a red backpack, loaded with books.

"Look!" she said. "A sure sign of spring! The L.L. Bean fishing catalog!"

"Feel free to read and drool. Just don't squirrel it away someplace in your room where I can't find it," I said.

Like I told the president, Elizabeth is quite the fly fisherman. She had a nice and delicate touch with the kids' starter fly rod we'd bought from L.L. Bean. We'd started out with pan fish and then graduated to smallmouth bass and trout. A little while back, all three of us took a two-day course on fly-fishing for stripers in Maine.

Maria came into the kitchen.

"You'll never guess what your father told the White House Chief of Staff," she said with a grin.

"What?"

"I can't repeat it," she said.

"Mom! That's *soo* not fair! Daring me to guess and then saying you can't repeat it!"

She turned to me.

"What did you tell him, Dad?" she asked.

I thought for a couple of seconds.

"I told him to do something unspeakably vile and physically impossible."

She lip-synched the words. Then she gasped. Just like her mother had an hour and a half ago.

"Dad! You didn't! The White House Chief of Staff!"

She had a sheepish grin on her face. It hadn't taken her long to break the code.

"I think your dad's waiting for the other shoe to drop," Maria said. "As in getting notice that he's fired."

"That is too funny!" Elizabeth said.

"You're not worried about me getting fired?" I asked.

"No, Dad. Not at all," she said. "The president really likes you—that was obvious at Camp David. And even if he did fire you, you could always get another teaching job. They always need math teachers."

Sometimes kids have the most amazing insights.

"Elizabeth. This is one of those 'family confidential' issues. Not to be aired out with Tala and Esmé or anybody," Maria said.

"Mom! Do you think I'm an idiot?"

"No, of course not," Maria said. "Just being careful."

"For what it's worth," I said. "Since the second shoe hasn't dropped yet, I think maybe it's not going to drop."

"You mean you're not going to get fired?" Elizabeth asked.

"I don't think so. I could be wrong, but I really think if it was going to happen, it would have happened already."

"I still think it's hilarious! 'Unspeakably vile and physically impossible.' You sure have a way with words, Dad!"

She giggled.

"I think I'll go for a run," I said.

"I've got to change. I'm due at Tala's at four to work on a science project," she said.

I was glad the subject had changed. She had figured out what I'd said a little too quickly for my comfort.

Twenty

As of noon the next day, there was no email or telephone message to the contrary, so I guessed my lunch date with Darps was still on. I kissed Maria and left in the Expedition, heading north.

The Globe and Laurel is an unofficial Marine Corps and FBI institution. Started and owned by a retired Marine Corps officer, it is named after the insignia of the British Royal Marines, which was also the first emblem of the U.S. Marines. Today's eagle, globe, and anchor came later. I am told the U.S. Marines and their British counterparts have a close and comradely relationship.

In its first life, the G&L had opened in the early seventies in Quantico Town as a beer-and-sandwich pub. A few years later, the building housing it had burned to the ground and the pub re-opened off base in the town of Triangle. The new place was larger and a bit more upscale and featured a fancier menu and atmosphere. It was at the new location that it started to attract instructors and students from the FBI Academy, which is located on the west side of the Marine Corps Base. And then, in the early twenty-first century, the place got shoved off the scene due to development and moved a few miles south to Stafford, putting it closer to the Marine Corps Officer Basic School and the FBI Academy. Not to mention fifteen-oh-six Prince Henry Street.

I arrived a few minutes before our agreed-upon time of twelve thirty. I looked around. I saw a lot of folks having lunch, but none of them looked like Darps. The good news was that the background noise level was high enough that I didn't think our conversation would be overheard.

"My name's Llewellyn and I'm meeting a guy named Taylor for lunch," I told the hostess.

"Sure, sir. I'll make sure that he joins you. Is he military or civilian? And could I get you a drink?"

"Civilian. Now," I said. "And could I please have a Bloody Mary?"

I'd had only two sips of the one I'd ordered yesterday before I'd walked out on Whitehead. A few minutes later the hostess re-surfaced with a Bloody Mary and a balding and bearded man in a tweed jacket and gray flannels in tow. The eyeglasses didn't hide the small brown eyes with the humorous glint. Even so, he looked a helluva lot different than when I'd seen him last.

"Darps!" I said.

"Shipmate!" he said. We shook hands and he ordered a Bloody Mary.

We made small talk till his drink came. I picked up mine.

"Cheers, Shipmate," I said. I took a swig of the Bloody Mary. It was even better than yesterday's.

"Cheers, Matey," Darps said and took a swig through his beard.

"What's up?" he asked, putting his glass down.

"Let me get it out on the table without any preliminary bullshit," I began. "I've been offered and have accepted a highly-classified, high-level U.S. Government assignment. I'm interested in having you join me. I'm asking you if you want me to continue this discussion or if you'd rather I switch the conversation to baseball spring training or the plans for our class's next reunion."

He took a sip of his Bloody Mary. The waitress showed up. He glanced at the menu in front of him. I'd already looked and decided.

"Prime rib sandwich," I said. "Coleslaw on the side."

"Same for me," Darps said.

"Oh, and I'll take a glass of the house merlot with the sandwich," I said.

"*Moi aussi,*" Darps added.

The waitress smiled.

"I'll get those orders right in," she said, without writing anything down.

"Okay, Shipmate. Back to my original question," I said when the waitress had gone.

"I sense a trap, but please continue," he said. "I assure you it'll go no further unless it's grossly illegal or gravely dangerous."

"It's not grossly illegal. But it might be slightly illegal. I haven't discussed the matter with any lawyers. And it could be a little dangerous."

"Okay. What the hell. Deal me in."

"Okay, Darps. Here goes. White House appointment. Set up a small, out-of-the-loop intelligence activity. To do a, quote, 'sanity check,' unquote, on the stuff that the big boys produce. That's my job. One-year appointment. Renewable after that."

The waitress showed up with our sandwiches and the glasses of wine. We polished off the dregs of the Bloody Marys and put the glasses down. The waitress smiled and picked up the empties.

"Enjoy your sandwiches, gentlemen," she said and was gone.

"You're shitting me," he whispered.

"No, sir," I said. "This is God's truth as I know it. Office on a nearby college campus. Fewer than thirty personnel. I'm the one who's setting it up. And I'm the one who reports to the boss man. That's Papa-Oscar-Tango-Uniform-Sierra himself. Directly, as in face-to-face. I need to hire someone ostensibly as a deputy. In actuality, you'd be an alter ego. Someone with whom to bounce ideas off, take over if I go down. The first person I thought of was you."

"Sweet Jesus," he said. "I've heard of some very squirrelly schemes in the U.S. Government before, but this one takes the cake. What'll they pay me?"

"One-hundred-forty K. Same as they pay me."

He took a bite of his sandwich and followed it up with a sip of merlot.

"Can I have a couple of days to think about it?" he asked. "The way I see it—through my eyeballs—the issue of whether I can turn over Savants, Inc., to my dash-two is the war-stopper. If I can work that out and not lose my ass, hat, and overcoat in the bargain, then maybe we can do business. For a year. Or maybe longer. And then there's the issue of whether Mama Taylor thinks we can survive a sixty percent pay cut. We can, but the issue is whether she thinks we can. Then, there will be a shitload of details. Stuff that you and I will have to work on. But the big enchilada right now is whether I can break loose and do it."

"There are a couple of complications," I said. "First one is that you can't tell Mama Tee about the White House connection unless and until you sign on the dotted line.

"The second one is the White House Chief of Staff."

"Whitehead? Jesus. How so?"

"I might get fired, even before I start," I said.

I was in the middle of telling him all the sordid details of my run-in with Whitehead yesterday when one of my new cell phones vibrated.

"Sorry," I said, taking the phone out. "I don't turn this one off."

It was Luke.

"Hey," I said.

"Your buddy got hauled off to the woodshed," Luke said. "I hear the boss worked him over pretty well and made a Christian out of him."

"Sweet," I said. "That means 'my buddy' will want to make *me* a Christian so he can toss me to the lions."

"I think it would be a good idea to watch your back. Remember what I said about politicians."

"Thanks. I'll talk to you soon."

"Stay well. And avoid dark alleys."

I pocketed the phone.

"That was one of the two Secret Service guys keeping tabs on me and keeping my line to the boss open. Luke Wallace and Mike Atwater. If you take the job, I'm sure you'll meet them soon. That was Luke. According to him, the latest chapter in the Whitehead saga is that the boss just chewed his ass for his muddling yesterday. So the part of Issue Number Two about me maybe getting fired seems to have gone away. For now."

"Are there any more?" he asked. "Issues that I should know about?"

"Yeah. There are one or two that are simmering. But not developed enough to talk about now."

I didn't get into any of the DiRienzo hit job details or the mole issue either.

"Are you really sure you want me to take this job?" he asked. "I mean, it seems like you're trying to put a really ugly face on it and talk me out of it."

"*Au contraire*," I said. "Just trying to be honest with you. And I'm being honest with you as well when I say I think we can have an ass-kicking good time doing this job. Even if you do have to take a pay cut."

I didn't tell him about the pay *raise* that I was going to get.

"When?" he asked.

"I started the day before yesterday. ASAP for you."

"Figured as much. Give me twenty-four hours. I'll email you. Blue if it's a go. Gold if it's not. Three-digit number will be the number of the day of this year that I can start. 'Blue zero-six-two' would be 'Yes. Can start March third.' Here's a card with home and cell phone numbers as well as email. Probably not a good idea to reach me at the office any more."

"Agreed," I said. "And Darps..."

"Yo."

He was standing up. I remained seated.

"Wanna split the lunch tab?" he asked, reaching for his wallet.

"No, no. It's on me. I dragged you down here."

"Well thanks. It was good. Like I said, I'll email you."

"Don't let me down, Shipmate. I don't have a backup plan," I said, stealing a page from Cheetah's notebook on arm-twisting.

Darps smiled.

I saw the waitress approaching with the tab. I reached for my wallet. By the time I looked up, my bald and bearded classmate was gone.

Twenty-One

Chestertown
March 3rd
Wednesday

I got home from lunch at the same time that Elizabeth got off the bus. The "little-girl-big-girl" syndrome kicked in again as I watched her walk to the house from the bus stop. It's a curse that fathers have to live through. The newly shapely legs. The kid's red backpack, loaded with textbooks. The gorgeous features. The sprinkling of zits. Still very much a kid, but womanhood was very much on the near horizon.

"Hi, Dad!" she said with a big grin. "Did you get fired yet?"

"Not that I know of, Sweetheart. I actually tried to do some hiring today."

I held the front door open for her.

"Hi, Mom!" she announced as she strode into the house.

"Hi, Mom!" I repeated.

"Well, well," Maria said. "The scholar and the spy are both home."

"You could write a poem with that line, Mom," Elizabeth said as she shrugged off her backpack.

"Yeah," I said. "Something like 'Home is the scholar, home from school. And the spy home from the snake pit.'"

"Bad day?" Maria asked.

"No, not really. At least I don't think so. Not yet, anyway. I tried to hire Darps at lunch. He was noncommittal, but he did tell me he'd have to take a sixty percent pay cut."

"Oh, the poor dear! How much will you pay him?"

"Uncle Sugar will pay him one hundred and forty thou, same as me."

"And did you tell him you'd be getting a raise that is more than one-hundred-fifty percent?"

"No. I don't want him to think that his new boss is a loser. By the way, Luke called. He said the boss chewed Whitehead out royally."

Elizabeth tittered when she heard me mention Whitehead's name and then went upstairs.

"Well, if he was angry at you yesterday, just imagine how mad he is today," Maria said.

"I know. Comforting thought. Guess I'd better check my email."

I did. The most recent one had been sent just three minutes ago.

From: roentgen86@ausable.com
To: allewellyn@ptolemy.com
Subj: Ahoy
Blue 068

Darps was a go. I checked the calendar. Zero-six-eight meant he could start a week from yesterday. I needed to line up the U.S. Government hiring machinery. It was a few minutes after three. I called Luke's cell phone number and got dumped into voicemail.

"Let's run at five," I said.

Loosely translated, that meant that I'd be running past the spot where he and Mike had intercepted me on the morning when this whole business started. One of the two would be there and ready to run, giving us a chance for a semi-private conversation. Unless they came back with a fallback.

There was another fly-fishing email. It was an ad for the "Grand Opening" of an online tackle store on March fifth. That meant the new office—my new office—would be ready Friday!

Luke was at the spot on the river where we made connections at five o'clock, and we started running.

After a few seconds, he said "I thought the plan was for us to talk, not to try and run poor old Luke's dick into the dirt."

I laughed and slowed down.

"Sorry. I guess I'm on a bit of an adrenalin rush," I said. Little did I know that said adrenalin rush was about to spike.

"That's better," he said. "What's—*get down!*" he yelled.

He slammed into me, and I tumbled into a patch of melting snow with Luke on top of me. I sensed a little burst of flame and a puff of blue smoke before I heard the gunshot. It came from a slow-moving silver-gray Honda Odyssey, and I'd bet my first government paycheck that it was the same van I'd seen on the girl's digital SLR in D.C. I rolled over as Luke got up on one knee and pulled out a handgun.

"Son of a bitch!" he said.

The minivan was accelerating.

"Too far! Fuck!" said Luke, more to himself than to me. He put the weapon back inside his jacket and gave me a hand up out of the snow patch. He tapped a little plastic gizmo in his right ear.

"Mike saw them moving in," he said. "He was too far back to get off a shot. But he gave us a warning."

"Who the hell was it?" I asked. "Were they trying to whack you or me?"

"My guess is that they weren't trying to whack anybody. If they were, one of us or both of us would be dead. I think they just wanted to send a message."

"I think that was the same van that left the scene right after DiRienzo was killed," I said.

"That may be part of the message, too."

"Are you going to call the cops?"

He paused. Listened for a second.

"Mike is doing that as we speak."

"Will we have to be interviewed? That would be the last fucking thing I need."

"You're telling me. But no. This baby will be kept very quiet. Let's run some more."

We started running again. Slowly. There didn't appear to be any eyewitnesses to our little encounter with the guys in the Odyssey. It took a couple of hundred meters for the adrenalin rush to subside—at least for mine.

"Okay Alan. This is your meeting," Luke said. "What was it you wanted to talk about?"

"Shit. I almost forgot. Some asshole shooting at me in broad daylight distracted me just a bit," I said. "Anyway, 'personnel' is the subject. As in HR. I just hired a guy who's going to start next week. The new digs are going to be ready on Friday. I need a contact that can get the new hires signed up and make sure they get paid, get their bennies, and that sort of thing. Not to mention me. Who started working yesterday."

"What position? The guy you just hired?"

"Deputy. Technically. He'll actually be my other half. Take over for me if something happens. And I need to hire an office manager ASAP, as well."

"I'll talk to our headquarters and get you a name and number of an HR pro at least. Maybe he or she will morph into another soul on board. Anything else?"

"Just that I got a fly-fishing email about the meeting next week. On base. The Lunga Recreation Area."

"Yeah. He's going for a run at Quantico. He wants Whitehead at the meeting. But Whitehead doesn't run. So the meeting will be at a picnic table back in the woods after the boss finishes his run. Wear running clothes and your badge. We'll go together."

We turned around and headed back. Mike joined us and the three of us ran to our pickup spot, and then I picked up the pace and ran home alone.

Twenty-Two

Chestertown
March 3rd
Wednesday

I decided not to mention the shooting incident when I got back to the house on Prince Henry Street. I think Maria felt that I was totally safe when I was running with a Secret Service agent, and I didn't want to upset that particular apple cart. I did change my evening cocktail from a light Scotch to a potent vodka martini. Maria had her usual dry sherry.

"I'm thinking of asking Judy Palladino to be office manager," I said.

"Have you asked her?"

"No. Darps will be on board next week. I think I'll talk to him first. Maybe he's got someone better."

"Somehow, I doubt it," Maria said. "Maybe in relevant experience. But I don't think you or Darps could find anyone with better judgment and more grace under pressure than Judy."

Maria knew Judy well from the family heirloom recovery adventure. Probably knew her better than I did.

"And, I would think that time is critical," she continued. "The sooner you get an office manager, the better off you'll be. And the better off your organization will be. By the way, have you figured out a name for it? The organization?"

"No. I haven't," I said. "Haven't thought about it, really."

"That shows that you need an office manager ASAP. To mind all the little details—and some of the big ones, like naming the place—while the boss does the grand strategy."

Elizabeth had appeared silently, thumbs no doubt exhausted from texting.

"I have an idea for a name," she said.

85

"What?"

"Bureau of International Affairs Studies. *BIAS*," she said.

"Hmm," I said. "Not bad. Innocuous. Which is good. A little ironic. Also good. I'll run it by Kehoe when I see him next week."

"I don't think you should 'run it by' him," Maria said. "Just tell him. *Fait accompli*. If you invite him to micromanage, you're asking for Whitehead to jump back into the game."

Elizabeth giggled but didn't say anything.

"Yeah, you're right. Best keep the creep at arm's length. Whitehead, not Kehoe. And, I'll email Judy about coming on board first thing in the morning," I said. "Run up the flag and see if she salutes."

"Time to start the pasta," Maria said. "Could I have another splash of sherry?"

Maria was fixing *Penne alla Arrabiata*. The blended aromas of pancetta, tomatoes, and chilies had me almost weeping. I poured Maria's splash of sherry and the dregs of the martini shaker for me.

Maria and Elizabeth left me alone in the living room and went into the kitchen to rattle the dishes. I sat there staring into the dead fireplace and wondered about getting lead "messages" fired from a gray minivan by people who had killed a U.S. congressman. I thought about the possible China connection. A Chinese mole. And wondered.

Dinner was drop-dead delicious. I violated the grain-no-grape rule and had a glass of decent *Chianti Classico* with my pasta. After catching the first fifteen minutes of the ten o'clock news on channel five I stood up and handed the remote to Maria.

"Bed time *pour moi*," I announced.

She clicked off the TV.

"*Anche per me*," she said shifting to Italian, which was certainly appropriate after the dinner we'd shared. Elizabeth was already in the rack, so we went around locking doors. After climbing into bed and turning off the lights, we said our bedtime Hail Mary and then she hugged me with a fierce intensity.

"Alan. I'm scared. I can't explain it. But I am scared. For you. For us."

"I'll be okay," I said, rubbing her back. "We'll be okay."

I moved my hand down.

"I'll be okay as long as you do that," she whispered.

I did and one thing led to another. The lost sleep was a tiny price to pay for the "another." But later, as I listened to her breathing slide into the sleep mode, I wondered about her exquisite intuition. I hadn't said word one about the asshole that took a shot at Luke and me during our run this afternoon, but *something* had spooked the main woman in my life.

Twenty-Three

Chestertown
March 4th
Thursday

Next morning, I decided not to email Judy but rather try personal contact instead. I knew she usually left her house about seven thirty, so at seven twenty, I kissed Elizabeth good-bye, then kissed Maria and told her I'd be back in thirty to forty minutes. The morning was chilly and there were patches of fog around, but there was a softness to the air suggesting a spring-like day in a little while. I jogged over to Judy's house and caught her as she was locking her front door.

"Hi, neighbor!" I shouted and waved.

"Oh, hi, Alan," she said with a smile. "How's everything going?"

I slowed to a walk as we both approached her red Infiniti coupe.

"Could I buy you a drink after work? J. Brian's?"

She raised one eyebrow.

"Sounds interesting. Sure. Five fifteen or so?"

"It is. Interesting, that is. See you at five fifteen," I said and started running again. We waved to one another and went our separate ways. I zigzagged through downtown and got back to the house thirty-five minutes after leaving. Maria had told me that she had an interview scheduled for this morning at the Imperium coffee shop and she was shrugging into her jacket as I walked in.

"I'm meeting Judy for a drink at J. Brian's at five fifteen," I said. "Other than that, I'll be home manning the computer all day. Unless you need me to run any errands."

"You're on the clock for POTUS. You shouldn't be running household errands."

Twenty-Four

She wasn't at J. Brian's at five ten when I arrived, but a lot of other people were. The place radiated good cheer. Lots of yuppies stopping by for a drink on their way home. Or maybe dinner. Fortunately, there was one table available, and I took it and ordered a Guinness and a small plate of hot wings. By the time the waitress arrived with my order, Judy had arrived as well. I stood up. We shook hands and exchanged pecks to the cheeks. She ordered a glass of sauvignon blanc.

Judy is a very good-looking woman in a no-nonsense kind of way. She's about average height, I'd guess five-five or so, and wears her black hair cut short. Purplish-blue eyes, very little makeup, which is a good thing because she doesn't need it. Pretty, refined features, just a step away from exquisite. She is quick to smile and comes across as one who doesn't take herself too seriously. A superior character trait in my values notebook.

"Good to see you, Judy."

"Good to see you too, Alan. God, I can't believe so much time has passed since *L'Aquila*."

L'Aquila was the city in Italy's *Abruzzo* region where we'd recovered Judy's family heirloom.

The waitress returned with her wine.

"Help yourself to the wings," I offered.

She did, nibbling at the chicken in an impossibly dainty fashion. I felt like an animal in comparison as I gnawed away on mine.

"Well, Alan. What's so 'interesting'?" she asked as she put down a totally clean wing bone and wiped her fingers with a napkin.

"A job," I said. "Actually two. Mine and the one I'm offering to you."

"Are you serious?"

"For once, yes. Let me tell you about mine first."

"I take it you're not talking about teaching."

"You're right. Totally new job. Very different. Hugely exciting."

"Okay. Let's hear it."

"It's classified," I said, *sotto voce*.

I leaned across the table.

"The very *nature* of this new organization is classified, that is. As well as its functions and its purpose. You can't share what I'm about to tell you with *anyone*. For the foreseeable future. Shall I continue or should I change the subject?"

She looked around the crowded watering hole. Then she wrinkled her brow.

"Aren't you going to have me sign an NDA?"

She was referring to signing a non-disclosure agreement, a standard practice when a person not "cleared" for a particular "compartment" is briefed on material in that compartment. The signer agrees not to disclose the material or face prosecution and imprisonment.

"No. No paper trails on this. Zero," I said.

She pursed her lips and closed her eyes for a second. Then she said, "Tell me."

"It's a White House appointment. The man offered it to me in person."

"Kehoe?" she whispered.

"Himself," I said. "Do you want me to continue?"

"Of course," she said with a grin. She took a sip of wine, put her elbows on the table and put her chin in her hands.

"Okay. This is the classified part. I'm in the process of setting up a small, 'private' intelligence office for the president. We're tasked with giving 'sanity checks' on official U.S. Intelligence Community products forwarded to the man himself. Twenty or thirty people. Here in Chestertown. I'm the top dog. I just hired a deputy dog that is really an alter ego. I need an office manager. That would be you. It would be more of a chief-of-staff position—you'll be doing a helluva lot more than ordering paper clips. I'm in the process of negotiating for a Civil Service

HR point of contact to handle the hiring and benefits details. My intention is to get you a promotion and/or pay raise and transfer your benefits from your current job."

The grin had faded.

"When?"

"ASAP," I said. "Interested?"

"I don't know. It's so—so totally out of the blue. Not to mention outrageous. Is it legal?"

"I don't know. Maybe not. Kehoe is a high school classmate of mine. On the other hand, we're not going to be doing data mining. No tapping phones or eyeballing people's credit card statements. Just looking at what's already out there. In the open market, so to speak. Our intel weenies—the bulk of the staff—will have regional expertise and will spend a lot of time on the road. And that will be out in the open as well. No clandestine or scurrilous stuff other than our connection to the White House. So maybe it is legal," I said, lamely.

She shook her head.

"I need a little time," she said. "To think about it."

"Of course. Today is Thursday. Tomorrow, I move into the new office spaces. Monday, the new guy—the alter ego—is aboard. How about you think about it over the weekend and let me know on Monday."

"I'll do better than that. Are you going to nine-thirty Mass at Saint Katherine's on Sunday?'

I thought about that for a nanosecond.

"Yes."

"I'll see you there after Mass. If I'm wearing earrings, the answer is 'yes.' If not, 'no.' Okay?"

"Earrings—yes," I said.

She stood up.

"Don't get up. I have to run. There's a lot to think about."

"I know," I said.

"Thanks for the wine and the nibblies," she said and was gone.

I finished the last two wings wolfishly and drained my Guinness. I paid my tab and walked home through the mild evening.

When I got home Maria said, "Dinner's in twelve minutes. Elizabeth and I are starving."

She plunged a couple of handfuls of fettuccini into a steaming pot of water and turned the gas on under an iron skillet that already held about a tablespoonful of olive oil. Then she scraped minced garlic and jalapeno pepper fragments from a cutting board into the oil.

"Oh, Alan. Mike, the blond Secret Service guy, stopped by. He left an envelope for you. It's on the hall table. Elizabeth, would you please hand me the clams?"

Maria pushed garlic and pepper pieces around in the hot oil with a wooden spoon.

Elizabeth interrupted her salad preparation and took a colander full of Middle Neck clams still in their shells out of the sink. She handed the colander to her mother.

"I think there are keys in the envelope," she said.

"No secrets in this house," I mumbled.

I poured myself a glass of Chianti and retrieved the manila envelope. Someone had scrawled, *Ripley Hall,* across the front. It contained six keys, which appeared to be identical, and which had the legend, "*Do Not Copy,*" etched on the key heads. By the time I got back to the kitchen, clams were starting to open in the skillet. The bouquet of olive oil, garlic, peppers, and fresh clams was enough to make a grown man drool.

Twenty-Five

I went into the new offices in Ripley Hall on Friday. The keys fit the identical dead-bolt locks on both doors. The brick building had two stories plus a basement. The latter looked to have been used for storage. It was semi-finished and had a lot of shelving. There were some rusty garden tools, some junky furniture, and a snow shovel. There were also two brand-new-looking, high-efficiency heat pumps for heating in winter and cooling in summer. Probably one for upstairs and one for down. The rest of the building looked to have previously been a combination of classrooms and offices. A guy from facilities was due to show up on Monday to talk interior doors and furniture. The place already had jacks for phones and computers. I was walking around with a notebook and a pencil when there was a pounding on the door. I opened it and Mike stepped inside. His face was red and sweaty and he wore a running suit. He was carrying a plastic grocery bag from the Giant Food Store.

"Thought I'd take a little break from my morning run," he said with a grin. "I take it the keys work okay."

"Yeah. Everything looks good. I'm just trying to figure out where to put people. Seems like there's plenty of room."

"Well, congratulations. You just got two more bodies."

"What?"

"I know. The boss said you have free rein on who and what goes into this little lash-up and you do."

"Then what's with the two new bodies that I know nothing about?"

"Luke and me. Security. I put in a report on that little ambush by the river the other day. In Secret Service channels. It set off some alarm bells. Went over like the proverbial turd in the punchbowl. So now you have a two-man security detail. Your old running buddies, Luke and Mike. I hope you have room for us. I'd hate to have to pitch a tent outside. Where's the coffee pot?"

He took a three-pound container of coffee out of the grocery bag.

"In the conference room," I said, thinking I could use a cup of Sumatran Breakfast Blend right about now. "What about cups and filters?"

"Oh ye of little faith," he snorted, taking a package of cardboard cups and a wad of filters from the grocery bag.

Once we had our coffee, I let Mike pick out where his and Luke's desks would be situated. Mike split them up. One on each floor at opposite ends of the building. Luke downstairs, Mike up. I gave him two of the building keys, one for himself and one for Luke.

"You guys aren't bodyguards, are you? That kind of security?" I asked.

"Not really. More threat analysis. And observation. I'll make some calls this afternoon and arrange for alarm and video surveillance systems to be installed next week. I'll also arrange to have the place swept for bugs on a regular basis. We'll check your home as well, since it's just a few blocks away. How's the hiring going?"

"Slowly. I do have a deputy. Darps Taylor. He'll be in on Monday. Made an offer to a potential office manager, named Judy Palladino. From Quantico. She'll let me know Sunday. Once they're here and I get a government HR guru to handle the hiring paperwork, things will pick up."

Mike glanced at his watch.

"Check your email. You might have something from Luke on the HR person. And speaking of Luke, I'm meeting him for lunch. At the 'Vine. Wanna come?"

The "'Vine" was local slang for the Grapevine Cafe, a neat little restaurant in Chestertown. But I demurred.

"Thanks, but no. I told Maria I'd walk home for lunch."

I did check my email. There was indeed one from Luke. It appeared I was getting another, unexpected addition to my staff. One Mrs. Rebecca Wolfe. She was a Civil Service HR ace. According to the classified email, she was an expert at cutting through bureaucratic red tape, was well connected, and knew where lots of bodies were buried. In the words of the email, she was a "fixer." I was to list her as "assistant office manager." She would be aboard within ten days.

I walked home for lunch, and Maria and I had tomato soup and salami sandwiches on rye toast. Even though I'd been home for lunch the past few days, walking home from the job and enjoying lunch with Maria was pretty special. She seemed to think so, too. I walked back to Ripley Hall and spent a solitary afternoon fooling around with a little PowerPoint presentation that I'd go over with Darps on Monday. I tried to fix it so that I could use it to bring Darps up to speed and then use it a couple of days later to brief Kehoe. I also made an appointment with the Martha Washington University president for a courtesy call next week. Then I knocked off early, locked up, and went home. I thought that it would probably be a while before I'd be able to do that again.

Elizabeth and I broke out our fly rods and drove out to a spot on the Rapidan River Saturday morning. The weather was chilly and drizzly and the water was running pretty high. There was neither insect life nor signs of feeding trout on the murky surface. We tried a few nymphs and, even with yarn strike indicators, got zippo action. Finally, we tied on orange, round flies that looked like salmon eggs. With a tiny *frisson* of guilt, I dipped them in clam juice. In the next thirty minutes, Elizabeth caught two nine-inch rainbows and I landed an eleven-incher, all three of which we released. We were freezing and were glad when the Explorer's heater kicked in as we headed for home.

"You know, Dad," Elizabeth said as we turned east on Route Three. "It may have been cold and rainy and we didn't catch many fish. But it was great that there was nobody else fishing. Just you and me."

It doesn't get any better than that.

On Sunday, I went to nine-thirty Mass as promised. Maria and Elizabeth were with me. Saturday's cold rain was continuing to hang around when we left for Mass and was still falling when we emerged at ten thirty. The area in front of the church was a forest of umbrellas. I finally spotted Judy. She had large gold hoops dangling from her earlobes. Bingo! *BIAS* now had an office manager as well as a director who had keys to the place.

When we got home, I jumped on my email right away.

From: allewellyn@ptolemy.com
To: jpalladino@vespers.com
Subj: Start
When?

Then I called Darps at home and left a voice mail message inviting him for coffee at the house on Monday morning. By the time I got off the phone, I had an email from Judy.

From: jpalladino@vespers.com
To: allewellyn@ptolemy.com
Subj: Start
The Ides of March.

Good enough. A week from tomorrow.

Then Darps called back.

"See you around eight thirty, Shipmate," he said after I'd given him directions to number one-five-zero-six Prince Henry Street.

I called a halt to *BIAS* activities and concentrated on the *Times Book Review* and *Travel* sections. Outside, the rain continued steadily and undiminished.

Twenty-Six

By Monday, the rain had quit and the streets of Chestertown were a little steamy or misty. I wasn't sure which. Perky Petra, the weather chick on the local morning news said we'd make it over seventy by noon. Darps showed up at the house a few minutes after eight. We had bagels and coffee in the kitchen and talked about various Annapolis classmates we had run into over the years. The conversation carried over into our walk to the new *BIAS* offices on campus. With his balding pate, his beard, and his tweeds, Darps looked like your typical, left-wing professor. With my short haircut and blue blazer, I probably stood out like the proverbial baboon's ass. What a team!

Once we were inside, we put the government laptop and the cell phones on the table that Mike and I had found in the basement on Friday morning. There were a few folding chairs that we'd dusted off. I put a carafe of coffee together while Darps wandered around. He wandered back at about the time the coffee was ready. I poured two cups.

"I have a meeting with the boss and Whitehead the day after tomorrow," I said. "Let me share with you what I'm going to tell him as a means of getting you up to speed. Comments and suggestions are welcome."

I pulled up the title slide on the laptop.

Bureau for International Affairs Studies (BIAS), it read.

"This is our name. It's unclassified. We'll probably have a sign made for the building. Regarding the rest of the stuff, I'm not sure what the classification is. If I had my way, everything we produce would be unclassified. On the other hand, our relationship with the White House and the fact that we're providing intelligence that amounts to second-guessing what the big boys give him is way classified."

I changed slides.

"These are the bullets I'm going to give him."

- Rules of the Game,
- Personnel/Manning,
- DiRienzo Assassination,
- Peoples' Republic of China, and
- A Mole.

"Jesus Christ!" Darps hissed. "We're not even up and running and you're giving the man multiple bombshells!"

"I know. He may fire me on the spot."

"Let's go for a little walk," Darps suggested, standing up.

I powered down the laptop, packed it up, and we got our jackets and stepped outside. The campus scene was what you'd expect for a small university in Virginia in the spring. Students in jeans and sweatshirts with backpacks. Flowering trees—dogwood, redbud, and magnolia—coming into bud. Red brick, white-trimmed buildings.

"What's up with the fucking mole?" Darps whispered.

"I don't know," I said. "But I'm pretty sure there is one. Working for the PRC. They're getting inside information. As in from inside the U.S. Government."

"Care to walk that cat back a little?"

"Sure. It's a very flimsy house of cards. Built by me. Alone. And it starts with us not even being up, running, or open for business."

"But—" he said.

"But, after DiRienzo was murdered, even though we weren't open for business, I got a tasking from the man to take a look at the hit job and tell him what I thought. I told you that part."

"Yup," he said.

"As part of my 'take' on the DiRienzo assassination, I looked at all the info I could get my hands on and did a crude little probability analysis. I concluded that there was a small but finite probability that the PRC Government was behind the hit."

"Right. And that's what got you crosswise in the breakers with Whitehead."

"Yes. And when I briefed Kehoe on the DiRienzo assassination—including my guess about the Chinese connection—he—Kehoe—told me that he'd discussed a possible vice presidential appointment for DiRienzo. With DiRienzo himself. Apparently Girtler has been having chest pains and is considering going over the side as vice. And by the way, I just violated a direct order from the President of the United States by telling you that. So you see what it means to be my alter ego."

"Jesus H. Christ," Darps muttered. "I'm not sure that I want to hear any more."

"Walking the cat back a little more, if the PRC took down DiRienzo, they must have known something of the vice presidential plans. Ergo, there's gotta be a mole."

"Not necessarily," Darps said, after a short pause. "The Chinese could have offed DiRienzo for a hundred different reasons. And nobody's even sure it was the Chinese. Hell, the shooter could have been a third-generation Korean-American with a couple of loose screws. Like an Asian-American Oswald. And let's not forget that it was just the driver that the nutty girl photographer claims to have seen. Nobody actually laid eyes on the shooter."

"I told you it was flimsy," I countered. "But there's more."

"What's that?"

"Last week, after I had lunch with you, I phoned Luke and left a message to meet me for a run. I wanted to get the hiring machinery in gear. Anyway, we went for our run and hadn't gone a hundred meters when some son of a bitch took a shot at us. Mike was running backup and gave us a warning over the radio and we hit the deck. But get this—the shot was fired from the same minivan that was seen leaving the scene after DiRienzo was whacked."

"Once again, that doesn't mean there's a mole. Let alone a PRC mole."

"You're absolutely right. But there *might* be one. And I think we've got to take it seriously. I just don't know what to do at this point."

"Yeah," he said. "It means we have to be very goddamn careful where and with whom we discuss him. Or her. The mole."

"Mike told me he's arranging to have the office building swept for bugs. Let's avoid mentioning the mole until that's done," I said.

"Let's not mention the mole at all—before or after the sweep—unless it's just you and I talking. Outdoors, like this. At random places. Where it's pretty hard to bug the conversations."

"Yeah. Good idea. And, upon reflection, I'm going to take it out of the brief for Kehoe. The issue is too much of a loose cannon at this point."

"I agree," Darps said, nodding his head several times. "If I were in your shoes, I don't think I'd bring it up just yet. Let nature take its course for a while."

"I do want to pre-empt nature a little and hire our China expert as soon as possible. Do you know any positive prospects?"

"Actually, I do," he said. "Old childhood neighbor of mine. Sammy Chen. Brilliant guy. Graduated from high school when he was thirteen. Taught me how to shoot a bow and arrow when we were about ten. Sammy went to RPI on an academic scholarship. We kept in touch, even though he always made me feel like a moron."

After hearing that from Darpley Roentgen Taylor, I wasn't sure I wanted to even *meet* Sammy Chen, much less hire him.

"What's he doing these days?"

"He's a senior fellow at the Zhang Foundation. Travels frequently to the PRC. Speaks Mandarin and Cantonese and a bunch of other languages. Lives in Florida."

"Could we be getting ourselves a second mole if we brought him on board?"

"I doubt it very much. He's every bit as American as we are. I'd be amazed if the Chinese had turned him around. As far as I know, his work is centered in getting American scholars into the PRC for advanced studies. Anyway, if you want to take a look at him, can't you have some of Kehoe's spooks check him out?"

By this time, we were back at Ripley Hall.

"I'm sure we could. What do you think?" I asked. "Would he be interested?"

"I can give him a call, offer to take him to lunch. Feel him out. If he's interested, I'll introduce you and you can take it from there."

"Florida's a long way to go for lunch. But, if he is interested, we can pop for a trip up here. Fly him up and take him to lunch. Here in C-town or in the nation's capital."

Twenty-Seven

Chestertown
March 8th
Monday

I unlocked the door and let us in, and we refilled our cardboard cups with strong coffee when Luke and Mike showed up. Luke had a laptop slung over his shoulder. Mike had two of them. One over each shoulder. I introduced Darps, and Mike handed him one of the computers after they shook hands.

"Here's your government laptop, Mr. Taylor," he said.

"Call me Darps. Please."

"No problem. I'm Mike. Did Alan tell you who we are and what we do?"

"Yes. I think we're very lucky to have you guys on board."

"Okay if we grab a cup of that coffee?" asked Luke.

"Hell yes. It's yours. Mike bought it. And the cups," I said. "Help yourself anytime. Let's agree among the four of us to keep the pot going till two or three in the afternoon, at least."

Mike and Luke poured themselves coffee and headed off in separate directions. I guessed to their new office spaces. A few minutes later, a government facilities guy with a fancy clipboard treated us to a visit. We spent the next hour and a half walking through the building showing the guy where we needed doors, workstations, phones, computers, and printers. I mentioned a sign for the building and he jotted something down.

After we finished and the facilities guy had left, I suggested to Darps that it was time for lunch. We walked past Mike's office and I poked my head in the door.

"We're going out for some lunch. Darps wants to ogle the coeds," I said.

"Understand. Today is a pretty good day for that, I think," Mike said.

We stopped for takeout Italian sandwiches at Federico's, a hole-in-the-wall dump just off William Street and brought them back to campus along with a couple of cold bottles of New York cream soda.

The weather weasel had it right again. It was over seventy. T-shirts had replaced the sweatshirts on many of the coeds and the ogling was fine.

"I've been thinking about this mole issue," I said.

"So have I," Darps responded.

We found a vacant bench, unwrapped sandwiches, and opened the sodas.

"There aren't a helluva' lot of possibilities," I mumbled.

"Right. Let's start at the top of the list. Whitehead."

"No question—he's a possibility. His reaction to the implication of the PRC in the DiRienzo hit suggests that he has some sort of hard-on about the Chinese."

"Yeah. But, if he *is* the mole, wouldn't it make more sense for him to *avoid* getting all bent out of shape over some Chinese issue?" Darps asked. "If I were a PRC mole, I sure as hell wouldn't draw attention to myself by chewing your ass for pointing a finger at the Chinese. In a public restaurant, no less."

"Good point," I said. "Plus, being an asshole doesn't automatically make him a mole."

"Okay. Where does that leave us? The president's wife?"

"Franny? Good grief! I don't think so. I dated her a couple of times in high school," I said.

Francine Kehoe, *nee* Belmont, the first lady, was a woman a year younger than I and still had the stunning good looks that she had back in the day.

"I don't think dating you in high school makes her immune to being co-opted by the PRC," Darps said. "Or being a spy, for that matter."

"You're right. But, for a first lady to have a clandestine relationship with a foreign intelligence service is beyond the pale."

"Probably. Probably," he said, nodding. "But not totally. She's still on my list."

"But a long shot. Very long. What about Girtler?" I asked.

"Hmm. He's interesting. Maybe bailing out of the administration sometime soon. Having chest pains. Looking his mortality in the face. What if the PRC promised him a bunch of money—a *huge* bunch of money—to keep them abreast of U.S. Government high-level goings on? That pile of money could go a long way in taking the edge off grandpa's passing for the kids and the grandkids."

"That would be an amazingly high-level penetration of the U.S. Government," I said. "Unprecedented. And, therefore, unlikely."

"'Unprecedented?' Are you sure?"

"Well, yeah," I said. "No vice president has ever been accused of— let alone prosecuted for—espionage. So, yeah, I'm sure."

"Well I'm not so sure," Darps said. "Just because it hasn't come to light doesn't mean it hasn't happened. Stranger shit has been covered up. I think Girtler's name has to stay on the list. At least for now."

I was beginning to learn that Darps was one suspicious son of a bitch. Paranoid, even. Which meant that he was a pretty good partner for me, one trusting son of a bitch.

We stopped talking and concentrated on leaning into our sandwiches. Kids were tossing a Frisbee on the grass.

"Do you have fond memories of throwing a Frisbee over the grass of the Yard in Annapolis with girls in t-shirts and shorts?" I asked, chewing on the sandwich.

"I think that activity is missing from my undergraduate experience on the banks of the Severn," Darps said. "Going after the advanced degrees in Cambridge was a different kettle of fish. Plenty of Frisbee time. Girls in t-shirts. With nice legs. No infantry drills. No parades. No Extra Duty."

"Who else is on our 'mole' list?" I asked.

"How about Luke and/or Mike?"

"Jesus," I muttered. "I think the clearance process for those guys is extremely rigorous. Unlikely. Very unlikely."

"But not impossible," he said.

"There are other possibilities that we don't even know anything about," I said.

"Like?"

"Like the Navy stewards at Camp David."

"They're probably scrubbed almost as much as the Secret Service. Very unlikely. But put 'em on the list."

"Marines in the security detail? Camp David and the White House?"

"Ditto."

"Then there are others that we *really* don't know anything about. Even who they are. Inner circle people. Like personal assistants. Assorted gatekeepers. Janitors. Girlfriends and boyfriends," I said, half to myself.

"Is Whitehead married?" Darps asked.

"Not anymore. Divorced. Don't know any details other than it happened before he came to Washington. He dates that Channel Fourteen anchor—Suzanne Racey."

"Well—he has good taste. She's pretty hot. 'Racey Suzanne,' as she's known. Is it serious?"

Once again, Darps surprised me. This time with his knowledge of the Washington social scene. "Racey Suzanne," indeed.

"I don't know," I said. "No idea. They've been seen together once or twice and photographed by the paparazzi."

"You know that column in the *Sunday Mirror—Morsels and Motes?*" Darps asked.

"Yeah," I said. "It carries the Washington rumors and innuendos of the week."

"That's the one. Word on the street is that Racey Suzanne writes it."

"No shit! I wonder how much of her stuff she gets from Whitehead."

I stood up.

"Watching girls chase Frisbees is fun, but I should get back. I'm no doubt behind on my email. And I want to get the HR hiring machinery going. Judy will be on our doorstep in a couple of days. Then there's your old buddy, Sammy Whatshisname, if he wants in," I said.

"Chen. With one 'n,'" he said, standing up.

Minutes later, we were back at Ripley Hall. A Budget rental truck was parked in front. A couple of guys were lugging furniture through the open front door while Luke sipped from a cardboard coffee cup and looked on.

"I just had another thought," I said and stopped walking. "More like a stream of thoughts, actually."

Darps stopped.

"What?"

"The 'mole list.' Franny. Whitehead. Girtler. Secret Service. Sailors and Marines. And unknowns. All tiny, minuscule probabilities when taken one by one."

"Yes. But taken altogether, they gotta add up to one-hundred percent. So they can't all be 'tiny and minuscule.' There's got to be a big boy or two in there. Mathematically."

"Correct. The big kahuna at this point has got to be the unknowns. The 'unknown unknowns'—not the 'known unknowns'—in Rumsfeld-speak. Anyway, unless something other than the DiRienzo hit and the shot at Luke and me surfaces, I think we should give the issue a rest. We don't have the resources to pursue it ourselves—and never will, even after we get to full strength. If I air it out with the boss, Christ only knows what he'll do. Maybe nothing. Maybe scream bloody murder to the Feebs, NSA, whomever. So let's move it to a back burner. Or off the stove. Until and unless something new drops out of the sky."

"I agree," Darps said. "Good call. Let's make the issue dormant. Not dead. But dormant."

Twenty-Eight

L ieutenant Colonel Yang Zemin removed his Burberry trench coat and hung it in a closet. Quing Maili waited until he was seated at his desk before entering with a tray containing a teapot and a cup.

"Thank you, Maili," Yang said as he turned on his computer. "Anything from *Mongoose*?"

"No, Comrade Colonel."

"Very well. I'll go through my email."

The colonel took a sip of tea. The first email was double encrypted.

He forwarded it immediately to Maili. A few minutes later she appeared carrying two manila folders.

"Here's your email message, decoded, and the file on the subject, Comrade Colonel."

One thin manila folder contained a single sheet of white lined paper. The message was in Chinese characters in Maili's neat calligraphy. The larger folder contained a dossier, including a number of photographs. Yang turned to the decoded email first.

From: KowloonStar@gwailow.com
To: HainanStrip@gwailow.com
Subj: Samuel L. Chen

We have confirmed that Darpley R. Taylor, a new member of the American Bureau of International Affairs Studies (BIAS), contacted the subject. Phone conversation implied BIAS is interested in hiring Chen as an intelligence specialist. Set up meet w/ Chen for our possible recruitment. Explore financial vulnerabilities. Report NLT 23 March.

The dossier pointed out that Samuel Chen was a frequent visitor to the Peoples' Republic of China and that his visits were academic and administrative in nature. He was listed in the Ministry of State Security Interagency Source Registry and had been given the code name, *Lynx*. The assessments of him conducted by a total of three different recruitment specialists during three separate visits to China were uniformly pessimistic regarding his suitability for recruitment as an agent.

"Idiots!" Yang muttered. "Not one, not two, but three professional recruiting specialists made passes at this Source *Lynx* and ran into a stone wall. In China! Now the imbeciles want us to *recruit* him! Here in the United States! Ridiculous!"

The dossier noted that Chen's only apparent "weakness" was in the area of gambling. He had shown no sign of a gambling addiction but had a photographic memory and had been kicked out of numerous casinos after winning large sums of money. He had not visited any gambling sites since his last eviction almost two years ago after winning a spectacular amount of money from a casino in Macau.

The dossier also contained personal data on Chen. It gave a home address in Jupiter, Florida, with a work address in West Palm Beach. According to the file, Chen was married. He and his wife had two children, both girls, ages ten and twelve.

"Idiots!" Yang mumbled again, under his breath. He closed the folder and tossed it into his *Out* box. Then he reached for it again and opened it, searching for something. The three assessments done in China—all three had been done by males.

"Maili!" he called. "Have you ever been to Florida?"

Twenty-Nine

Chestertown
March 12th
Friday

When Darps and I walked into Ripley Hall, Luke gave me a little nod. He made a little gabbing motion with his hand. He wanted to talk. I got to my office on the first deck. Darps was with me. His office was on the second deck. As was Mike's. Luke was babbling into his cell phone. By the time I got my jacket off, Mike was coming through the door with Luke. He was carrying a file folder. All four of us crowded into the office and sat on the new chairs around the new glass-topped table.

"We did a little security survey of your house. Fifteen-oh-six Prince Henry," Luke said.

"Ever see this guy in the neighborhood?" Mike asked, flashing an eight-by-ten color photo that he'd pulled from the folder. The photo was a head-and-shoulders shot of an Asian man in his early thirties. He reminded me of an Oriental version of Mike and Luke. Heavily muscled neck. Massive shoulders. A scraggily mustache and a little vee-shaped beard. In the photo's background were bare branches of oaks as well as a beech tree or two with only a couple of brown leaves showing. The picture could have been taken on Prince Henry Street. In front of my house. Yesterday.

"Nope. Never," I said, honestly.

"How about her?" he asked, flashing another photo.

"Oh yeah," I said. It was the young, good-looking Asian woman who walked the corgi and the baby and carried groceries. "I've seen her three or four times in the past few weeks. Walking a dog. Pushing a baby. Maria has seen her, too. We figured she's a new neighbor."

"Classic *Guoanbu* cover. Dog walking and baby pushing. For casing and surveillance."

"*Guoanbu?*" I asked.

111

"It's an acronym for *Guojia Anquai Bu*. Ministry of State Security. PRC's version of the old Soviet KGB. How about this lady?" Mike asked, pulling another photo out of the folder.

I looked at the next photo. It was "the empress." The older woman.

"Her too. Walking the same dog," I said.

"We're pretty sure they're part of a team that is keeping an eye on your house—and you," Luke said. "One of them circles your block roughly every two or three daylight hours. Sometimes they'll have the dog, sometimes the baby, sometimes they'll pick up something at the store. At night, they seem to back off to every four or five hours. With the dog. The little beast has probably lost four or five pounds since they moved in. With all those walks."

"Okay. Who are they? *Guoanbu*? In practical terms, what's it all mean?"

"We don't know," Luke said, shaking his head. "We can't even be sure that they're Chinese, at this point."

"It *does* mean that *BIAS* is probably blown. Or at least, you're blown, Alan. To the Chinese, the Taiwanese, the Koreans or whoever's watching your house. Quite possibly the rest of us are blown as well. We should know who the watchers are from the photos by tomorrow, latest," Mike added glumly.

I didn't like it. This meant that my family was being roped into some sort of dangerous game.

When Darps and I locked up and left, I still wasn't feeling too great about the situation. Darps had left his wheels around the corner from my house that morning. We walked back to the house together.

"I just got through to Sammy Chen," Darps said. "He's in Beijing."

"Now?"

"Yup. Flying back to D.C. on Sunday. He has a meeting at Georgetown on Monday morning. Then he's meeting us at noon for lunch at the Army-Navy Club. We'll drop him off at Reagan National after lunch."

"Sounds good," I said. "Are you a member at the Army-Navy Club or is he?"

"*Moi*. I joined when I was a Mid."

We reached the side street where his car was parked.

"See you tomorrow, Shipmate," he said.

"Maybe we can finally get the goddam paperwork done so we'll both get paid," I said. "If they don't shut us down."

As I turned back towards the house, two things—actually, two people—caught my eye. Elizabeth was number one. She was approaching the house from the direction of Esmé's house, stopped and fished our mail out of the mailbox, and then turned onto the little brick sidewalk leading to our front door. The second person was the big Chinese guy in Mike's photo who appeared to be snapping pictures of Elizabeth and our house with his cell phone from across the street. I broke into a run and then a sprint and lowered my shoulder just as he started to become aware of my approach. Too late. I knocked him flat on his ass and the cell phone flew into the street. I jumped into the street, grabbed the phone, and, keeping one eye on the photographer, who was getting to his feet, hit the *review* button on the phone. The last picture showed Elizabeth retrieving the mail. I dropped the phone in the road and stomped on it twice.

"I'm calling the police!" he hissed.

"Not with that phone, you're not!" I said. "See if you get through to them before I do. Taking photographs of children without their knowledge. They'll haul your sorry ass into police headquarters and book you in a New York minute."

That just pissed him off, and he came at me swinging. Like someone who's never seen the inside of a boxing ring. I stepped back, left, and forward and drilled him with a two-punch combination just forward of his right ear and down he went for a second time. I looked around and didn't see anyone who might have been watching our little one-sided affray. Most importantly, I saw no curtains or blinds being pulled aside in any of the windows of number fifteen-oh-six.

My new friend was getting to his feet. Very slowly. Didn't look like he was ready for another boxing lesson. I picked up his ruined cell phone and tossed it to him. He caught it awkwardly with both hands.

"Here's a souvenir, asshole. Now get lost. And stay lost. If I see you sniffing around my home or my family, you'll end up in the fucking river. Tell your two girlfriends the same thing."

He turned and left. I rubbed my knuckles and considered my options.

I could go inside. I was more than just a little agitated. More like really highly pissed. Probably a little red in the face. Maria would sense that something was amiss immediately. I'd have to explain a fistfight in the street in front of our house and that would set the cat amongst the pigeons, domestically speaking. Or I could walk back to the office and calm down for fifteen or twenty minutes. I opted for the office. Earlier in the day, Darps had parked a liter and a half of Dewar's scotch in one of the new file cabinets.

"In case of emergency," he'd said with a grin.

I figured this was our first emergency.

Thirty

Quing Maili heard her cell phone's chime signal that a text message had arrived. Irritated, she retrieved the text. She had been on her way out the door. She gasped as she read the message and immediately went into Colonel Yang's office without knocking.

"What is it, Maili?" he asked.

"Kehoe's spy, Llewellyn, 'made' his surveillance! He beat up Kwan and trashed his cell phone in the street in front of his house!"

"Kwan! That incompetent, bumbling dildo! Ship his worthless ass back to the homeland at once. And shut down the overt surveillance of Llewellyn immediately. Leave the electronic apparatus in place for now. When did this fiasco take place?"

Maili looked at the text.

"This evening, Comrade Colonel. Just under half an hour ago."

"Who reported it?"

"The text message doesn't say. *Kowloon Star* was the originator of the text."

Yang picked up the porcelain bell and shook it roughly.

The steward appeared instantly.

"Bring me cognac and cigarettes!" Yang ordered.

The steward bowed and left and returned almost immediately with a red lacquer ware tray. On it were a bottle of Martel cognac, a freshly opened pack of Marlboro Reds, a box of matches, a crystal ashtray, and two crystal tumblers. He set the tray down on a coffee table, poured an inch of cognac into each of the two glasses, set the bottle down, and silently left the office. Yang picked up a glass.

"Help yourself, Maili," he muttered. "Cigarette?"

"Yes, please, Comrade Colonel."

He drank off half the cognac, put the glass down, and lit both their cigarettes. Maili noticed that his hand shook. Yang smoked only when his stress level exceeded some arbitrary threshold of which only he was aware. Maili smoked only when the colonel did.

"Do you have a plan yet for this *Lynx*?" he asked, changing the subject.

His respiration rate appeared to be returning to normal.

"Yes, Comrade Colonel," Quing replied. "But I have serious misgivings about achieving success."

"And why is that?"

"As you know, Comrade Colonel, Source *Lynx* has been assessed in China on multiple occasions. Every time, the assessment was negative. Trying to actually recruit him here in the United States makes no sense."

"Maili, we don't have any knowledge of his vulnerability to an approach by a female. That's where you come in."

"I understand, Comrade Colonel. *Lynx* is in our homeland as we speak, overseeing some Sino-American student exchange activity. He is due to return and is scheduled to land at Dulles at eleven a.m. the day after tomorrow. I hope to join him for cocktails in Washington that evening. A trip to Florida would be nice, but my presence there would doubtless arouse his suspicions. Llewellyn and his assistant, Taylor, have scheduled a luncheon date with Chen at noon at the Army-Navy Club in Washington the day following his return. He flies out to West Palm Beach that evening."

"Is it your hope to compromise him?"

"Not necessarily, Comrade Colonel. My hope is to get a commitment from him."

"Excellent, excellent, Maili. Commitment. That's what we need. Would you care for some more cognac?"

"Yes. Comrade."

"Excellent," he repeated.

The colonel poured Martel.

Thirty-One

When I got home forty-five minutes later, I didn't say anything about the fisticuffs in the street in front of the house. Maria didn't say anything about the bouquet of scotch whisky on my breath. I'd had barely more than a tablespoonful of Darps's Dewar's mixed with a generous jolt of cold water, anyway, as I cooled down in the office, so maybe there wasn't anything to notice. I did observe that there was more than just a bottle of scotch in Darps's "emergency" drawer. There was an M1911A1 forty-five-caliber handgun complete with two loaded magazines and a black shoulder holster.

Monday morning, I walked to work. An icy, damp wind was blowing out of the northeast. The spring seemed to have died. I unlocked the front door of the office and let myself in, and the place felt only slightly warmer than the street. I went to the thermostat on the first floor. Punched in *Heat, Auto,* and *72* and heard a low rumble from the basement. Then I felt warm air coming from somewhere.

I was scooping coffee into the filter when I heard someone come in. Finishing up with the coffee I turned and saw Luke's formidable shape filling the doorway.

"Gotta start getting in here earlier," he said, with a grin. "It's bad news when the boss is the first one in and has to make the coffee."

I laughed.

"Let me tell you about Friday evening," I said. "Do you still have the pictures of the Asians who were surveilling my house? The big guy, in particular?"

"Yeah. Let me go get 'em."

He left and was back in a couple of minutes with a folder. I poured coffee into cardboard cups for both of us.

"Let's take a look at the dude with the mustache," I said.

Luke got the picture out.

"Bingo!" I said. "That prick was taking pictures of Elizabeth in front of our house when I got home Friday afternoon. I knocked him on his ass and stomped his cell phone camera. He got pissed and took a swing at me, and I clocked him. Fortunately, Elizabeth was already inside, and I don't think she or her mother or anyone else saw anything. I told him that if I saw him around the house or family again, he'd end up in the river. Told him the same thing went for his two girlfriends. I haven't seen any of them since."

"What did you hit him with?"

"Left-right combination. Back when I was a callow youth, I did some time as brigade light-heavyweight boxing champ at Annapolis."

"Boss, you are just one surprise after another! Do you have the guy's cell phone?"

"No. I totally destroyed it when I stomped on it. I gave the wreckage back to him."

I heard the door rattling again. This time it was Darps and Mike. Judy Palladino followed them almost immediately.

"I'll talk to Mike and we'll get online. I'll get back to you as soon as we get anything," Luke said. "Too bad you didn't keep the asshole's cell phone."

"Yeah. Sorry. I was so pissed I couldn't even see straight. Wasn't thinking."

"You guys have to clean up your language," Judy declared. "I've been working with the Marines for almost twenty years, and they know how to clean up their act when I'm around. So you clowns need to square away!"

We males looked sheepish.

"Gentlemen," I said, with an air of humility. "This is Judy Palladino. She's our combination chief of staff and office manager. Hear her and heed."

I showed Judy into her office—which was right across the hall from mine.

"Here you are. And welcome," I said. I handed her a folder bulging with papers that had been accumulating for the past couple of weeks. "Relax, have a cup of coffee, look through this stuff, and we'll have a meeting in a little while. It'll probably be during a walk outside."

Darps was shadowing me and followed me into my office.

"What was all that about?" he asked. "The 'asshole's cell phone' and you being pissed off," he whispered.

I sat down at my desk and he sat down on the couch.

"On Friday, right after you turned off to go to your car on George Street, I caught that big Asian guy—the one that Mike had the picture of—snapping pictures of Elizabeth right in front of our house with his cell phone. I kicked his ass and smashed his cell phone. Luke and Mike are going to see what they can find out. I didn't see any of my Chinese neighbors for the rest of the weekend."

"Speaking of Chinese, remember we're having lunch with Sammy today."

"Yeah. Looking forward to it. The Army-Navy Club is a lot more posh than places where I usually have lunch. Oh, and by the way, after I thumped that dirtbag in front of my house, I came back here to cool off."

Darps held up a hand.

"Let me guess. You polished off my scotch."

"No, no," I said, laughing. "Barely broke the seal. Had maybe half a shot."

"Well, I got it for emergencies. A fistfight in front of your house certainly qualifies."

"Is that forty-five in the drawer for emergencies, too?" I asked.

Darps grinned his shark smile.

"Contingencies," he said. "It might be good to be strapped if we're carrying sensitive material for the man."

"Let me talk to Luke or Mike about getting some sort of permit," I said.

"I already have," he said. "Luke should have some sort of federal conceal-and-carry permits for us in a couple of days."

I used the time before we had to leave for Washington to talk with Judy. I gave her more or less the same PowerPoint presentation I was planning to give the president on Wednesday. Then we went for a walk. I told her of the suspected Chinese surveillance in our shared neighborhood, to include the Friday evening festivities in front of my house. Then I told her about my mole suspicions. I explained the evolving security situation. She was amazed that Kehoe had me give him my thoughts on the DiRienzo assassination before I had even started the job.

"But he did pay me," I said.

"I have a ton of questions," she said. "But, you're short on time. I'll jot them down while you're in D.C., and we can air them out later."

Darps drove us in his Saab convertible to the nation's capital. He found a parking space a lot faster than I would have, and we hit the *maitre d'* at eleven-fifty-five.

"Taylor," he said. "Table for three. Don't know if our guest is here, yet."

"Right this way, sir."

He showed us to a table. Darps and I both ordered a Samuel Adams. The waiter was delivering the beers when the *maitre d'* showed up with a bespectacled Asian man in an exquisitely tailored dark blue suit, a blazing white shirt, and a dark red tie.

Darps jumped to his feet.

"Sammy, you old hound! Great to see you! Allow me to introduce my boss, Alan Llewellyn!"

I stood up and we shook hands.

"Great to meet you, Mr. Chen. Darps has a lot of great things to say about you," I said.

"Darps and I go way back, Mr. Llewellyn. Back to when we were nine or ten-year-old pipsqueaks in Valhalla, New York. I think he knows all my secrets. I go by Sammy."

"Please call me Alan," I said.

Sammy ordered a Manhattan from the hovering waiter. When the waiter left, Sammy turned to Darps.

"Speaking of secrets," he said, quietly. "Just so you know, I think the Peoples' Republic tried to recruit me yesterday. Again."

After retaking our seats, Darps and I leaned in closer.

"Again?" I asked, feeling stupid.

"Oh yes. This makes attempt number four. But this one was the first try on American soil. And I have to wonder why. I had just spent the last five days in China. Why didn't they troll for me over there like they have in the past?"

"Care to share any details?" I asked.

"Sure," he said.

The waiter showed up with his Manhattan. He took a tiny sip.

"I checked into the Mayflower about noon, had a room service salad and a glass of tea, and took a nap. Then went for a jog. Came back, showered, and went to the bar about five thirty. Sat at the bar and ordered a beer. About five or ten minutes later, an attractive Chinese girl comes over like she's recognized her long-lost brother. She's wearing a little gold ID bracelet with 'Sin' engraved on it. 'Sammy Chen!' she says. 'Isabel Sin! Remember me? Last year in Hong Kong? The Scholarship Conference?' Well, I was in Hong Kong last year. And I remember the Foundation Scholarship Conference. But I sure as hell didn't remember any Isabel Sin. She was really quite good-looking. Nice boobs for an Asian woman. And perfect English. I'm pretty damned sure I'd have remembered her."

He patted his pockets.

"She gave me a card. It's probably still in the pocket of the shirt I wore yesterday. It didn't say much. But *she* did. 'You don't remember me,' she says. 'I was in the background. Doing translation for Dr. Jin.' There was a Dr. Jin. I don't remember an attractive female interpreter. Let alone one with nice boobs. But then, I started doubting myself. In China, she'd probably be frumpily dressed, wearing a ratty hairdo, so maybe she was in the background and I didn't notice her.

"You know, when I told my parents I was going to marry Alicia, the first thing my father asked was 'Is she Chinese?' When I told them 'no,' it was a huge disappointment for them. I was sure I'd be disinherited. I may have been and just don't know it, yet. I have to wonder how'd they react if I showed up now and introduced this Isabel Sin as my Chinese mistress."

"If I remember your mom accurately, she'd carve out your heart with a fish knife," Darps said. "Especially now that she's a grandma."

"Yeah. You're probably right," Sammy said. "Anyhow, no danger. I'm happily married. Hope to stay that way. Forever. Anyway, I'd bet the rent check that Isabel's *Guoanbu*. I blew her off. Politely."

"I have an idea," Darps said. It was barely a whisper.

"Ready to order, gentlemen?" asked the waiter, reappearing. "Or would you like a little more time?"

We were ready. Sammy ordered a steak sandwich, Darps went for crab cakes, and I went for the seared tuna with wasabi. Darps and I ordered refills on the Sam Adams and Sammy asked for a glass of the club pinot grigio.

"So, Darps, old buddy—what's your idea?" asked Sammy.

"Too early. Way too early," Darps said, almost like he was talking to himself. "I'm way ahead of myself."

He took a healthy swig of his beer, precluding further talk for a few seconds.

"Did Darps tell you what we're up to?" I asked, filling the void.

"A little. You're heading up a presidentially appointed studies group that does work for the Office of the Secretary of Defense. On the Martha Washington campus. Overseas issues. You need somebody with China experience. He thought about me. That's about it."

"He hit all the high points. Are you in any way interested? Do you have questions? Or should we just talk baseball?"

"I *am* interested. Mildly, at this point. I've enjoyed working for the Foundation, but I don't see any upward mobility. Unless someone croaks or bails out. And that doesn't seem likely anytime soon. This sounds like a whole new opportunity set. There are plenty of issues, of course. Compensation, for one. And relocation. I don't really have any feel whatsoever for the Chestertown area housing market. The girls are in a Catholic school in Jupiter—and all four of us—parents and girls— are quite happy with it. So, yes I'm interested, but there's a lot I need to know before I'm anywhere close to being able to make a decision. Not to mention conferring with Alicia and the girls down in Florida."

Darps and I drove Sammy to Reagan National Airport after lunch. We shot the breeze about his "issues" and I took notes while Darps drove. I mentioned that Elizabeth attended All Saints Academy, a Catholic school for girls in Chestertown and that we were quite happy with it. I told him

I'd put something in writing about the position and have it to him within the week.

As Darps piloted the Saab into the airport complex and headed for *Departures*, I brought up Isabel Sin—again.

"Did this Isabel seem to know anything about *BIAS*?"

"No. She talked like an American with university connections. Didn't say whether she was faculty or a graduate student. Nor did she cite a specific university. Her card said she was affiliated with a, quote, 'American-Chinese Cultural Exchange Association,' unquote. In Richmond. Virginia."

"Are you *sure* she wasn't at that conference in Hong Kong last year?" Darps asked.

"No, I'm not sure," Sammy replied. "I am sure that we were never formally introduced. Even if she looked dowdy then. There's no way I'd forget a name like Isabel Sin!"

"I can see your point," I said. "I'll probably remember that name for the rest of my life. And I've never even met the woman."

After we dropped Sammy off, Darps headed south on I-95.

"What was your idea that you suppressed before lunch when Sammy told us about Isabel making a pass at him?" I asked.

"I'm an idiot," he said. "You'll recall that I mumbled something like 'too early.' At first, I was thinking it might make sense to have Sammy make a run at Isabel. Manufacture some worthless info to pass along to her and see what happens. But hell, we don't know if Sammy is going to take the job, let alone be willing to act as a *de facto* double agent. Plus, pulling something like that off would require some detailed planning to make sure it wouldn't blow back on us. So. Shitty idea all the way around. I'm glad I caught myself before I opened my fat mouth."

"Maybe not. Not shitty, I mean. Maybe it's just a little premature. You have to wonder what made the Chinese decide to go after Sammy. Here in the States. Like he said, there were all kinds of opportunities for them to do it risk-free over in China last week. Why risk Isabel's ass here in Washington? For all they knew, Sammy would call the FBI. Hell, for all we know, maybe he did. Or will."

"But you gotta wonder," Darps said, half to himself.

"Wonder what?" I asked.

"How the hell the Chinese knew that Sammy was going to be staying at the Mayflower and how they were able to wind up Isabel and shoot her at him so fast. And—even though Sammy didn't see any connection between Isabel and *BIAS*—could there be a connection?"

"You said you talked to Sammy on Friday afternoon," I said. "That would be Saturday morning in Beijing."

"Yeah. Woke him up. It was five a.m. over there. He was kind of pissed."

"*Guoanbu* could have copied that phone call. I'd guess the probability is pretty high that they did. That would explain a lot," I said.

"So would a mole," Darps muttered.

I thought about that for a few seconds.

"I don't think so," I said. "You and I are the only people connected with *BIAS* who knew when Sammy was due in D.C."

"Good point. It's gotta be the phone call."

When we got back to Ripley Hall, Luke was waiting for us.

"Your three Chestertown neighbors are PRC. *Guoanbu*," he said.

He handed me a folder. "Their bios are in here with some other photos. We've been watching the house where they were staying. No activity all day. No corgi. No baby stroller. Nada. Looks like they up and left."

"But they're definitely Chinese?"

"Definitely. Check the folder."

I did. There was no doubt. Not only Chinese, but *Guoanbu* as well.

I spent a good chunk of the next day addressing Sammy Chen's questions and concerns and putting *BIAS* positions on them down on paper. Darps and I kicked them around for a while. I made a few changes, attached it to an email, and shipped it off to Sammy in Jupiter.

Thirty-Two

Quantico
March 17th
Wednesday

Wednesday was B-Day. B as in "briefing." The Main Man. POTUS. "Cheetah." It was also Saint Patrick's Day. Luke and I drove back to my house from the office in our Government-Issue Expedition. I stepped inside to make a quick change into running gear. I donned a green t-shirt in honor of Saint Paddy. I grabbed my Secret Service ID and gave Maria a smooch on the nape of her lovely neck as she talked on the phone. She gave me a wink and a thumbs-up for good luck and Luke and I hit the road for Quantico. Luke drove.

The weather seemed fickle. Humid, warm, and cloudy with fitful gusts of wind popping up, seemingly from nowhere. There were extra MPs and firepower on the gate at Quantico. A corporal, armed with a Beretta nine-millimeter handgun and a slung M-Four carbine, compared our IDs with our faces and found our names on a list before saluting and waving us through. Luke seemed to know exactly where to go. We passed the lake's spillway, which had tons of water thundering over it, and then Luke turned left onto a muddy road into the woods. I could see the gray waters of the lake through the trees to our left, little whitecaps curling across the surface. Occasionally, I saw a cammy-clad Marine with a rifle in the woods. We parked in a little clearing on the lake. The grass was winter-brown. There were four or five picnic tables scattered about the clearing, each with a black iron charcoal grill planted in the ground alongside. Four males and one female, all wearing windbreakers and blue jeans, were scattered about the clearing. There were four black Expeditions—clones of mine—parked around the edge of the picnic area.

We climbed out of my SUV. I slung the laptop bag over a shoulder. The air smelled like rain.

"Hi, Luke," the guy nearest the vehicle said.

"Hey, Kenny," Luke replied.

Secret Service. No doubt.

I spotted the white thatch of hair immediately. Whitehead was seated at one of the picnic tables along with a woman. The chief of staff was wearing a dark gray trench coat over a suit and tie and also wore rubber overshoes. There was a folded-up, short umbrella on the picnic table in front of him. The woman, attractive in a severe sort of way, reminded me of pictures I'd seen of Jean Harris, the slayer of the Scarsdale Diet doctor years ago. I couldn't tell whether her silvery hair was blonde or gray, and her skin appeared almost transparent. Neither could I tell how tall she was, but she was slight, almost to the point of frailty. I remembered that Jean Harris was very slight, had a high forehead, and had pumped four or five rounds into her diet doctor lover. Frailty can be deceiving. This woman wore a dark green raincoat; apparently over a black pant suit and boots. There was an open laptop on the picnic table in front of her. Whitehead half-stood up, waved, and smiled. Not knowing what to expect, I returned the wave.

"Hi, sir," I said.

"Hi, Alan. Good to see you again. Allison, this is Alan Llewellyn. Alan, this is Allison Jenkins, President Kehoe's personal assistant."

Not a sign of the "unpleasantness" about my reporting of Chinese involvement in the DiRienzo killing.

"It's a pleasure, ma'am," I said.

She held out a slender hand and smiled thinly. We shook hands briefly.

"You and the president must be very good friends," she said. "He speaks of you frequently."

"No old secrets from our misspent youth, I hope," I said.

"No, no, not at all," she said with a little chuckle. "He talks about you only in very flattering terms."

I felt my face blush. Whitehead seemed to sense my discomfort and appeared to savor it. Fortunately, the presidential running gaggle chose that moment to come flooding into the clearing with President Kehoe in the lead. Whitehead and Ms. Jenkins stood up.

"Thanks, everybody," the president said to his fellow runners, most of whom I assumed were Secret Service. Judging from the haircuts, two of them must have been Marines. All of their legs were spattered with mud and most of them—including the president—wore long-sleeved tees and cotton gloves. He pulled off a glove and shook hands with everyone and they disappeared down the trail.

"Hi, Alan," said the president.

"Good afternoon, Mr. President," I said.

We shook hands

"Alan, if I'd been thinking, I'd have invited you to join the run. But then you'd have kicked my ass."

Everybody laughed and I could feel my face reddening again.

"Next time, come along," he said. "But only if you'll promise to go easy on me."

And just what am I supposed to say to that? I asked myself.

"Works both ways, Mr. President," I said lamely.

"Have a seat, Alan," Kehoe said. "What have you got?"

I sat on the empty side of the picnic table. President Kehoe climbed in beside me. He didn't say anything about my calling him 'Mr. President,' so I figured it was kosher with Allison and Whitehead present. I opened the laptop and turned it on. Whitehead and Allison sat down in their original seats on the opposite side of the table. Whitehead looked slightly vexed at not being able to see the laptop's screen.

"Okay, Mr. President. Here goes," I started.

The title slide appeared. I let it linger on screen for five or six seconds. "Bureau of International Affairs Studies," I said. "That's us. *BIAS,*" I added, before flipping to the next slide. "*Rules of the Game,*" it said. Followed by bulletized items, including, "*POTUS Eyes Only*" and "*Tightly Compartmented,*" among others. My cue to launch my little spiel.

"My understanding was that *BIAS* would provide you with alternative intelligence viewpoints, Mr. President. My understanding was also that these viewpoints were to be closely held and not shared with the Intelligence Community. If I remember correctly, you used the phrases 'closely held' and 'sanity check' in describing the role of *BIAS*. I understood that to mean that whatever product *BIAS* provided to you would be private and compartmented and not shared beyond your office. Sir."

"That's absolutely correct. The relationship between *BIAS* and the White House is classified. As is the role of *BIAS* in the intelligence production process. *BIAS* products are for my eyes only, unless I am out of the country or otherwise unavailable, in which case you're to brief Walt."

"Thank you, sir. There was a misunderstanding. Between Mr. Whitehead and myself. Over my view of the issues in the DiRienzo assassination—mainly the Chinese involvement."

The president held up both his hands.

"I don't really give a rat's ass about that," he said.

"Mr. President—you'd better give a rat's ass about it! Or you'll have to find a new guy."

I think Allison Jenkins turned even paler than normal, if that was possible. Whitehead grimaced. I continued.

"You just used the phrase 'for my eyes only.' Either you mean that or you don't. If Whitehead here goes running off to the Secretary of State or the Director of the CIA and runs his mouth about what I'm telling you, the whole premise of having a *BIAS* is undermined. So I may as well go home. I'd be wasting your money—taxpayer money, actually—and nothing's changed. You'll still be getting the filtered bullshit that you're getting now. Or 'flapdoodle,' as you so elegantly put it."

"What I'm telling you—both of you—is I don't have time to referee pissing contests," the president said, slowly and deliberately.

"I understand, Mr. President," I said. "And I don't want to get into pissing contests with your chief of staff or anybody else. I had enough of those goddamn government turf battles at the Pentagon years ago. I resigned from the Navy because of them. As I told you, I'd be delighted to bust my ass to provide you with the service that you said you need. But only on the terms you described. The 'rules of the game' are your terms."

"Mr. President!" said the chief of staff. "All I've been trying to do is ensure that the information that lands on your desk is of the highest quality."

He sounded like a preacher of lousy sermons.

"I appreciate that, Walt," the president said. "But remember. *BIAS* and Alan are providing me with a different pair of eyeballs. I'll consider it and evaluate it. I need it unfiltered and un-spun. And it must remain unshared. Everybody understand that?"

The president looked at the three of us at the picnic table. The use of the word "everybody" and the eye contact with the three of us was a slick way of making his point without accusing Whitehead of anything.

"Yes, sir," we all said.

That was probably the best I'd be able to do under the circumstances. I clicked the mouse for the next slide and went through the personnel situation. Bottom line was that *BIAS* had six or seven souls on board or at least lined up to come on board. That was out of an eventual total of nineteen. Thirty or thirty-five percent. I listed the names, positions, and a few vital statistics on a couple of slides. I also told him that we had a government HR pro to navigate our way through the thickets of rustling quality people out of their current jobs and into the *BIAS* fold.

The next slide contained one word: "*DiRienzo.*" I told the president that nothing had changed since I'd briefed him on board *Eliza Dee* last month—with one exception. I'd revised my estimate of PRC involvement upwards. From one-tenth of one percent to five-tenths of one percent. It was still tiny but five times higher than my earlier estimate. I glanced at Whitehead and Jenkins. The chief was expressionless. A hint of color had returned to Allison's features.

"Which leads me to the Chinese," I said, clicking on the next slide. "They seem to be sniffing all around *BIAS*. 'They' being *Guoanbu.*"

"You're shitting me," said the Leader of the Free World.

"No, sir," I said.

I clicked the mouse for the next slide and sneaked a glance at Whitehead. Same expression or lack thereof. The slide's title was "*PRC Activities.*" The first bullet read, "*Prince Henry Street Actions.*"

"Prince Henry Street is my street. 'The Street Where I Live,' to paraphrase the old song title. I noticed the presence of some apparently new Asian neighbors. Luke and Mike investigated and said it appeared that they were surveilling my house. Then, I caught one of them taking pictures of Elizabeth and the house. I kicked his ass and stomped on his camera right there in the street. Meanwhile, Mike or Luke ran the photos of the neighborhood Asians and they're definitely *Guoanbu*. But they stopped surveilling the house after I kicked the guy's ass."

The president chuckled and raised an eyebrow.

"Does that mean the PRC ambassador is going to be raising hell with the secretary of state?" he asked.

"Probably not, sir," I answered. "We're pretty sure they're here illegally. They disappeared after our little confrontation."

I clicked the mouse again. The next slide was the same as the previous one except that it had an additional bullet: "*Beijing/Washington Actions.*"

"Darps contacted an old friend to recruit for the *BIAS* Chinese desk. It turned out the guy was on a trip to Beijing, and Darps called him there about having lunch with us when he got back. He came back to D.C. a couple of days later and hadn't been back for more than a few hours when a Chinese female contacted him and claimed that they'd met in Hong Kong. Darps's friend was pretty sure she was a *Guoanbu* recruiter and the story about having met in Hong Kong was bogus. Sammy—Darps's friend—has a photographic memory."

"Have you hired this guy yet?" the president asked.

"No, sir. I made him an offer. His name is Samuel L. Chen. I'd like to have a background check run on him."

The president turned to Allison Jenkins.

"Allison," he said. "Make it happen."

She tapped the keys on her laptop.

"Found him. Zhang Foundation. We'll run the check," she said.

"He's going to talk to his wife about the job," I said. "They live in Florida and would have to relocate. My guess is that he's interested enough to take the position unless his wife really pours cold water on it. But that's just a guess."

"Do you see any connection between the stuff on your street and the recruitment attempt?"

"Yes, sir. Two of them actually. *Guoanbu* and *BIAS.*"

The president nodded his head a couple of times.

"So," said the president. "The bottom line is that the PRC Ministry of State Security not only knows of the existence of *BIAS*, but seems to be very interested in its activities. Possibly to the point of trying to recruit a prospective employee."

"Yes sir. Possibly. Even though it's a bit of a stretch. In a nutshell, that's it," I said.

"Okay. The only problem with that is if the PRC leaks information about *BIAS* to the press, various governments, elements of our own government, or whoever. If not, no harm, no foul. You guys must be—in their eyes, at least—pretty damned small potatoes. Or small rice. I can't see the PRC Government standing on its hind legs and braying about *BIAS* to the usual propaganda targets worldwide. And in the meantime, we can take all appropriate protective actions and maybe even go over on the offensive. A little bit. If *Guoanbu* keeps trying to make contact with *BIAS*, perhaps *BIAS* can float a little horseshit their way. Muddy their waters a bit. That'll be your call, Alan. Just keep the horseshit morsels small. No major geopolitical or nuclear policy stuff. And keep me posted. That's all. I gotta run."

He stood up.

"Do you really think that's wise, Mr. President?" asked Whitehead. "I mean, if *BIAS* is running independent intel operations against the PRC—"

"Damned right I think it's wise, Walt. Otherwise I wouldn't have suggested it."

I couldn't believe my eyes and ears. Whitehead was acting like he *wanted* to have a few pieces of his ass chewed off.

The president climbed out of the picnic table bench and headed for one of the black SUVs. The Secret Service agents bounded for others. In the distance, I could hear a helicopter start running up. Even Whitehead and Allison Jenkins got up and headed for a black SUV. Whitehead looked a little chastened. As if on signal, the rain started, just a hesitant few drops at first and then a serious downpour. I slammed the laptop closed and zipped it into its case.

"C'mon Alan!" Luke shouted. "Or you're gonna drown!"

I ran for the Expedition. As I slammed the door of the SUV, I had to wonder how the hell the Chinese had come to be interested in an obscure, low-rent operation like *BIAS*. The M-word kept popping up in my mind.

Thirty-Three

Chestertown
March 17th
Wednesday

It was still raining heavily and the wipers were slapping madly when we got to Chestertown, so I had Luke take us directly to Ripley Hall. We ran in through the rain and he flipped me the keys.

"Talk to you later, Boss," he said.

I grabbed a cup of coffee, trotted upstairs, and popped into Darps's office. He looked up and took off his glasses.

"That coffee smells good. Let me grab a cup, and then you can tell me how it went with Cheetah and Whitehead," he said.

I sipped coffee and he returned, steaming mug in hand. I gave him a run-down of the meeting. He chuckled a couple of times. I saved the part about going on the offensive against the Chinese for later when we could talk outdoors. Luke had assured me that the place had been swept and was clean as a whistle, but I harbor healthy amounts of paranoia about some things. Discussing possible offensive intel ops against the PRC headed the list.

"Oh, and by the way, Kehoe's 'personal assistant' was there. Allison Jenkins. Looks like Jean Harris. The woman who went to jail for offing the Scarsdale diet doctor."

Darps reached for his notebook.

"I think she's out of jail. Pardoned by the New York Governor. 'Personal assistant' as in 'secretary'?" he asked.

"Yeah. My guess is that he's got a half-dozen secretaries. And that this one is the first among equals," I said.

"Allison. One 'l' or two?" he asked.

"I don't know," I said. "Not sure if it's an 'i' or a 'y,' either."

Darps scribbled in his notebook. Then he held it up with the page he'd written on facing me. *Allison/Alyson Jenkins – Possible mole???* was scrawled across the notebook page.

I shrugged and held my hands up in an *"I-have-no-clue"* gesture.

"By the way," Darps said. "It looks like Sammy is coming aboard. He emailed you and cc'd me. He also sent us a copy of Isabel's card. He was right. It doesn't say much."

He tore the page with his note about Allison from his notebook, folded it, and stuck it in a pants pocket. I stood up and made a sign for walking with two fingers of one hand. Then I pointed at the window.

"Later?" I said. It was still raining pretty hard.

"Sounds good," he said.

At three thirty, a sunbeam crossed my desk. I looked out the window. No rain. Plenty of sunshine. Clouds seemed to be breaking up, and the wind was bending the trees and starting to dry things out. Good time for a walk. I went up to Darps's office.

"Let's go out for an espresso," I said.

"Sounds good to me."

We left Ripley Hall and headed for the nearest campus gate, on William Street.

"Couple of things came up," I said.

"I figured," said Darps.

"First of all, the old man liked your idea about running something back at the PRC. If they keep sniffing around. So let's put our heads together on that and get Sammy into the fold as soon as we can.

"Secondly, there's Allison Jenkins. Kehoe's secretary or admin assistant or whatever. My gut tells me she's not a mole—she seems totally loyal to Kehoe. But stranger things have happened.

"Finally, we need to dissect your phone conversation with Sammy when he was in Beijing. We need to figure out if you guys talked enough about his trip for them—*Guoanbu*—to have picked up enough to run Isabel Sin at Sammy at the Mayflower Hotel so quickly. If not, then we have to try and figure out how they got the scoop."

"How close do they—the White House—watch our expenditures?" Darps asked.

"I'm not sure," I replied. "I'm supposed to do an expense summary at the end of the month and send it electronically to a 'black' White House address. It's pretty gross and I haven't had any feedback. I've only done one. At the end of February. And that was almost zilch, really. My expenses and pro-rated salary for looking into the DiRienzo execution. I wasn't going to claim anything, but I got a fly-fishing email asking me for a claim. I sent it in and got a check a few days later. It totaled around seven hundred and twenty dollars. So I think we'll get paid, even though we still haven't jumped through the government HR hoops yet."

"Do you think we could rent an off-campus site? *Really* black? Nobody in the loop but you and me. Like a studio apartment. Or a little hovel. Way off the skyline."

"Yeah," I said. "I could probably bury it in 'miscellaneous.' The amount would be so small that I doubt it would catch anybody's eye. And even if it did, I think I can bubble dance around the issue well enough to keep us out of the slammer. And we'll probably need to keep Judy in the loop as well."

"Yeah. We'll probably need her help to avoid said slammer. Especially with you violating rules hand over fist," Darps said with a chuckle.

"Hell, the safe house is your idea, Shipmate," I said. "As the old naval saying says, 'If the mast goes...'"

"I know, 'We go with it.' But seriously, we—you and I—need a place where we can talk. With no Secret Service. No place that the Chinese know about. No place that Whitehead and/or Jenkins know about. Way off the fucking grid."

"You're right. And that's why I hired you. For exactly that kind of idea. Let me give it a bit of thought."

We entered Imperium and ordered espresso. The place was nearly empty. The barista handed us our coffee, and I handed her our money. I shoved two bucks into the tip jar. We sat down in a far corner of the coffee shop. I had an idea.

"Do you know where Chancellorsville is?" I asked.

"The Civil War battlefield? Someplace west of here?"

"Right. Around ten miles west. How about the Wilderness?"

"Another battlefield. In Virginia. Same general area?"

"Close. A little farther west. Maybe fifteen miles. Spotsylvania County. Astride Route Three."

"What's with the history and geography lesson?" Darps asked.

"Well, Elizabeth and I drove through there the other day on a trout fishing expedition. We drove past a house with a *"For Rent"* sign out front. A little dump. Between the Wilderness and Chancellorsville. And it's definitely off the skyline. Probably affordable, too."

"Habitable?"

"I don't know. I just got a glimpse of the place—the 'For Rent' sign caught my eye. I can run out there on Saturday with Elizabeth and throw a line in the river. On the way, I'll take a closer look at the place, get the phone number, and see what's up."

When we walked back to Ripley Hall, the streets were dry.

Once back in the office, I ran through my email.

From: SChen@Zhang.org
To: allewellyn@bias.gov
Cc: roentgen86@bias.gov
Subj: Commute
Attachment: Scan173

Alan,
    It is my intention to accept the position under the terms you described in your email. Alicia wants the girls to remain in school here in Jupiter through the end of the school year in June and I support that. If there is any way BIAS can get me a small, temporary crash pad in the C'town area as part of the relocation package, it would be very helpful. Studio is fine. My plan is to commute to Florida on those weekends when I'm not otherwise engaged. Of course, I'll handle the airplane tickets myself.
    I found Isabel's card and am attaching a copy.
    Cheers,
    Sammy

```
┌─────────────────────────────────────────────┐
│                                             │
│                                             │
│                  Isabel Sin                 │
│              American Chinese               │
│            Cultural Exchange Ass'n          │
│                                             │
│   703-555-5555              PO Box 4771     │
│   isin@accea.org      Richmond, VA 23804    │
└─────────────────────────────────────────────┘
```

I forwarded the email to Mike and Luke. They'd tried to track down Isabel after Sammy told us about her. There were a number of Sins in *Guoanbu*, but none of them was named Isabel, they'd said. Maybe they'd be able to do something with the card, the email, and/or the phone number, but I doubted it.

I could hear doors closing and keys snicking in locks. I glanced at my watch. Ten till six.

Luke poked his head in the door.

"You and I are the only ones still here, Boss. If you want to head for home, I'll lock up and set the alarms behind you."

"Good deal," I said.

I headed for home.

Thirty-Four

Chestertown
March 18th
Thursday

I got into the office at seven thirty the next morning. The coffee was already made and smelled good. There was nobody downstairs, so that either meant that Mike or Darps was in upstairs. I hadn't seen Darps's Saab outside, so that probably meant Mike. I poured a cup of coffee and turned on my computer and heard footsteps pounding down the stairs. Seconds later, Mike was standing in my doorway.

"Seen your email, yet?"

"No. Just started booting up."

"You'll see one from 'PackageStore.com.' Subject is 'Parcel Pickup.' That means we've got an assignment. I'm going up to Quantico to the Air Station. There's a Marine helo bringing down the goodies—whatever they are—from the White House aboard an HMX-1 bird. I'll pick 'em up and be back here in an hour."

Then he was gone. HMX-1 meant Marine Helicopter Squadron One. The guys who fly the prez around. I was puzzled and a little pissed. I mean, Kehoe knows that I'm less than forty percent organized and manned, he knows I've got zero intel analysts, unless he counts Darps and moi—which is a non-starter in my case. And now, just like with the little DiRienzo shitstorm, he's throwing another tasker my way. Christ knows what this one will be about. At least I was on the clock and—presumably—getting paid.

Meantime, I had some other stuff to worry about—*and* address. First of all was Sammy Chen. I sent him an email saying that *BIAS* could pay him a grand a month for temporary living quarters in Chestertown for April through June. I suggested he coordinate with Judy in finding a place. Then I started to scheme a little. I thought about the little place out on

137

Route Three between Chancellorsville and the Wilderness with the *"For Rent"* sign. Darps and I wanted an off-site, off-the-grid hole in the wall where we could meet from time to time. Maybe we could park Sammy in the same place—at least until his commuting to South Florida was done. Then there was the issue of the inbound HR ace—Rebecca Wolfe. She was due on Monday. And she should be able to help me with the relocation of Sammy and maybe his temporary housing needs.

"Hi, Alan!" Judy said, poking her head through the doorway.

Just seeing her face jacked up my confidence. I needed that. The day was developing into a ball-buster.

"Got a minute?" she asked.

"Yes I do," I said. "Let's take a walk. Outside."

"Sounds good. Looks like a gorgeous day."

She headed for the door.

"When Mike gets back, I have a feeling that a lot of our minutes are going to be spoken for."

I told her about the mysterious, inbound assignment.

She nodded that she understood.

"Sorry about my casual attire," she said as we stepped outside. She was wearing a flannel shirt, jeans, and running shoes that looked like they had a fair amount of mileage on them.

"There are a few things that need to be done to make this place fit for human habitation. I've got to check out the stuff in the basement and might get dirty. But first, our little chat yesterday generated a bunch of questions in my poor little brain. I have a list."

She tapped a pencil on a yellow legal pad that already had a lot of scrawling on it.

"Go for it," I said. "Let's hope you're going to bring order to what's been a lot of chaos here."

By the time Mike got back a few minutes after ten, we had covered a lot of ground. I—and Maria—had been right about Judy. She was well organized and quintessentially sensible. During our walk in the sunshine, she convinced me that Sammy Chen and an off-campus safe house should remain separate.

"If *Guoanbu* has tried to recruit him four times, then he's already on the skyline. Your so-called safe house will be blown before the electricity is turned on," she said. And she was absolutely right.

"Also, while we're talking about a safe house, I think *I* should be the one who checks it out and rents it. I'll take pictures and give you a description, not to mention my opinion. That way you and Darps stay more or less out of sight. Which is the whole idea."

When we got back to the office, she had me dig out Rebecca Wolfe's email and phone number.

"Hell, the president put you to work while you were still teaching. We may as well start tapping into Miss Rebecca's expertise by putting her to work right away."

She convinced me that I needed to hire two geeks for our technology as well as a budget analyst/accountant. Plus at least two administrative specialists.

"Jesus. I just told the president yesterday that *BIAS* would have a total of nineteen souls on board. Now we're up to twenty-four."

"Like the Leader of the Free World really gives a darn about five down-in-the-weeds government drones," she said, a little acerbically. "Besides, his guidance to you originally was to hold the total at or below thirty. You're at twenty-four. No problem."

I had to admit that her point was well taken.

Then she hit the really important key.

"I'm going to order a coffee catering service," she said. "We don't need to drink this swill that you and Luke and whoever concoct. We'll get a couple of blends and decaf for those who need it. The vendor will supply self-contained coffee maker-thermos combinations. They'll supply the coffee. All we have to do is dump the package and add water. And pay. Everything'll be taken care of."

When Mike came back, he was carrying a rigid briefcase. There was a four-digit combination lock on each hasp. The hasps were locked. There was a brass plate on the case under the handle that said, *AL-1*. I guessed it meant, "*Alan Llewellyn dash One.*"

"Did anybody give you combinations?" I asked.

"Not *per se*," Mike said. He handed me a slip of paper folded in half.

"The Marine who gave me the briefcase handed me this."

I unfolded it. It had a logo of a coat of arms at the top with "KEHOE" in block letters underneath the crest. Then, "4 X 8 Relay Record—JMK" scrawled in pen.

The four by eight-hundred relay. We had set the school record. Eighteen years ago. Seven minutes, fifty-two point six seconds. All of us under two minutes! The record time was burned in my memory forever. Seven-five-two-six. I set the numbers on the left hasp lock and tried it. *Click!* It opened. I tried it again on the other lock. Same result. I opened the briefcase.

At first, I thought it was empty. Then I poked around in the little pen-pencil-calculator-cell phone pockets. There was a USB flash drive—one of those little data storage gizmos about the size of a pack of chewing gum—in one of the pockets. There was a yellow post-it note on the drive with the words: "Llewellyn's eyes only - No copies. JMK," scrawled in black Sharpie.

"Sorry," I said. "I gotta look at this in private. More later."

Everybody left. I stuck the little drive in one of the laptop's USB ports. There was only one item on the drive—a scanned document. I opened it. The first half-dozen lines had been redacted with a black marker. The next several lines had been circled with the same marker. The circled paragraph read as follows:

> One well-placed source reports that the PRC has a sophisticated network in place that has as its aim the manipulation of the upcoming presidential elections in Argentina. These efforts are all false-flag operations, ensuring their deniability. Large sums of money have been laundered and disbursed to political parties and politicians who, if in power, would presumably act in ways that are sympathetic to the Government of China. There is no collateral on this issue.

In the margin, the words, *"Loose: Tell me what you think. Keys,"* had been handwritten. The writing appeared to be the same as that on the tape. I remembered the relay team. We had nicknames that were variations or corruptions of our actual names. Larry Graham the leadoff man was "Cracker"; John Scully was "Skull." Kehoe was "Keys," and I was "Loose" Llewellyn. I called Darps on the phone. And disobeyed another presidential order when he popped in the door.

"Take a look at this," I said, turning the laptop so he could see it.

"Jesus Christ," he said. "'No collateral' means there's no sources other than the one quoted. That's no doubt why your buddy wants us to take a look at it."

"We need to get Sammy up here now!" I said.

"You're right," he said. "I'll call him right away."

He pulled out his cell phone and punched in numbers.

"Sammy!" he said. "You're hired. You need to get your ass up here ASAP! We've got a major issue brewing. *BIAS* will cover the airfare and any other travel costs. You'll be on the clock, pro rata, as soon as you hit the road. We'll be finished in a day—maybe less. Rent a car at Reagan National and drive to Ripley Hall on the Martha Washington University campus. If you get in late or early, go to a motel and crash and we'll see you at sunrise tomorrow."

He listened for thirty or forty seconds.

"No sweat," he said into his phone. "You can go right back and clean up whatever you need to in the way of loose ends. You can be in and out of here in twenty-four hours or less. But now, we have an issue brewing and we need you!"

He listened for a few more seconds and then hung up the phone.

"He's on the way," he said.

"Keep me posted on his timetable," I said. "Do you have any thoughts on the PRC trying to influence Argentine elections?" I asked.

"Actually, I do," Darps replied. "They're not particularly well-formed thoughts. More lizard-think than anything else."

I thought about Maria and her "gut-think." Which was always pretty good. I hired Darps because I felt the same way about his.

"Talk to me," I said.

"Think about Spain," he said. "Those Arab swine blew up the Spanish trains. And Bingo! The Spaniards immediately caved and elected a new government that was soft on Arab terrorism. Because they're scared shitless. Regardless of how fucking good their soccer team is. So now we have a Western democracy—Spain—that has a government handpicked by Islamist terrorists. Think about it. Spain! Moorish chickens coming home to roost! That lesson can't have been lost on the Chinese. But they're a hell of a lot more subtle than the Arabs. Not to mention smarter and wealthier. They don't have to blow up subways. They can just spread their money around. They know it will work. And so they try it in Argentina where their influence is waxing. If it works there, then what?"

"So, do we already have an answer to the boss's question?" I asked.

"Not really!" Darps replied. "That's just gut-think. *My* gut-think. We need some boots-on-ground expertise. Or at least loafers-on-the-ground. Let's wait till Sammy gets here."

An hour later he was back in my office where I was finishing up a pile of email.

"Sammy's at Palm Beach International," he said. "He just went through security and is due in at Reagan National at sixteen-forty five. From Atlanta."

That was at four forty-five this afternoon.

"Call him back. Tell him to forget the rental car. We'll meet him at the airport. That way we can shoot the shit about the Chinese while we're stuck in traffic."

He did. And spoke to Sammy.

"We'll meet you at the baggage claim and give you a lift to your hotel. We'll also get you back to your return flight to Florida. And, of course, we'll pick up the tab."

He nodded.

"Later," he said, pocketing the phone. "They're getting ready to push back. He has to turn off his phone," he explained.

Thirty-Five

Richmond
March 18th
Thursday

Quing Maili cleaned off her desk, which was not a difficult task as she kept it neat and chaos-free throughout the day. Two file folders needed to be put away. Her notes were headed for the shredder. She took care of the loose ends. She felt relaxed. Colonel Yang had gone home—or wherever. He was gone. She was looking forward to a quiet evening in her Richmond apartment—a little farther out on the Fan. First she would go to her gym. Do her evening "triathlon." Twenty minutes on the elliptical trainer, twenty more minutes on the exercise bike, and finally, twenty minutes swimming laps in the pool. A solid hour of vigorous exercise. It helped with shedding the stress associated with working for a self-absorbed ass like Lieutenant Colonel Yang Zemin. At home, there was an American microwaveable Dinty Moore Beef Stew dinner in the little pantry. Maili wasn't crazy about American cuisine, but had an inordinate fondness for Dinty Moore beef stew. There was a bottle of Smoking Loon Merlot. There was NCIS this evening on the television.

She was locking her file cabinet when her cell phone chimed for an inbound text message. She turned her phone off. *Workout time, followed by Dinty Moore and Smoking Loon time,* she thought happily. She locked the office door and walked down the stairs to the street entrance. Her Mini-Cooper was parked two and a half blocks away. The gym was another ten blocks. She often thought about walking the whole way. Glancing at her watch, she opted for the walk.

Thirty-Six

I drove the Expedition. I had the classified briefcase with the POTUS flash drive with me. It wasn't handcuffed to my wrist but it did feel like an albatross around my neck. The flash drive probably would have been just as secure in my trouser pocket, but I carried it in the super briefcase anyway. Darps had the forty-five. The trip to National was easy enough. But already we could see that the trip south would probably be the usual nightmare. A lot of D.C.–Northern Virginia commuters must leave work well before three thirty, and a lot of them were packing I-95 South already. Maybe by the time Sammy's plane got in, the I-95 mobs would have thinned out a bit. I hoped but doubted it. I parked in short-term parking at the airport and we went directly to the baggage claim area. According to the monitor, Delta Airways Flight 1838 was on time and landing. Ten minutes later, Sammy appeared.

"Hello chaps! I only have carry-on," he said. "Let's go."

We avoided I-95 and took the George Washington Parkway to Mount Vernon, then Route One to Woodbridge before we came to a complete stop where Route One linked up with I-95. Darps drove on the return trip. It was stop-and-go from there to Stafford, so we had plenty of time to pick Sammy's brain.

"There's an intel report floating around that says the PRC is spending big bucks trying to influence Argentine elections," I said. I opened the laptop and popped in the flash drive. I passed it back to Sammy. "Supposedly, they're doing it on the sly, laundering the cash before it ends up in the hands of politicians—to include a presidential candidate. Do you think that's credible?" I asked while Darps concentrated on the traffic.

Sammy pondered for about a microsecond.

"Hell, yes," he said. "It sure as hell is credible! I'm surprised that the story is buried in a single, presumably classified, intel report 'floating around' rather than being a lead story in *The Economist*. And I'll bet that, sooner rather than later, you'll see reports of the same sort of thing going on in Chile, Venezuela, and Brazil. And after that, probably Panama and Mexico."

"Holy shit," Darps muttered. "Where do you get that kind of info? Or maybe I should say, from whom do you get that kind of info?"

"Um, I hesitate to give specific names as I would probably attribute at least some of the stuff inaccurately or incorrectly. Plus, the names aren't household words. But this is stuff I hear about all the time in China. It comes from academics—university professors. And also newsmen and women. Reporters, columnists, and editors. And some businessmen, for that matter. It's talked about quite openly—as long as *Guoanbu* spooks aren't sniffing around. Also, I think the guys who are running their mouths tend to forget I'm an American. I speak the lingo and am the same color. And besides, those folks don't see meddling in another country's political processes as something at all shady or sinister. Rather, they seem to look at it—influencing politics and elections—sort of like plowing profits back into an enterprise to make more and bigger profits. And profits are what we're talking about here. Money. Dollars. Yuan. Whatever. Ideology isn't really a factor."

Well, I thought. Now at least I have a meaningful response to Cheetah's question. The response cost the American taxpayer just over fifteen hundred bucks. The tab for Sammy's trip. That seemed pretty pricey to me, but in the grand scheme of things, it probably wasn't.

We parked Sammy in a Best Western in Stafford, just north of Chestertown. Darps worked his cell phone, and Sammy got online with his laptop. Sammy was able to change his flight reservations for earlier in the day tomorrow, and Darps arranged for Luke to get him to the airport. Once we had that nailed down, we walked across the parking lot to Rooney's Irish Pub for a pint of Guinness. I called Maria from the bar and told her I'd be home in forty-five minutes—that would make it close to eight. I was glad I didn't have to make that Washington commute every day.

Thirty-Seven

Chestertown
March 19th
Friday

March nineteenth. The feast of Saint Joseph and the day that the swallows return to Capistrano. The mission of San Juan Capistrano in California, that is. Here in Virginia, the doors were unlocked, the lights were on, and I smelled freshly brewed coffee when I arrived at Ripley Hall at seven thirty. Right outside the downstairs conference room there was a table set up with dark brown urns with glowing orange lights on them. Above the shiny metal spouts. One of the urns was labeled "French Roast," another was labeled "Breakfast Blend," and the last was labeled "Decaf." In green.

I grabbed my mug, held it under the spout with the "Breakfast Blend" label, and pushed. Delicious smelling coffee sloshed into my cup. Judy's idea about the coffee service caterer was a definite winner.

I took my steaming mug into my office. Judy followed me in. I noticed that she was carrying one of the super briefcases—the twin of the case that had flown to Quantico from the White House in an HMX-1 helo. For a second, I thought that she'd lifted mine but mine was under my desk where I'd put it a couple of minutes ago. She must use the same supply catalog as the White House.

"Good morning, Alan," she said. "Do you have a minute?"

"I always have minutes for you," I said. "And by the way, good catch on the coffee caterer."

She smiled and sat, held the briefcase in her lap, fiddled with the little combination gizmos, and popped the lid open. Then she put a manila folder on the middle of my desk. It was labeled "12335 North Plank Road." I opened the folder and saw a photo of the dumpy little white house between Chancellorsville and the Wilderness with the "For Rent" sign out in front.

The next photo was a closer-in shot of the house. Then, there were several exterior shots of the house from various angles. After that, there was a series of interior shots. The rooms were mostly empty and appeared to be relatively clean. Under the photos was a yellow legal pad note with perfect Palmer Method handwriting.

I called the number on the sign. A man said the house is an old guesthouse on his farm. We can get it for $650 per month including utilities, but we pay for telephone service. This place is Spartan but very clean. Should work as S.H. unless you require luxury. There's none of that. No A/C. There is heating and it works. There is also minimal furnishing as you can see in the photos. Two chairs in the "living room," a table with three chairs in the kitchen. Top of the stove works, but I didn't check the oven. I didn't figure you guys would be roasting turkeys or rib roasts out there. There is an ancient microwave, which is really small but works. There are two twin beds and a dresser in the downstairs bedroom. Nothing in the upstairs bedroom, which is tiny. There's an old TV set on a stand in the living room and the plumbing all works. One full bath and one powder room. The owner says he can keep an eye on the house from his farmhouse on the hill and will be happy to do so. My recommendation is that the place is ideal for what you need and we should grab it while you can. Just give me the word and I'll set it up.

Cheers,

J

I gave her a "thumbs up" sign.

"Good to go," I said. "Don't worry about getting the phone turned on. We'll use mobiles. If anything."

She returned the thumbs up, smiled, and left. It felt odd talking to her in these truncated sentences. But it seemed necessary.

Darps popped in the door.

"Sammy is on the way home," he said.

"Time for me to write up what he told us and send it to the old man," I said. "It'll be interesting to see if Whitehead gets involved," I added. "After all, it was the question of Chinese involvement that got him all spun up the last time."

"Yeah. We'll see how much control your buddy Kehoe has over his staff, too."

Darps left and I started typing. My memo to POTUS would be short and sweet.

Mr. President,

We dragged our soon-to-be China desk guy up from Florida and asked about the likelihood of the PRC trying to influence internal politics in Argentina. Conversations w/ Chinese academics, businessmen, and journalists in China strongly suggest to him that this sort of thing is not at all rare—and is definitely going on in Argentina. He's convinced that there will be more of this kind of activity elsewhere in Latin America—Chile, Brazil, and Venezuela— and also Panama and Mexico as well.

Very respectfully,

Loose

I saved the note on the same little flash drive on which he'd sent me the original intelligence report. Then I buzzed Darps.

"If you've got a minute, I'd like to get a sanity check from you," I said.

"Be right there," he said.

I showed him the note on my laptop. He read it in about ten seconds, leaned back, and stared at the ceiling. Then he looked at me.

"It answers his question. But it begs another one," he said.

I knew what he meant immediately.

"Are they doing it here?"

"Bingo," he said.

"Wanna take a walk?" I asked.

Outside, the clouds were thick and low and the temperature must have been hovering around freezing. March in Virginia. One never knows.

"Two things," I said. "Judy's getting the safe house. The one I told you about between Chancellorsville and the Wilderness. Six-fifty a month. It has heat but no A.C."

"Heat is good—today. But we'll roast in the summer. I assume the second thing has to do with the Chinese."

"Yeah. We can put in a window A.C. unit before it gets too hot. Can you send Sammy an email with your phone?"

"Of course."

He pulled out the phone and glanced at it.

"I'm guessing he's on the ground in West Palm," he said. "Maybe texting him would be faster if it's not too long."

"Ask him 'can they do it here?' He'll know what we mean."

Sammy's answer came through before we arrived back at Ripley Hall. And we hadn't gone far because of the cold. Darps handed me the phone.

Hll yes! Probly alrdy r.

"Well, there you have it, sports fans," I said. "Methinks I have material for an add-on to my little note to the man."

"I'm glad we're getting that heated dump. Since I've been here, I feel like I've walked more than the Welsh corgi that the Chinese were using to case your house," Darps muttered. "And I'm really getting tired of being out in this freakin' cold."

He followed me into my office. I opened up the laptop and inserted the flash drive. When my note showed up on the screen, I typed, adding a new, final sentence:

When I questioned our expert if he thought that the Chinese could do the same thing in CONUS, he advised that they probably already are.

Darps read over my shoulder.

"That says it all in a nice neat nutshell. Answered the man's question," he said. "And something else just occurred to me. It has to do with what we were discussing outside. I'm thinking it might be good if we lawyered up."

"You mean hire a lawyer?"

"Maybe not full-time. But somebody on a retainer, at least. Maybe some K-Street type who's retired but knows his or her way around the government and can keep our young asses out of jail."

"Lemme think about that one," I said.

I saved the new version of the memo, pulled the flash drive out of the laptop, and put a strip of masking tape on it. Then I printed, *"Cheetah Eyes Only"* with a black Sharpie on the tape. I stashed the drive in the pen pocket of the super briefcase and locked it up.

"Now we just have to get the damned thing up the road."

Darps took the briefcase.

"I'll talk to Mike. We'll figure something out."

They did. Mike made a phone call. He grabbed the briefcase and Darps drove him to the Chestertown railroad station where he boarded a Virginia Railway Express train for Washington. He got off at the National Airport stop where he passed the briefcase to a Secret Service buddy who had taken the Metro to National and would ride it back to the White House. Mike had to cool his heels for forty-five minutes before catching a southbound Amtrak train back to Chestertown. He was gone a little less than three hours. Not terribly efficient, but not bad with airtight security. And there was a bonus. He brought back another super briefcase that his

Secret Service buddy had passed to him. The brass tag on this one said *AL – 2*. The Kehoe memo said, *"Same Record."*

I understood. Sure enough, seven-five-two-six, our high school record, worked the locks. Inside, the only thing was another Kehoe memo that read:

Nothing this time. But I do think you need a second secure briefcase. Have a great weekend.

Keys.

I was shrugging into my leather jacket prior to walking home when Judy popped into the office. She held up a key.

"What's this?" I asked.

"Take it," she said. "I'm sure you'll have it figured out by the time you get home. I'll give one to Darps. Spares in my safe."

She squinted her lavender eyes and gave me a sly-and-silly grin.

"Thanks," I said, taking the key to the safe house. "And have a great weekend."

Thirty-Eight

Chestertown
March 19th – 20th
Friday-Saturday

Having fed the Cheetah with, what I felt was, high-quality, lean red meat of information and informed opinion, there was a spring in my step as I walked home to fifteen-oh-six Prince Henry Street. When I tried to let myself in, the front door was locked. I took out my keys, unlocked it, and went inside.

"Hello? Anybody home?" I called.

Silence.

Damn. I was looking forward to boasting to Maria about a successful day doing stuff for the President of the United States. I went into the kitchen.

"E & I are @ Giant. Back by 6," was scrawled on our white message board. A glance at one of the multiple clocks in the kitchen told me it was five thirty. I knew from my walk home that it was still damp and raw outside. I kindled what could be the last fire of the season, poured myself a scotch, and studied various stored takeout menus. My boasting would have to wait a little.

The fire was blazing merrily, and I had just taken off my shoes and put my feet up on the coffee table when my all-purpose phone vibrated.

Damn again, I thought. I should have turned the freakin' thing off when I'd exited Ripley Hall.

It was Darps. A text.

Chk email

I did, shifting the phone to *Mail*. Darps was jerking me around.

152

From: **roentgen86@bias.gov**

To: **allewellyn@bias.gov**

Subj: Big One

Have a pretty firm line on a possible legal beagle. You won't believe who it is! It is someone who has major league clout and definitely knows where the bods are buried. Keep your phone turned on over the weekend.

I heard a car in the driveway, then a bunch of giggling, and the mudroom door opened. Four females burst into the kitchen and then into the family room where I sat with my open phone in my hand and an untouched drink. Maria, Elizabeth, Tala, and Esmé. Elizabeth was toting a Giant plastic grocery bag.

"You don't have to go out for takeout," Maria said, eyeing the menus on the couch beside me. "Giant is having a sale on tuna salad subs, so we got a bunch of them. I also got some tomato and basil soup, today being a Lenten Friday. The girls are having supper here," she added.

"Sweet!" I said. "That way, I get to have dinner with four beautiful women instead of just two."

Elizabeth made a gagging motion with her finger and her mouth. Esmé and Tala giggled. Maria rolled her eyes.

I poured a glass of sherry for Maria and added ice cubes to my watery scotch. The three chicklettes scampered upstairs, and Maria was giving me a funny look.

"What's the matter?" she asked. "You had the weirdest expression on your face when we walked in the door."

I pointed to the phone.

"Nothing's really wrong," I said. "My old Navy classmate is jerking me around a little bit."

"Darps?"

"The same. Take a glance at the email," I said, handing her the phone.

She sat and took a sip of sherry.

"Tchh!" she snorted. "What a tease!"

"I was thinking of another word. It begins with a 'p,'" I said. "And rhymes with 'sick.'"

"But he's your friend and confidant," she said.

"Yes, that's very true. And, because we're shipmates, he thinks it'll be fun to jack me around over the weekend. I've half a mind to shut down my phone and not turn it on till Monday morning just to piss him off."

I sat down on the sofa, turned her head gently toward me and planted a kiss on her lips. That made me forget about Darps and his hotshot lawyer.

"How was the rest of your day?" Maria asked.

"Pretty darned good, actually," I said. "We put together a short but to-the-point paper for our main customer. It was a good thing that we were able to pick Sammy's brain yesterday. Most of our competition apparently isn't seeing what Sammy has been seeing, nor hearing what he's been hearing. So I feel like I've really been earning the king's shilling today."

"Good for you," she said, patting me on the knee. "Pour me a splash of sherry while I put the soup on."

I freshened up her sherry, as requested, and dumped a little dollop of scotch on the diluted remains of my drink.

Dinner was a learning experience for me as it always is when Elizabeth's friends are there. It's surprising how smart twelve-year olds can be. But, then again, there are some stunning gaps in their overall awareness. These girls are articulate, well read, and clever to a fault. The awareness gaps are widest when it comes to non-popular-culture happenings in the real world. But then, they are still kids. And one would hope that a bit of innocence went along with that. In any case, it was fun to share a Lenten meal with them. At one point in the conversation, I did express my hopes for warmer, drier weather and improving fishing conditions. Elizabeth shared my hopes for same. Esmé and Tala, not being angler women, looked at us like we were speaking Lithuanian.

Saturday morning's weather was a continuation of Friday's. Both Llewellyn women had the good sense to sleep in. I had started my second cup of coffee and the crossword puzzle when my "special" phone vibrated on the counter. It was a text message:

Run 2day @ 12n @ LZ Hornet. Keys

"Jesus H. Christ," I muttered. Kehoe himself was "inviting" me to run with him. I wondered what that was about.

Thirty-Nine

Quantico
March 20th
Saturday

It was still raining pretty hard at eleven fifty when I parked the Expedition off the road at Landing Zone Hornet. There were three Marine Humvees and two more Expeditions parked in front of where I parked. There were Marines in ponchos with rifles and civilians in raincoats standing around the LZ. One of the civilians approached, and then I realized it was Mike.

"Hi Alan!" he said. "Ready to run?"

"Sure," I said. "Where the hell are *your* running duds?"

Mike was wearing a tan trench coat over a tie-less blue Oxford shirt, gray civilian dress slacks, and black penny loafers.

"You guys are too fast for me," he said with a sheepish grin.

"Oh bullshit. You just don't want to run in the rain, you pussy!"

Five minutes later I heard and then saw two HMX-1 helicopters landing steeply into the middle of the zone.

Jim Kehoe was the second one off the lead helo after a Marine. He was wearing a Yankees ball cap and a Mindzenty High School sweatshirt. He saw me right away.

"Hey Alan!" he yelled, waving. "Let's run. Everybody is telling me I'm too dumb to come in from the rain!"

I slipped alongside him as a big Secret Service runner pulled out in front of us. As we reached the road, a Marine Corps military police sedan, followed by a Humvee full of riflemen, pulled in front of us. I glanced back over my shoulder and saw that six runners were behind us. Three of them had black Secret Service ball caps and three had red Marine Corps ball caps. There was another Humvee behind the runners. It was like running in a Memorial Day parade.

155

"So, what's up, Mr. President?" I asked.

"Damn it, Alan," he snarled. "How many times do I have to tell you? We're classmates and relay teammates. I'm Jim. If you insist on formality when we're in a crowd, I can live with that. But when it's just us two jerk-offs running in the rain, you're 'Alan" or 'Loose' and I'm 'Jim' or 'Keys,' just like the bad old days in high school."

I laughed.

"You're a piece of work, Keys," I said. "So why the hell did you drag me out here to run in the rain with you on a Saturday afternoon?"

We crossed over the roaring Lake Lunga spillway outflow. The president glanced at the water rushing through the culverts beneath us.

"Several reasons. An invitation, for starters. You and Elizabeth are invited to wet a line at Camp David next Saturday. My original plan was for the three of us to fish together, but it turns out that I won't be able to join you—I have a couple of meetings with folks that I don't want to bring out to Camp David. So I'll stay in Washington. And hopefully the weather will be better than today's. Luke or Mike will go over the logistics with you. And the kitchen staff will fix lunch for Elizabeth and you before you head back to Chestertown."

"Wow!" I said. "She'll go absolutely nuts with excitement. Thanks."

It felt like we were doing a little bit over eight minutes per mile. 'Keys' seemed very comfortable with that pace and showed no indication of wanting to crank it up faster. That was fine with me.

"I also wanted to tell you how much I appreciated your quick response on the China-Argentina business. On top of that, I needed a good long run today. And finally, I felt badly about forgetting to invite you to run when we had our little meeting with Walt and Allison. So this is a make-up run. How're things going with *BIAS*?"

"Pretty well, actually. We hired two more intel weenies. Middle East and Central Asia specialists. And Sammy, our China specialist will be aboard full-time starting Tuesday. Darps thinks we need a lawyer."

"Uh-oh. Needing a lawyer. Should that cause me to lose sleep?"

"No sir. I think we're just being prudent. Making sure we stay away from stuff that might cause you to lose sleep."

We turned left and headed down a long, washboard road toward Camp Barrett. The rain continued, cold and steady. I thought that yesterday's fire was definitely not the last one of the season for the Llewellyn hearth in Chestertown. After clearing Camp Barrett, we went down a long, straight hill, giving us ample opportunity to visually survey the long, straight hill opposite, which we would have to run up. We crossed Beaver Dam Run at the bottom and started up the hill. I resisted the temptation to jack up the pace and bust the president's balls. In fact, as he slowed down about two-thirds of the way to the top, I slowed with him.

"This hill is a ball-buster," he hissed.

"You've got that right," I told him.

Our little running convoy trundled past the rifle range and the FBI Academy in the rain. It was gently rolling terrain, and we both seemed to recover from the hill—somewhat.

"Alan, there actually is something I'd like you to take a look at," he said.

Uh-oh, I thought.

"The goddamn Chinese have me worried. I'm getting zilch—zippo—nada—from the U.S. Intelligence Community about the PRC meddling in the politics of other countries. I get tons of stuff on their naval modernization, their research, their petroleum import plans—you name it. Except for their dicking around in other countries' politics. Other than that one report I cited to you. It came from a CIA case officer in Hong Kong who seems to have a pretty good Chinese source. I only got the report by accident. Somebody mistakenly attached it to another, bigger report on China. But it did catch my eye. Your guy, Sammy, on the other hand, says it's common knowledge in Beijing that they're playing around in South America's politics. Why the fuck doesn't the CIA or the State Department or DIA or NSA report anything about China spraying money around South America to try and influence elections? I mean, Jesus Christ, we have a two-hundred-fifty person staff at the U.S. Embassy in Buenos Aires! Not to mention the huge staffs we have in Beijing, Shanghai, and Hong Kong! We've got all kinds of collection assets worldwide. Plus the technical stuff! And nobody knows that the Chinese are buying Argentine votes? I need a dozen or so sheets of paper from you guys—a follow up on your recent excellent piece. Give me an overview of Chinese meddling in political processes worldwide. Try and emphasize what may be happening here in the good ole USA. With attention on their inclination to use violence as well as cash. Does that make sense?"

"I can get you something by C.O.B. Tuesday," I said. "We need Sammy for this," I added.

"Tuesday or Wednesday will be fine. There's another issue. Syd is in Bethesda this morning. More chest pains. I don't think he's at death's door or anything. I spoke with him on the phone—he called to say that he was more or less okay. But, if the Chinese popped Rick DiRienzo to keep him off the ticket—you can see where I'm going with this."

"Yes sir. At least I think I do."

"I don't want to put another life at risk by making another VP announcement."

"If memory serves, there was no announcement about Congressman DiRienzo being named VP," I said.

"Yeah. I thought about that, too. Somebody must have leaked that information."

"Yes sir," I said again. "Or there may be no Chinese connection whatsoever."

"I know. But I just have a funny feeling about this stuff. And it was you that surfaced the possibility of a Chinese connection with DiRienzo."

"But with very low odds," I said.

"Yeah. I remember."

"Mr. President—Jim—let me kick the whole Chinese thing around with Darps and Sammy in a couple of days. Shooting a U.S. congressman is a far cry from laundering money to give to Argentinean political action committees."

"Sounds good to me. Just get me something by mid-week."

"We'll get you something. I just don't know how good it'll be."

"Right now, anything is better than nothing, Alan."

We were approaching LZ Hornet and we both slowed down. The entourage slowed with us.

"I don't know whether that's true or not, Jim," I said as we slowed to a halt at the edge of LZ Hornet. I was thinking, *What if what we give him is totally wrong?*

A Marine materialized out of nowhere and handed Kehoe a white towel. Then the Marine held out a white towel to me.

"Here, sir," he said, simply.

Kehoe wiped his face and head. I followed suit and handed the towel back to the Marine.

"Thanks," I said.

Kehoe and I shook hands.

"Thanks, Loose," he said and turned and jogged to the lead helo.

Both birds spooled up their engines. I watched them take off in the rain and then went home soaking wet.

Forty

Chestertown and Chancellorsville
March 20th
Saturday

I was still soaked when I got home and chilled to the bone in the bargain.

"How did it go with the main man?" Maria asked.

"Mainly wet," I said. "Let me poach myself back to ninety-eight-point-six degrees in a hot shower. Then I'll fill you in while I fix myself some lunch. I'm starved as well as cold and wet."

At the top of the stairs, I heard cackling from the direction of Elizabeth's room, so I walked down and poked my head in. Sure enough, the three musketeers were having some sort of digital gabfest. All three were pushing keys on cell phones. Okay, it was a text fest.

"Hi, Dad! Hi, Mr. Llewellyn!"

"Hi, ladies!"

"Dad! You're all wet!"

Raucous laughter ensued.

"I wish I could tell *my* dad that he was all wet and not get in trouble," Esmé said.

"Just wait until he comes in from running in the pouring rain," I advised.

"Did you really run with the president, Mr. El?" Tala asked.

"Yes, I did. And got cold and wet for my troubles. I'll tell you about it—after I'm dry and warm."

When I got downstairs wearing ratty but dry corduroy slacks and an equally ratty Augustine Washington High School sweatshirt, I was delighted to see that the Faire Maria had whipped me up a roast beef-with-lettuce-and-horseradish sandwich on pumpernickel and poured me a glass of red wine in the bargain. She had garnished the sandwich with a pile of potato chips. I nibbled one. Salt-and-vinegar. Things were looking up. I tasted the wine and recognized an inexpensive but robust and chocolaty Chilean merlot. Things were really looking up.

"Thank you, Sweetheart," I said, sincerely. "This hits the spot."

"It's a bribe," she said. "Now tell me what you guys talked about during your run."

The texters were clomping down the stairs, no doubt hungry for White House gossip tidbits as well. I took a bite of the sandwich. Seconds later, the sub teens had joined Maria and me at the kitchen table.

"Well—and this will probably be on the evening news—Vice President Girtler is in the Bethesda Naval Hospital," I said. "It may be online already. Chest pains. The prez didn't seem to think it was all that serious, but apparently he and Girtler have chatted about retirement. Girtler's. This isn't the first indication of heart problems."

"Wow! Is that top secret or can we tell anybody?" Esmé asked.

"You can tell your parents—but nobody else. Of course, after it's on the news, you can tell anybody you want."

I was on solid ground telling the kids about Girtler. No real secrets involved. On the other hand, the China stuff was way off limits, so I avoided that completely.

"What else did you and the president talk about, Dad?"

"The lousy weather, running up big hills, the Washington Nationals' spring training in Florida. That's about it. Oh, I almost forgot. He invited us up for some trout fishing next Saturday morning. He won't be there. But we can still fish and then have lunch there."

Elizabeth beamed.

"How could you 'almost forget' something like that?" she asked.

"That is so awesome!" Tala said. "Even though I don't fish. Fishing in the president's private trout stream is way cool!"

My phone gave a little growling noise as it vibrated on the counter across the kitchen. Everybody looked at it. I got up and picked it up. A text. From Darps.

New place @ 1500!? Y or N?

Uh oh, I thought.

I glanced at my watch. One fifty. With Saturday traffic, it would take thirty or thirty-five minutes to reach the new safe house. I had time to finish my sandwich and could easily make it by three. I texted a *Y* to Darps's phone and took another bite of my sandwich. Esmé stole a few of my potato chips. I wondered what was up.

It was fourteen fifty-five when I pulled off the main road and went slowly down the muddy driveway toward the little white house. The rain had quit for now, but it was still gray and clammy. I parked in back, out of sight of the main road. Darps's Saab was already there. There was a light on in the kitchen. The back door opened and there was Darps, looking very much the country squire in flannels, lamb's wool, and tweed.

"Hi, Shipmate!" he said.

"Hi."

I stepped inside.

"Jesus," I said. "This place feels like a morgue. We could store dead bodies in here."

"Not to worry. I just got here and turned on the heat. There's no stiffs lying around and there's warm air coming in from the furnace. Meantime, we can have a wee dram to take the chill off."

He pulled a bottle of Dewar's and a package of paper cups from a shopping bag and poured each of us an inch.

"Cheers. Sorry no ice."

"Cheers. Just as well. It's so damp and cold in here that the very thought of ice makes me shiver. What's up?"

He held up a hand and walked over to the antique television and turned it on. There didn't appear to be a remote. There was a Yankees Grapefruit League game in progress being broadcast from Tampa. He revved up the volume a little.

"Hiring a lawyer," he said.

I took a sip of the whisky.

"That's what you hinted at in your email on Friday," I said. "I've got no objection to running out here for a nip of scotch on a weekend and on short notice. But talking about hiring lawyers would be something that would seem to be a natural for Monday morning coffee in Ripley Hall. Or am I missing something?"

"If we decide to make this move, we have to move fast," he said. "And I'm not talking about generic lawyers. I'm talking about Miles Guilfoyle."

"Are you shitting me?"

Miles Guilfoyle was a Washington household name. He had been an adviser to several recent presidents, including the incumbent, and had been mentioned for various cabinet-level posts. Word on the street was that he'd never become a finalist because he'd banged scores of Washington A-List women over the years. He'd been working in the White House since completing a successful tour as U.S. ambassador to the Peoples' Republic of China a couple of years ago.

"He retired a few weeks ago. There was a news item in the *Post* about Kehoe giving him the Medal of Freedom. So I called to congratulate him. He didn't say so, but I'm betting Whitehead pissed him off and that's why he bailed out. He and I did some work together on a project on East Asian power shifts while I was at Savants. He knows his way around the Far East. He knows Sammy, too. I thought with all this presidential interest in China—not to mention the Chinese interest in *BIAS*—he might be a good guy to have on the team. And, as we've talked about, we do need a legal counsel."

"I don't get it. Why in hell would a hotshot like Guilfoyle want to come out of retirement to work in a low-rent operation like *BIAS*?"

"Honestly, I think he just wants to keep his hand in. You know, 'the grand game' and all that. We can get him for a retainer of a thousand a week. That buys us one day a week of his time for forty-eight weeks a year. He and his wife do Christmas in London for two weeks and two weeks on Martha's Vineyard in the summer."

"Must be nice. But that still seems cheap for a high roller like him," I said.

"He's not in it for the money. His family already has plenty. Being a White House counsel or an ambassador doesn't make one wealthy. Necessarily. He defines himself as a true patriot. He'd prefer to work at home in Alexandria as much as possible but he can come to campus whenever we need him to. He and I clicked pretty well in the past. But don't expect him to run with you and Kehoe over the moors and fens of Quantico. He's eighty-two years old. He is very spry and alert for his age, but he's rather large, to say the least, so I doubt he runs. He's married to a Malaysian woman fifty years younger than he, the sly dog. He needs to know by noon tomorrow. He's got another offer on the table, but says he'd prefer to go with us."

The little house's gas heater was starting to work. I could no longer see my breath. I took another pull of the tepid scotch. Then I made a quick decision.

"Sign him up. You've worked with him. You know him. You think highly of him. If you think he'd be a player, let's get him. But I need to meet him soon."

"How about Monday? For lunch?"

"Sounds good. Since he lives in Alexandria and since I didn't get lunch the last time I was up there, let's try the Afghan place. *Buzkashi.*"

"Just so long as you don't tell *him* to go fuck himself like you told Whitehead."

"No sweat, G.I.," I said.

"I'll call him this evening and try to set it up," Darps muttered. "Probably be a good idea to avoid any electronic emissions from this place. Want another inch of scotch?"

"Where's the crab dip? The smoked salmon?" I hectored. "Half an inch," I added.

He poured into our white cups.

"Got a text from HRH this morning. We went for a run on base in the pouring rain," I said.

"No shit? What was that about?"

"PRC. Specifically about them fucking around with other countries' politics—worldwide. He wants a follow-up to the memo we sent him yesterday."

"All the better to have Guilfoyle at the table," he said. "Want me to try and move the lunch up to tomorrow?"

I took a sip of his booze and thought for a couple of seconds. Kehoe had said he wanted about a dozen pages on Tuesday or Wednesday. No reason to start screwing up peoples' weekends. I was sure there would be plenty of that down the road.

"Nah. Let's stay with Monday. Tomorrow, stay home and chase your wife around the apartment."

"Xi xi," he said. "That's Mandarin for 'many thanks.'"

Forty-One

Chestertown
March 20th
Saturday

I rolled into the driveway at fifteen-oh-six Prince Henry Street at sixteen forty-five.

Maria and Elizabeth were watching golf. Neither one plays, but they love watching the big tournaments. Tala and Esmé had apparently gone home.

"Darps says 'Hi,'" I said.

"So that's where you were," Maria said. "With Darps."

"Right. With Darps."

"On campus?" she asked.

Maria had been on the phone with her mom when I left. I'd scrawled, "*back @ 1630,*" on the family message board and blown her a kiss, but hadn't said where I was going.

I don't lie. To anybody. Ever. That was drummed into my skull many years ago. Besides, I'm sure that I'd step on my schlong and screw it up if I tried it. So no lying. In the twenty-first century, that probably makes me a weirdo, eccentric anachronism.

"No," I said. "Not on campus."

Her eyebrows bounced up about a quarter of an inch.

"Well where, then?" she asked.

I walked over to our messages white board and scrawled the words, "*Let's go 4 a walk,*" thereon. Both women reached for their coats. I was still wearing mine. Seconds later, we were out the front door.

"Now that we're outside, I can explain. Up to a point," I said. "We have a safe house. *BIAS* has a safe house, that is. Only Darps, Judy, and

166

I—and now, you two—know that we have it. We never refer to it indoors. *Never*. Not at home. Not in Ripley Hall. Never indoors."

"Where is it?" Maria asked. "In case of emergency."

"About halfway between here and Culpeper. Just off Route Three," I said. I recited the address. "One-two-three-three-five North Plank Road. If there is an emergency, your best bet is to call Judy. Darps is next choice because he's usually there with me. But we usually turn our cells off when we go there. Except for the one connected to the boss."

I had already given Maria my number on the presidential phone. The one I never turned off.

"Is our house bugged?" Elizabeth asked.

She doesn't miss a trick.

"I don't know," I answered, honestly. "But we have to assume it is."

"So even the president doesn't know of this safe house," Maria said.

"That's right," I said. "Look, I can't emphasize too much how sensitive this is. To buy your silence, I'll spring for takeout sandwiches at Federico's. And I'll even throw in an order of fried calamari," I added, solemnly.

"And an order of wings?" Elizabeth asked sweetly.

"Yes, Sweetheart."

Federico's was less than half a block away.

"What we—Darps and I—talked about there this afternoon was retaining Miles Guilfoyle as the *BIAS* legal counsel."

"That name sounds very familiar," Maria said. "Isn't he some sort of Washington big shot?"

"Yup," I said. "Besides being a lawyer, he was the U.S. ambassador to China and a presidential adviser. Darps knows him from some study the two of them worked on."

That observation seemed to spark a recollection by Elizabeth. Her eyes opened wider.

"Dad, remember when you were talking about Chinese women walking up and down our street?" she asked. "Well, now there are Asian-looking college kids walking up and down Prince Henry. At least I assume they're college kids. They're young. They have backpacks. They go by when the other college kids are walking to and from campus."

"Hmm," I said. "Thanks for sharing that. Let me know if you see them again. Now let's order our sandwiches."

I held the door to Federico's open for the two of them.

Forty-Two

The day was the polar opposite of the day when I met Whitehead at the *Buzkashi* restaurant. Sunny, dry, and warm. There was a light, spring-like breeze out of the south. I parked the government Expedition around the corner from the front entrance. A tall, broad-shouldered man with a wavy mop of white hair was preceding us into the restaurant.

"Hi, Miles!" Darps called. "Miles!" he called a little louder.

The big man stopped and turned.

"Darpley," he said with a warm smile and held out a beefy hand. His expertly tailored blue suit couldn't completely hide his ample girth.

"Hi Miles. This is Alan Llewellyn. Alan, this is Miles Guilfoyle."

We shook.

"Pleased to meet you, Mr. Ambassador," I said.

"Same here. Please call me Miles. And you're 'Alan'? 'A' or 'e'?"

"'A,' with one 'l,'" I said.

"Very good, Alan."

I estimated his height at about six-four and his weight in excess of three hundred pounds. That, plus his feet were on the large side. He was wearing highly polished, black wing tips that appeared to be size fourteen's or maybe even larger. The overall effect was that he seemed larger than life—like an NFL lineman. The shirt was white and a muted blue silk tie disappeared into the buttoned suit jacket.

We were blocking the doors and another patron was seeking to gain entrance. The same well-dressed *maitre d'* I'd seen when I'd met Whitehead at the restaurant broke the logjam.

"Right this way, gentlemen. Mr. Ambassador, it's good to see you, sir. Nice to see you again, Mr. Llewellyn."

"Excellent memory. I'm impressed," I said.

The *maitre d'* smiled his dazzling smile.

He whisked us expertly to the same table I had briefly shared with Whitehead. The establishment's *Stammtisch* for Washington Big Dogs, perhaps? Not that Darps or I qualified as Big Dogs. But Whitehead and Miles certainly did. Or was it a bugged table? Or both?

The *maitre d'* took our drink orders and passed them to the bartender. Guilfoyle ordered a double scotch-and-soda, Darps a Ketel-One martini, and I a Bloody Mary. After a minimum of hemming and hawing, we placed our lunch orders. Guilfoyle and I both ordered a lamb kebab with grilled eggplant and rice pilaf. Darps chose a roasted half-chicken, which also came with the grilled eggplant. We opted to split a bottle of a dry, Turkish red wine with the lunch. The waiter brought us a basket of fresh, warm *Naan*, the Afghan flat bread that we nibbled on while we waited for our entrees.

"Mr. Ambassador," I began. "I assume that Darps has covered what *BIAS* needs from you to your satisfaction. Is there anything that I might be able to help you with?"

Guilfoyle took a healthy sip of scotch and put down his glass.

"Do you play tennis, Alan?" he asked.

Startled, I shot a quick, sidelong glance at Darps who had a little smirk on his face.

"I play, sir. But not very well, I'm afraid. It's been a few years since I stepped on a court. My wife Maria plays often. And she's pretty good."

"I try and play three or four times a week. Perhaps we could get together and hit some from time to time. Perhaps your wife could join us once in a while?"

Darps was still smirking.

Eighty-two years old and three hundred pounds, I thought. *The mind boggles.*

"Perhaps," I said. "And perhaps Darps could add to the mix. I know he used to play when we were at the Naval Academy."

The smirk disappeared.

"Darpley gave me some namby-pamby excuse of having a bad knee," Guilfoyle said. "I told him that it would be at least another thirty years before he really knows what bad knees are."

"Well, then. We'll have to put something together, especially now that the weather is turning nice," I said. "Meantime, I wonder if we could hijack some of your time and East Asian expertise tomorrow. In Chestertown."

"Certainly," he said. "Darpley mentioned that."

"It'll be for most of the day—let's say nine thirty to five or so, with a break for lunch. And this time we'll need your regional expertise rather than your legal background."

"Of course. Darpley made it very clear that that might frequently be the case."

"It's a matter of some urgency, sir. Probably won't be time for tennis," I added, hoping to not piss him off.

"Understand. I'll try and get a quick set in early in the morning. With my wife. She's pretty good."

We passed on dessert, but had Turkish coffee, medium sweet. Between the concentrated caffeine and the sugar, I anticipated no problems with getting drowsy during the drive back to Chestertown.

Forty-Three

Chestertown
March 23rd
Tuesday

I left the house about seven ten. It was semi-dark, but it still felt like we were in for a warm spring day—just as the weather guy had predicted on TV. Two young women walked past number fifteen-oh-six as I approached the sidewalk. Both wore "hoodies" and jeans. Both were carrying what looked to be heavy backpacks. And both were Asian. I thought of Elizabeth's observation a couple of days ago and wondered if we had a new team of watchers keeping an eye on us.

I waited for them to pass and then fell in behind them, not sure whether or not they had seen me emerge from the house in the half-darkness. They proceeded down Prince Henry Street and entered the Martha Washington campus from William Street. I followed, thirty or forty yards back. They went past Ripley Hall, where I saw Darps's Saab parked, and I continued in trace of the two women. They crossed the campus diagonally and exited on Route One where they turned south. One of them appeared to be talking on a cell phone, hardly unusual for a student—or anyone else for that matter. I followed, falling way back, but keeping them in sight. They appeared to be moving in a large circle—or trapezoid, actually, and I confirmed this to myself when they passed fifteen-oh-six Prince Henry Street—again! As we approached campus—again! —I snapped a couple of photos of them from behind with my phone. Then I accelerated and passed them as we went through the gate. By the time I estimated I was seven to ten feet in front of them, I turned and snapped another photo, head-on. They appeared somewhat startled but made no protest, preferring to turn their faces away and taking the first opportunity to change course away from me. I headed back to Ripley Hall.

Mike was in his office.

"Hey, Mike. Got a minute?"

"Sure, Alan. What's up?"

"Elizabeth told me a couple of days ago that she had noticed some Asian female college students walking past the house. This morning, I noticed these two chicks going past the house toward campus. I fell in behind them and they walked past Ripley and then left campus. They circled around past my house again and headed back to campus. I took their picture. Now they're probably telling the campus police about some pervert with a short haircut taking their picture. Could you check them out?"

I handed him the phone. He looked at the head-on photo, squinting.

"Kind of weasely-looking," he mumbled, almost to himself. "Let me download this from your phone, send it in, and see what they say up the road. They look a little older than your average undergraduate, but it's hard to tell with Asians. I'll get back to you."

Mike had no sooner left my office than Darps popped in.

"Sammy's here. Checking in. Judy is taking care of him, shaking him down for his coffee mess dues, important stuff like that. She worked a two-month deal with Guest Suites hotel in Stafford for him, so he's set until he brings the wife and kids up in June. I'm going to run down to the station to meet Miles whose train is due in ten minutes."

Yesterday, after lunch, I had searched the Internet for news on the Peoples' Republic of China dicking around in other countries' politics. Perhaps the ink-stained wretches of the Fourth Estate were too polite to mention it—I didn't believe that for a moment—or maybe there simply wasn't any evidence pointing that way. But there was nothing in the mainstream media or the blogs. Whatever, our little ten- or twelve-page paper for the man would depend wholly on what our two resident experts came up with.

We started the meeting with bagels from Einstein Brothers and our catered coffee. On our SMART board, I listed the names of countries in which our experts—Sammy and Miles—believed that the PRC was spending significant amounts of cash trying to influence elections or other parts of the political process. The list was surprisingly long. I saved and erased. The second list was the names of countries in which the PRC had used violent means for political objectives. Neither Guilfoyle nor Sammy had any candidates. They kicked it around for a few minutes between the two of them and came up with zilch. I scrawled *USA* on the board and they both looked at me like I'd just grown a second head. Darps was sitting behind them and looked like he was enjoying himself.

"In this country?" Sammy asked, his voice dripping with disbelief. "I can see maybe one or two crazy *Americans* maybe using violence to swing political things here, but not the Chinese."

Miles just shook his head.

"DiRienzo," I said.

"The New York congressman? The Chinese took him out?" Sammy asked. He seemed to be gasping for air. "Do we know that for a fact?"

"No," I said. "We do not. But, in my mind, there's a small but finite probability that they did. And since coming to that conclusion, I've revised the probability upwards. It's still very small, but think about it. If the PRC is willing to spend a million bucks to swing an election in Argentina, why should they hesitate to clip a potential vice presidential candidate in the U.S. of A?"

Sammy looked like he was in a state of total concentration, his eyes wide. Miles had a slightly puzzled look on his heavy features. I thought of sending Darps for his Dewar's emergency rations but demurred.

"DiRienzo? Vice? What in God's name are you talking about? When?" Sammy seemed to be hyper-alert, totally focused.

Miles swigged from a bottle of water and didn't say anything.

"Let's take a fifteen-minute break," I said. "I'll try and put the pieces all together when we come back."

Both Miles and Sammy made a beeline for Darps in the back of the room. I went to the head. While I was washing my hands, Mike came in.

"How's the China meeting going?" he asked.

"I honestly don't know," I said. "I mentioned my idea about the Chinese whacking DiRienzo and, for a couple of minutes, I thought Sammy was going to have a heart attack. Miles was able to take it pretty well in stride, but he may have been in on Cheetah's chat with DiRienzo about possibly replacing Girtler."

"Lemme know when you have something ready to go up the road," he said. "I'll make it happen."

"Thanks, Mike. I'm shooting for mid-morning, tomorrow. Let's plan on a launch between ten and ten-thirty. If anything changes on that, I'll let you know right away."

"Um, Alan. The other day when you ran with Cheetah, did he mention a potential replacement for Chipmunk?"

"No, not specifically. I think he may have been a little goosy about it because of what happened to DiRienzo. Why?"

"Well, there's a rumor floating around the Secret Service that he's thinking of and talking with Michelle Hookes about it."

"No shit," I said, stupidly.

Michelle Hookes was an elder stateswoman. She was the widow of a zillionaire who had started with selling bottled tap water and ended up owning an NFL team and a major league baseball franchise simultaneously, among other money generators. A few years after hubby went to his eternal reward, Michelle had been named ambassador to Turkey where, from all reports, she had done an outstanding job. Since then, she was a Washington fixture for most of the year, showing up at high-rent social functions and giving the occasional speech and major-league dinner party. She spent her Julys on Martha's Vineyard. One year, she gave a speech that I had attended when I was still in the Navy. It was at a seminar at Monterey. The speech was entitled, *Thinking about Thinking about Foreign Aid,* and was one of the few speeches I've heard over the years that I remembered. It was clear, articulate, and elegant. And it made perfect sense. That was about ten years ago, and she was in her sixties then. I wondered if Miles Guilfoyle had boffed her. Michelle was tiny, maybe five feet, one inch tall. Oh, the horror.

"That's some rumor," I said.

I got a Breakfast Blend refill and went back to the conference room and went to the white board and picked up a SMART marker. Miles and Sammy went back to their chairs and picked up their pencils.

"There were rumors," I said. "Rumors that Girtler might step down because of a heart condition."

I looked at Guilfoyle. He remained impassive.

Girtler's chest pains and visits to Bethesda had been reported widely in the news media.

"There were other rumors. That somebody in the Kehoe administration—maybe Kehoe himself—had contacted DiRienzo about being appointed vice upon Girtler's resignation and then being on the ticket with Kehoe in the next election."

Miles simply gave his rather bushy eyebrows a little lift but said nothing.

"I don't know how widespread it was," I said. "But it was out there. And then, when DiRienzo was murdered, it was just a matter of reading the tealeaves to suggest that the PRC may have had a hand in it. After all, the Chinese Government has been pretty hostile towards the Kehoe Administration."

"And that shouldn't come as a surprise," Miles said. "If a government wants to incite hostility in Beijing, cozying up to the government in Taipei is a sure way to do it."

"True enough," Sammy said. "But to go from there to suggesting that the PRC is willing to assassinate a U.S. congressman just because there's a flimsy, not to mention obscure, rumor floating around that he might become vice president is a huge leap of logic. I agree with Miles that the current administration's flirtation with Taiwan is pissing off the powers that be in Beijing. And I don't doubt that, if *Guoanbu* felt that one of *their* agents in place in the U.S. was doubling up on them, throwing them under the bus would be almost automatic. The agent in question would simply meet with an untimely end or disappear. But the public assassination of a U.S. member of the House of Representatives is beyond the pale."

I scrawled *Beyond the Pale* on the SMART board. My little three-by-five card with which I'd briefed Kehoe on board the *Eliza Dee* a month ago was starting to seem very flimsy indeed.

I wrote the paper for Kehoe using the saved SMART board notes after lunch. It was ten pages long. I told him that there was a high probability that, as U.S. elections approached, the PRC would spend freshly laundered money on trying to influence the outcomes. And that their preferred outcome would be Kehoe's opponent. I also told him that the probability of the Chinese Government using violence to influence those elections was quite small. I wasn't particularly happy with the paper, but felt it was the best we could do on short notice with limited resources. I did not print "the paper" but saved it on a flash drive after having Darps, Miles, and Sammy take a look at it. Then I called Mike.

"We finished the paper. Can you get it up the road by noon tomorrow?" I asked. "I want to let it stew here overnight and then take a fresh look it first thing in the morning."

"No problem," he said.

We hung up, I returned to the computer and typed one last morsel: "PS: Keys: Suggest any VP change idea be closely-held for now. Keep your head down. Loose."

I put the "Cheetah's Eyes Only" tape on the little flash drive and popped it into the briefcase. Then I locked the case and stashed it in the safe.

Forty-Four

W ednesday started out fine and then things turned bizarre. I arrived at Ripley Hall at about seven twenty-five a.m. Didn't see any Asian girls en route. Judy was already there, messing around with the coffee.

"Hey, Kiddo," I said.

"Darps called in. He said he'll be in around nine," Judy said.

"Did he sound hung over?" I asked, ever the caring, sensitive boss.

Darps usually showed up at about the same time Judy and I did. Around seven thirty. The nine o'clock arrival puzzled me.

"No, not at all. He sounded fine. A little tense, maybe. But other than that, fine."

I went to my office with a mugful of Breakfast Blend, booted up, and started out on my email.

I scrolled through the subjects and one entitled, *Mountain Fly-Fishing Deal!* Jumped out at me. I opened it.

Father-Daughter Special! This weekend only. Lunch in main lodge—Free! Bring five-weight rods. Flies supplied. Lost flies and tippets $1.50 each. Fishing hrs 7:00-11:30. Lunch 11:45.

I wondered if I was supposed to drive to Camp David with Elizabeth to arrive by a fishing start time of zero-seven hundred, or whether Luke and/or Mike would let me know. And Kehoe was a cheap bastard. Charging his guests a buck and a half for lost flies!

Three more guys—actually, two guys and one gal—were due to check in this morning and I thought I heard the process starting in Judy's office.

Just then Rebecca, our new HR guru, showed up at the office door with three people. Rebecca is a slender woman with ginger-colored hair and a perpetual smile.

"Alan, I'd like to introduce three new staff members," she said, gesturing them into the office.

I stood up. The guys wore "sincere" suits—one gray, the other dark blue—over button-down Oxford shirts and conservative ties. They appeared to be about twenty-five. The young lady appeared to be about the same age. She wore a navy blue suit with light blue piping on the lapels. Underneath was a pale, yellow blouse, open at the neck.

"Jason is our network specialist, Eddie is one of the administrative techs, and Samantha is our Central Asia desk officer," Rebecca said.

I shook hands with all three of them. I'd glanced at their bios earlier, but left the hiring to Darps, Judy, and Rebecca. They looked good on paper and even better in person. Especially Samantha. Which meant I was a sexist swine to even think that way. But she reminded me of a particularly attractive anchorwoman who is one of my TV favorites. And I don't have many of those.

After the introductions, Rebecca took them down to the conference room to start some paperwork. Judy showed up at my office a few seconds later.

"Alan, I just got the strangest call from Darps a few minutes ago."

"What do you mean 'strange'?" I asked.

"He sounded panicky," she said. "Darps never sounds panicky. But he did just now. He asked me if Miles had called in today."

"Why was he panicky about that?"

"I don't know. I told him I had unlocked the place and opened up and had taken all the phone calls. None was from Miles. He said, 'Jesus Christ,' and hung up. That's so unlike Darps."

"Is he still on the way in?" I asked.

"I don't know," she said. "He didn't say one way or the other. I assumed he was on his way, but..." she glanced at her watch and I did the same thing.

"No reason to panic," I said. "It's not even nine o'clock. He'll probably show up in a few minutes. If not, I'll call his cell."

Then I wondered again about Darps and Miles. *What the hell was going on?*

My phone bugled. It was Darps. His voice sounded tight.

"Have you heard from Miles?" he asked.

"No," I said. "Should I have? I wasn't expecting to."

"Goddamn it. Something's wrong. I got a call from his wife, Jeanette, thirty or forty minutes ago. She doesn't know where the hell he is," he said.

"He's probably out playing tennis someplace," I said. "Or maybe getting laid."

"Let's hope. I'll be in within five minutes or so."

It was more like two and a half minutes.

"The problem is he doesn't have his cell phone with him," he said.

"Maybe he just didn't turn it on," I said.

"No. I tracked it on the computer. It's at his house in Alexandria."

"Well maybe he's there."

"No. When I located the phone, I called it. It dumped me to voice mail. Then I called Jeanette back on the landline. She said he'd left an hour and a half ago and told her that he was on his way to D.C. I asked her to see if he left his cell phone and sure enough, it was there. Still is, as far as I know."

"Well, then. No problem. He's probably playing tennis with one of his girlfriends."

Darps shook his head.

"Jeanette says he never forgets his phone," he said.

"Never say 'never,'" I said, hating myself for the cliché.

Then his phone buzzed. He groped for it and glanced at it before answering.

"Taylor," he said.

He nodded his head a couple of times and his expression brightened.

"Great. Thanks for the heads up. Maybe he's got a lot on his mind because of our meeting yesterday. Thanks again."

He hung up.

"That was Jeanette. She said Miles just walked in. He did have a tennis date. With some Chinese guy. Not a girl, according to him. Said he'd forgotten his phone."

Half an hour later, I took a phone call from Miles.

"Sorry about dropping out of sight on you, Alan," he said. "Really stupid of me. I managed to forget my tennis date till I woke up this morning and then just went to the courts while Jeanette was still asleep. And didn't take my phone. Not smart."

I felt stupid and silly, accepting an apology from a guy like Miles Guilfoyle.

"No problem, Miles," I mumbled.

Actually, I think my subconscious makes me forget *my* cell phone occasionally in an effort to gain a little degree of freedom. Maybe Miles was the same way, limiting all this twenty-first-century connectivity. We exchanged goodbyes and hung up. Then Mike popped into my office and handed me one of the twin briefcases.

"Just back from delivering your paper. Used Reagan National to trade briefcases again. Zorn, the agent I swapped with, said there's a blurb on the two Chinese women in here. You know, the 'students' whose picture you took."

I popped the combination. There was a manila envelope with a yellow sticky note affixed. I read the note.

Loose: Thanks for the China paper. I looked at the pictures of these Chinese chix. Your taste in women has really gone south. Keys

I had to laugh as I slit open the envelope. Good old Kehoe could bring us back to the carefree days of high school with a few strokes of the pen. Inside the envelope there were two little stacks of paper, each one held together by a paper clip. The first one had a blow-up of the snap I'd taken of the two Asian girls. The head and shoulders of the one on the left were circled with a yellow highlighter. Underneath were several other photos of the same woman. Then there was a page with a smaller photo and a biographic sketch. She had an overbite and a face that brought rodents to mind. Bottom line: She was a known *Guoanbu* case officer, twenty-six years old, fluent in English and Russian. The second stack was much thinner, containing another copy of my photo with the other woman circled and a terse note. She wore glasses and looked determinedly unpleasant.

No info on unsub. Probably a recent recruit. Will start building file and will let you know what develops. Well. The bastards were keeping an eye on us again. At least they were yesterday. And I had to hand it to Elizabeth for spotting them first.

I handed the stuff on the Chinese women to Mike.

"Don't know if you realize how much of a wiseass Cheetah really is, but take a look at this," I said, handing him the sticky note.

He chuckled.

"I told you they were kind of weasely-looking," he said and handed me back the sticky.

I wondered if I could find a frame to fit the note in the little frame shop down the street in Chestertown.

There was something about the little disappearing act of Miles Guilfoyle that bothered me. And something Darps had said about it pulled a little wire in my head. But I couldn't get my arms around it. At all.

Forty-Five

We left at four a.m. Mike drove the Expedition. Elizabeth fell back to sleep by the time the SUV had cleared the driveway. Having anticipated this, I, as a thoughtful father, covered her with a "throw" I'd snagged from the family room on the way out. The fly-fishing gear was in the back. I'd already ensured that she was carrying her All Saints ID card. Mike had the all-news station on the radio, and he and I slurped coffee in silence. The weather woman said the temperature in D.C. was forty-five now and was bound for the low seventies. I wondered how things were in the mountains of Western Maryland. As if reading my mind, Mike said, "I checked the computer before we left. Temperature at Thurmont was thirty-seven. They're expecting a high of sixty-eight." We continued slurping coffee.

Dawn started coming on a little before six thirty. Elizabeth woke up, and we entered Maryland. The woods looked wintrier than they had looked back in Virginia, but there were still plenty of signs of spring. And the hills were getting steeper.

It was six fifty-eight when we stopped at a gate. We held up our IDs, and Mike lowered the windows on the driver's side. A guard in a black uniform took the IDs and checked them against a monitor in the guard shack. He handed the IDs back to Mike. A Marine in digital cammies stepped out of the guard shack.

"Corporal Strong," he said with a grin. "I'm your guide for the morning. President Kehoe said that Elizabeth is one of the world's great fly fishermen. Or fisherwomen."

Elizabeth's Cheshire-cat grin lit up the morning and Corporal Strong, who was carrying a broken-down, three-piece fly rod as well as a camouflage bag on a shoulder strap, got into the truck in back, alongside Elizabeth. He directed us down a narrow, wooded road to a parking spot in a little clearing. I could see a dark but tiny stream through the trees.

"We'll rig our tackle here," the corporal said. "We'll start with nymphs. Maybe when things warm up a little, they'll start feeding on a surface hatch and we can have a little fun with that."

He groped in his bag and came up with coiled tippets complete with nymphs and yarn strike indicators already rigged.

"You guys use uni-knots?" he asked.

"Does the Pope eat bratwurst?" I asked, ever the wiseass.

"Good to go, sir," he said. "Let me give you a quick demo here."

He tied a tippet and fly to his leader using, I assumed, a double uni-knot and stepped over to the stream bank. The stream itself was narrow—maybe ten or twelve feet wide—and was running slowly but steadily.

"I'll fish this nymph pretty close to the far bank," he whispered. "And I'll watch the strike indicator and pop the rod as soon as it stops."

He tossed his fly against the far bank. The yarn started downstream and then stopped and he lifted the rod tip.

"Rats!" he said. "Too late."

"Rats," indeed. I thought that maybe Corporal Strong had been chosen to be Elizabeth's guide because he—unlike many Marines—apparently eschewed profanity.

He retrieved the fly and dumped it into the same spot and this time, when the strike indicator hesitated, he raised the rod tip and we all saw the silvery flash of a hooked trout. He brought it in, unhooked it, and released it immediately.

"Brookie," he said. "We usually release them. These flies are tied on barbless hooks. Sometimes the boss likes to serve trout to company and we'll keep a bunch for him. There are rainbows and browns here, too."

"We'll release them," I said. "We were here a few weeks ago and had a delicious fish dinner. Maybe you caught them—he said that Marines had supplied the trout for the meal."

I never thought the day would come when I got tired of catching trout on flies. I'd lost count by ten thirty. That's when I started seeing dimples on the surface.

"Try this," I heard Corporal Strong say to Elizabeth about twenty yards upstream. "It's size-sixteen Humpy. A dry fly. It'll be exciting if the trout take it."

"Here's another one that seems to work," he said to me. "A Sulfur Dun. Size eighteen."

He clipped off my nymph and handed me the tiny fly.

By eleven fifteen, my wrist and shoulder were killing me. The action had been fantastic. Both Elizabeth and I were getting strikes on virtually every cast. Unlike the nymphs, just about every strike on the dries resulted in a hook-up, although sometimes the trout got off, probably due to the barbless hooks.

"We should probably shut down and head for the house," Corporal Strong announced. "They're expecting you for chow at eleven forty-five and you probably want to clean up a little."

Mike joined us for lunch. There was a fire in the fireplace. But no Sham. And no Kehoe.

"This is nice," Mike said. "I usually eat in the kitchen."

We had hot-and-robust minestrone followed by club sandwiches with thick slabs of turkey and hefty rashers of bacon. I enjoyed a glass of sauvignon blanc while Mike and Elizabeth had sweet iced tea. On the ride back to Chestertown, I stayed awake to make sure Mike stayed awake. I needn't have bothered. As we turned off I-95 going into Chestertown, he told me that he'd slept the whole time Elizabeth and I were fishing. For her part, Elizabeth slept the whole way back. I reached back and tugged her foot as we turned onto Prince Henry Street.

"Wake up, Kiddo," I said. "We're home."

She stretched like a cat, emitting a little squeak.

"You know, Dad," she said. "The fishing is really good when it really tires you out."

Words to live by.

Forty-Six

Chestertown
March 29th
Monday

Sammy showed up for work on Monday morning in a state of extreme agitation. I was usually one of the first people in, although once in a while, Judy or Luke got in before I did. This morning, Sammy was waiting for me.

"I almost called you at home last night," he said. "But I didn't want to discuss what happened over a phone."

"If that—whatever 'that' is—happens again, call me anyway. We can always meet here or somewhere outdoors," I said.

"Well," he said. "Upon reflection, I cooled down and figured there wouldn't be anything that anyone could do last night."

"Let's get Darps and then you can tell us both what's got you so jacked up."

The three of us got coffee and sat in my office.

Sammy took a sip of his coffee and said, "You're not going to believe this."

"Try us," I said.

"Remember Isabel? Isabel Sin?"

"Yeah. I remember telling you I'd remember her name for the rest of my life," I said. "Even though I've never laid eyes on her."

"Well, you might get your chance. To lay eyes on her. She's in Stafford."

"You've got to be kidding! Or hallucinating," Darps said.

"I shit you not. Yesterday evening, I went to Carlos O'Kelly's for dinner. There were no empty tables in the restaurant, so I took a table in the bar. I sat down, ordered a beer and was looking at the menu when in walks Isabel. Then she turns and leaves, just like that. But I'm *positive* it was her."

"Probably just a look-alike," Darps said.

"No way," Sammy said.

"Hmm," I said. "Do you like Mexican food? Or faux-Mexican?"

"Yeah," he said, wagging his hand to indicate "so-so."

"Go back to Carlos O'Kelly's again this evening. See if she shows up again. If she does, make eye contact and show recognition. Chat with her; maybe even buy her a drink. See what happens and where she's coming from."

"I don't know if that's smart. If I'm right about her being *Guoanbu*, and fifty percent of that restaurant's customers are FBI, I could end up on somebody's shit list."

"Not to worry," I said. "We're not asking you to go home with her. Just find out what her game is. If she's even there. Besides, the boss has already okayed *BIAS*—and you—making a run at her."

"If she *is* there, it might get interesting," Darps interjected. "For example, it would be very interesting what sort of a story she spins about being in Stafford. Not to mention how it is that she runs into you in two different bars forty-five miles apart."

Sammy seemed uneasy.

"I don't know," he said.

I had an idea.

"How about this? We'll have Luke or Mike act as your backup. If things look at all dicey, one of them will be there and intervene."

"I have a better idea," said Darps. "We can still have Luke or Mike lurk in the background and have Judy break in after ten or fifteen minutes. Like she's Sammy's date."

"Jesus Christ," Sammy said. "Now you're setting me up to get on a shit list at home in Florida."

"Time out," I said. "We're putting something together on the fly. Totally winging it. Let's go back to square one. Sammy, let's plan on you *avoiding* Carlos O'Kelly's tonight. Go out west on Route 610 and find some restaurant out there. Stay the hell away from Carlos O'Kelly's. That might translate into your staying away from Isabel. Which is fine. Unless *Guoanbu* spooks are following you. If they are, we need to know that too. So we'll have Luke and/or Mike or somebody they line up check you for surveillance. Meantime, we can think about just what the hell we're trying to do and come up with a little game plan that makes sense. You can go back to Carlos's Wednesday evening and if she shows, we'll have a plan ready to go that we've thought out."

Darps and Sammy both seemed to relax.

"Good point," Darps said. "Winging some half-assed operation against *Guoanbu* probably ain't a real good idea."

"No shit," Sammy said.

"Let's reconvene in twenty-four hours. I'll nail together a strawman for a run at Isabel. You guys jot down any thoughts or ideas you have. We'll start with everything on the table. Sammy, talk to Luke or Mike about what you're doing this evening."

They left and I started wading through my email.

Forty-Seven

Maili saw Colonel Yang park his black Lexus and start to dismount. She poured tea from a kettle into a small, light-blue teapot and poured hot water from a different kettle into a matching blue cup. When she heard the click of the door lock, she discarded the hot water from the cup into the wet bar's sink and filled the cup with pale, fragrant jasmine tea.

"Good morning, Comrade Colonel," she said.

"Good morning, Maili."

The short colonel wore no overcoat. He walked without perceptible motion of his upper body, almost as if he were gliding across the room on wheels. Maili followed him into his office, towering over him and carrying the tea tray.

"There is a report from *Mongoose*. It came in late on Friday. After you had gone. *Lynx* is back in Virginia. And *Mongoose* visited the *BIAS* office in Chestertown last week. And finally, Llewellyn made our new surveillance team."

"Those fucking *idiots*! Did he beat them up and trash their cell phone like he did with Kwan?"

"No, Comrade Colonel. He took pictures of them with *his* cell phone."

"The worthless, incompetent sows! Am I to assume that they have been pulled off the surveillance?"

"Yes, of course, Comrade Colonel. They are en route to Nevada as we speak."

189

The American *Guoanbu* headquarters were in the mountains outside Reno, Nevada, where they masqueraded as the *Jackalope Ranch*, a legal brothel. Almost all the "patrons" were *Guoanbu* members, as were the "associates."

Yang sipped tea daintily.

"And what of *Lynx*?" he asked.

"He has come without his wife and children. He is staying at a motel in Stafford, just north of Chestertown. I confirmed this myself."

"It seems the Politburo wants us to continue to try and penetrate *BIAS* by recruiting *Lynx*," Yang muttered.

"Why, Comrade Colonel? Especially if *Mongoose* has the place penetrated already."

"Because *Mongoose* has gone into semi-retirement. His access will be only part-time. Occasional."

"I'm still not at all confident that trying to recruit *Lynx* is a workable strategy, Comrade Colonel."

"Nor am I. Nor am I," repeated Yang. "But they are forcing our hand. We need to try again."

"Those silly bitches that I sent to Nevada are compromised. They won't be of any use whatsoever," Maili said.

"No," said the colonel. "It must be you. 'Isabel Sin.' What a delightful, revisionist name!"

The colonel picked up the porcelain bell.

Maili glanced at her watch. It was nine fifteen.

"Don't you feel it's a bit early in the day for cognac, Comrade Colonel?"

"Yes, but it's never too early for champagne. We'll toast to the health and success of Isabel Sin."

Forty-Eight

Chestertown
March 30th
Tuesday

Sammy probably weighs about one-forty, soaking wet with his clothes and his wingtips on, and is one of the smartest people in the world, so it made perfect sense that he would bypass Einstein Brothers' Bagels and stop by Dunkin' Donuts to pick up a box of their most lethal gut-bombs on his way in to our meeting. I took a maple glazed, Darps glommed a jelly-filled beast, and Luke grabbed the other one in the box. Sammy had a huge chocolate donut with chocolate chips embedded in the chocolate frosting. Judy rooted around till she found the only plain donut in the box. She plucked a crumb-sized morsel from the donut and popped it into her mouth. Then she appeared to abandon the rest of the donut on a paper napkin.

"Here's what I slapped together for a plan," I said. "Anyone feel free to jump in at any time."

My team chomped donuts and swigged coffee. Except Judy. Who sipped coffee delicately, like a hummingbird tasting nectar. And left her donut, minus the tiny fragment she'd eaten, on her napkin.

I stepped to my SMART board with a fistful of notes on three-by-five cards. I was sure my comrades were thinking unkind thoughts of my Luddite tendencies because I wasn't doing this in PowerPoint on the projector.

"Sorry, no PowerPoint," I said. "I do brainstorming better on a white board."

I drew an oval. Labeled it, "*C. O'K's,*" for Carlos O'Kelly's.

"If she shows, all we want to do at this point is see where she's coming from. That's all. If she wants to continue talking with Sammy, then we'll decide whether to toss a few softballs her way and see what happens. But that will happen later. We'll do nothing more than keep the ball in play right now."

After that clumsy mix of metaphors, I drew an arrow going into the oval from the right. Above the arrow's shaft, I printed, *"Sammy-1800-Bar."*

"Okay. This evening, Sammy shows up at Carlos's at exactly six. On the dot. Goes into the bar and takes a seat. Orders a drink. Savors his drink. If nothing happens in ten minutes, he orders an appetizer. He munches thereon, enjoys his drink. If nothing happens in the next twenty minutes, he pays his tab and leaves. Goes home to the motel. No Isabel. If still hungry, he telephones for a pizza. Or whatever."

I drew another arrow, this one leaving the oval. I printed, *"Sammy-1830-out?"*

"At the twenty-nine-minute mark, Judy enters the bar. If Sammy is alone and getting ready to pay his check, Judy turns around, leaves and goes home. On the other hand, if Sammy is 'involved' with someone—as in Isabel Sin—Judy moves in. 'Hi Sammy. Ready for dinner?' or words to that effect."

I drew two more arrows leading into the *"C. O'K"* oval, labeled one shaft, *"Isabel?"* and the other shaft, *"Judy-1829."* Then, I drew a diamond and labeled it, *"Isabel there?"* With a *Yes* and a *No* coming out of the diamond. On the *Yes* side, I wrote, *"Disrupt."* On the *No* side, I scrawled, *"Depart."*

"Meantime if sweet Isabel has shown up, Sammy recognizes her, invites her to take a seat and have a drink and listens to her tall tale about how she happens to be in Stafford. If she asks him what he's doing, he tells her he's part of a team doing foreign policy issue papers for DOD—our normal cover. Just keep the talk small. How long is she in the States, blah, blah. And then Judy comes to the rescue. Whole time, Luke is sitting at the bar watching everything in the mirror.

"In any case—Isabel there or not—Sammy's out of there in thirty minutes. Either of his own volition or with Judy's help. If Isabel is there, he can shoot the breeze and see if she wants to reconnect. Exchange phone numbers, see what happens. If Isabel isn't there, oh well. In any case, Sammy leaves. And orders out. And Luke is watching his back the whole time. We reconvene here tomorrow morning and take things apart."

Judy picked another tiny crumb from her donut, sucked it in and washed it down with a tiny sip of coffee.

"Question," she said. "Suppose Isabel—or anybody else, for that matter—is there with Sammy. I disrupt, remind Sammy of our dinner date, and we leave. What then?"

"Okay. You said 'anybody else.' Excellent thought. If Sammy has been joined by *anyone*—other than his wife or mother—go ahead and disrupt and leave together. After that, go ahead and let Sammy buy you dinner someplace else."

"Hey!" Sammy said.

"*BIAS* will pay, you cheap bastard," I said. "As long as dinner is in Stafford. No trips to *le Citronelle* in Georgetown."

Forty-Nine

Stafford
March 30th
Tuesday

At five o'clock, I followed Sammy to his motel in Stafford. We got there about five twenty-five. He got us each a bottle of Samuel Adams from a miniature fridge in his room and then turned on the TV. For a few amazing minutes, I watched Sammy in action. He was a compulsive, information-sucking machine. It almost made me dizzy. He cycled from CNN to Headline News to CNBC to MSNBC to Fox News, all the while flipping the pages of *USA Today*. Next he checked out two weather channels and ESPN. Then he surfed through a few websites on his laptop. A copy of *The Economist* was on the coffee table. He must have read it already, as he didn't touch it. About halfway through his beer, Sammy excused himself.

"I'm going to grab a shower and change clothes," he said, putting the laptop down and clicking through some more channels.

"Okay. I'll be gone by the time you get out," I said. "Thanks for the beer."

We had arranged that I would be a secondary backup outside the restaurant. I drank the rest of my beer as I heard the shower start to roar and then let myself out.

Sammy went into Carlos O'Kelly's at exactly six o'clock. I was sitting in my battered Explorer in an adjacent parking area, feeling that the government Expedition might attract undue attention. Luke walked in at six-oh-one. About a minute later, I got a text message from Luke.

Izbl alrdy here, was all that it said. I wondered how he'd been able to recognize Isabel.

So she was already in the bar. I wondered if or when she'd approach Sammy. About ten minutes later, I got another text from Luke.

194

Sam and Iz r chttng lk long lost sibs.

A few minutes went by, then another text.

Orders her drnk.

Silence for a couple more minutes.

Margrta.

Then I saw Judy climb out of her red Infiniti and head for the front door of the restaurant. I checked my watch. I needn't have. It was exactly six twenty-nine. Five minutes later, Judy and Sammy exited the restaurant. Judy led the way to her coupe and they climbed in. She fired up the car and they were gone. I waited in my spot in the other parking lot. About four minutes later, an attractive Asian woman came out of the restaurant. A Kia SUV stopped in front of the door and picked her up. The vehicle and the woman disappeared into the night.

Less than a minute later, Luke emerged, crossed over to my Explorer and climbed in.

"Nothing much," he said. "They shot the shit like old friends. Judy barged in, as planned. End of story. Except that Isabel was there, waiting. Oh, and Mike is watching their backs for any surveillance."

"Was that woman that just came out Isabel?" I asked.

"I assume so. She was the chick that was talking to Sammy until Judy interrupted them. Attractive. And a nice figure."

"Must be her. We'll get together as planned tomorrow morning to kick this around. Sammy can tell us for sure if she's Isabel."

"Sounds good, Alan," he said and let himself out of the truck.

I was home by seven fifteen. Maria and Elizabeth had already eaten dinner.

"I wasn't sure when you'd get home," Maria said. "There's a plate of liver and onions and mashed potatoes that's ready to be nuked. And kale. Elizabeth is doing homework."

I poured a scotch. Light on the ice, heavy on the scotch. God help us. As they say, some days you eat the bear, other days the bear eats you. At least I was home with the women I loved. Even if dinner was liver and onions with kale. I took a healthy tug of the scotch and wondered a bit wistfully where Judy and Sammy had dinner.

Fifty

Richmond
March 31st
Wednesday

Quing Maili was the first person to enter Lieutenant Colonel Yang Zemin's Richmond office, which wasn't unusual. She savored the quiet as she set the thermostat at seventy-two and the air conditioner clicked on and started clearing the stale air with a gentle hum. She filled a small, stainless steel kettle with tap water, set the kettle on the two-burner stove on the wet bar, and turned on the gas. Then she turned on her computer. It was seven forty-five. Li, the steward, probably wouldn't be in for another fifteen minutes; the colonel wouldn't be in for another half-hour, she guessed.

She went over in her mind last evening's contrived rendezvous with Source *Lynx*. She had been waiting for him to show up at Carlos O'Kelly's. He did and had sat down in the bar. She had gone to his table.

"Hi, Mr. Chen! Remember me?"

"Um, yes. Of course. Ms. Sin. We met at the Mayflower last week."

He had stood up at the table, politely but awkwardly.

"Yes. And before that in Hong Kong, last year," she said, brightly.

And she remembered that she'd told him that she was meeting with "university officials" about scholarship opportunities in the Peoples' Republic. He had seemed to accept that.

She heard the front door of the office open and close and Li appeared. Early.

"Good morning, Comrade Quing," he murmured. "Thank you for starting the tea."

They both heard a car door slam out front and the front door opened again. The colonel was early too.

"Good morning, good morning. Maili please come into my office. Li, please bring us both tea as soon as it's ready."

Yang glided across to his office door. Maili waited a few seconds, allowing him to be seated and then followed.

"Please have a seat, Maili," Yang said. "Tell me how it went with Source *Lynx*."

"It seemed to go well, Comrade Colonel," she said.

"'Seemed to'?" queried the Colonel, lifting his eyebrows.

"Yes, Comrade Colonel. Seemed to. He didn't try to get rid of me like he did in Washington. He seemed to buy my explanation of why I was in Stafford—for cross-cultural contacts with the university in Chestertown. And that cover is very shallow and could easily collapse if he tries to check it out. I asked what he was doing there and he said he was working on, quote, 'foreign issue papers for the Department of Defense,' unquote."

"No details? Subjects?"

"No, Comrade Colonel. He volunteered none and I didn't press him."

"Good. How about future contact?"

"I have his phone number. He has my mobile phone number. I asked him to call me."

"If he doesn't, what then?" asked Yang.

"I'll go to Carlos O'Kelly's. On Friday. There's usually a good crowd there on Friday evenings," she said. "We'll see what develops then, if anything."

"Good," said the Colonel. "Put together a contact report by noon."

"Yes, Comrade Colonel."

"And also, Maili, do not be overly pessimistic about your contact with Source *Lynx*. I think it went as well as we could have expected. Better, actually."

Maili stood up and gave a slight bow just as Li entered the office with the tea tray. She left the office silently and sat down at her computer to begin composing her "contact report." Li silently brought her a cup of tea.

Fifty-One

A t the office, we had an excellent wash-up of the Wednesday evening encounter with Isabel Sin. Bottom line: she was nibbling at our bait and probably thought that Sammy was nibbling back at hers. We'd have to wait and see how things developed. After leaving Carlos O'Kelly's, Sammy and Judy had gone to a Japanese place out on Route Six-Ten and had sushi, steak, and shrimp. I thought of the liver-and-onions-and-kale at fifteen-oh-six Prince Henry Street last evening and allowed myself a twinge of self-pity mixed with envy.

I debated with myself for a while over whether I should do a memo for Cheetah and decided not to. I'd do one for the file and let it go at that. Sammy's encounter with Isabel Sin didn't reveal anything new about the Peoples' Republic or anything else on the world stage.

After the meeting, Darps followed me into the office, looking worried. He was carrying a small white board like the one Maria and I had in our kitchen for messages. He held it up. *"New place? Now?"* was scrawled diagonally across the board. He raised his eyebrows. I gave him a thumbs up and he turned to go upstairs, erasing the board with a Kleenex as he went.

"Lemme grab a jacket and I'll be right down," he said.

Donning a Navy windbreaker, I stepped into Judy's office and told her that Darps and I were "off." She knew that "off" means Chancellorsville. Darps came rumbling down the stairs, twirling car keys.

"I'll drive the Expo," he said. "Unless you want to."

"No. You drive. I'll steal us some coffee."

I grabbed a Breakfast Blend catered thermos that felt like it was about half-full. We climbed into the GI Expedition and headed west. I didn't think the SUV was bugged, but we didn't take chances.

"This is really fucking bad," was all Darps said.

When we got to the safe house, Darps parked behind the little dump. The morning was bright, and the sun was warming things up quickly. Once we got inside, I poured coffee and Darps turned on the heat and the ancient TV. And jacked up the volume. *Sesame Street* was on.

"Guilfoyle's name has shown up in Chinese chatter," he said. "In the same paragraph as *BIAS*."

"How in the fuck do you know *that*?" I asked.

"Old girlfriend," he said.

"Shit!" I said.

"You know what that means?"

"Is there any of that Dewar's lying around?" I countered.

He opened a dish cabinet and grabbed the jug. He splashed a spoonful of scotch into my coffee and then into his own. I sipped. He sipped.

"The mole is alive and well," I said.

"Yup," he said. "No doubt."

I took another sip.

"You know who it has to be," I said.

"Yup," he said. "Mike-Golf."

"Jesus Christ," I muttered. I stepped outside the door into the sunshine and sipped the scotch-flavored coffee from its cardboard cup. Darps came out, joined me in the sun and sipped.

"It gets worse," he said.

I thought that the mole could only be Mike. Mike—a Secret Service agent! He was the only one who knew about the Guilfoyle-*BIAS* connection that could have reported that back to the Chinese. Other than Guilfoyle himself. Jesus, I thought.

"I wonder if you and I are thinking of the same person," I said.

"No doubt. Hence my grievous—heinous—embarrassment," he said. "I was the guy who recommended we hire him, remember?"

My mind was in a state of semi-paralysis. It had fixated on the "Mike" part of what Darps had said.

"What are you talking about? The man himself—Kehoe—dictated the hiring of Mike. And Luke!"

"No, Shipmate! You're not listening. I said 'Mike-Golf.' As in 'm-g.' Our great big elder statesman lawyer. Miles fucking Guilfoyle! It's got to be him! The *asshole*! He's been the mole all along!"

Jesus, I thought. Miles Ass-Man Guilfoyle. Advisor to presidents. U.S. ambassador to Beijing. Cozy with the PRC and a battalion of PRC Government drones. He had White House access. Probably heard about plans for *BIAS* from the get-go. Including about me. Before I did, even. Probably heard about my three-by-five card about the DiRienzo killing. It explained a lot of things. As if reading my mind, Darps started talking again.

"It explains a lot of stuff. The leaks to the Chinese. That little absence the other day when he 'forgot' his cell phone. I'll bet that was an emergency dead drop to tell the Chinese about our report on them messing around in American politics. The prick!"

"You're right," I said. "It explains a lot."

Miles Guilfoyle, a Chinese spy, a mole. A mole in the fucking White House. And by extension, in the State Department. And lately, into *BIAS*. The bastard. Eighty-two years old and betraying his country. I wondered how long that had been going on.

"Do you have anything besides your intuition and this juxtaposition of Miles with *BIAS* in the PRC chatter pointing at him?" I asked.

"I think that's probably enough, but yeah. I do," he said. "I tried to call him at home the other day. He wasn't there. Jeanette, his wife, took the call. She volunteered information that she didn't think Miles had played tennis the morning he went missing. He had worn his tennis togs, taken his briefcase, but left his rackets at home in the garage. She was thinking about another woman. I was thinking about the Chinese. Later, I met him for drinks in Alexandria. Asked him about it. He got all pissy and angry. Gave me some bullshit arm waving. But I think my questions made him nervous."

"Why the hell didn't you tell me?" I asked.

"At that point I didn't think there was enough there to say that *THE* Miles Guilfoyle might be betraying his country. Pretty fucking stupid. Sorry."

"Okay," I said. "But no way am *I* going to cast the first stone at you. If you had told me, I'd probably have come to the same conclusion as you did."

"The war stopper was my old girlfriend who knows whereof she speaks, if you get my drift. She knew we'd hired Guilfoyle and she saw his name linked to *BIAS* in the Chinese chatter. More than once. But I only got that word this morning. That pretty much clinched it for me."

"Jesus Christ," I said again. "Let's go back to the office. Maybe talk with Luke. This isn't something that we can sit on."

I finished my coffee. Darps was already inside turning things off and retrieving the coffee thermos. We hit the road.

Fifty-Two

At first, we left our little hovel fast, bouncing down the dirt road to Route Three and then breaking the speed limit as we headed east toward Chestertown.

"What are we going to do?" Darps asked.

"Damned if I know," I said. "It's a pretty fucking dicey situation. At this point, I don't think we can cite your ex-girlfriend's info, much less take that to court."

A little beep sounded from in front of the steering wheel.

"Shit!" Darps hissed. "The fucking low-fuel warning light just came on."

"Go ahead and stop for gas at the next station. Filling up will give us a few minutes to think," I said.

After a couple of miles, Darps slowed down and pulled into a gas station in a grungy little strip mall. I got out of the truck and started pumping gas. Then I speed-dialed Luke. Thank the Lord he picked up after the first ring.

"Can you track down Miles—or, at least his cell phone? I need to get a hold of him ASAP," I said, my voice cracking a bit.

"No sweat, Boss. Call you right back," he said.

Several minutes passed. Then the ring tone chimed in. Wynton blowing the opening bars of the *Prince of Denmark's March*. It was Luke.

"Yeah, Luke."

"All I'm getting is his voice mail. After three tries at calling him, I went to the computer to track his cell phone. The computer puts his cell phone in the park at Great Falls."

"Great Falls?"

"Yeah. The park on the Virginia side of the Potomac waterfalls. Above Chain Bridge."

"Okay. I know the place. Been there a few times. Darps and I are going to head that way now. Do me a favor. Get on the computer and interrogate his cell phone's location every ten minutes or so. Let us know if there's any change."

"Got it."

The gas pump shut down. I replaced the hose. *The hose,* I thought. *First the smoke. Then the fire. Now the hose.*

The pump beeped at me, and I grabbed the receipt.

Darps jackrabbited out of the gas station and hit Route Three East.

"Get on I-95 North," I said. "We're going to Great Falls. The park."

"Roger that," mumbled Darps.

The community of Great Falls is a high-rent D.C. suburb in Virginia, upstream from the District of Columbia. There is a park there where the Potomac tumbles over a rocky escarpment with a roar. It isn't Niagara, but it's still pretty impressive. Darps turned onto I-95 North and headed for the Capital Beltway.

"Luke's computer shows Miles's cell phone in the park at Great Falls," I said.

"Meaning Miles is in the park at Great Falls," he said.

"Maybe," I said. "It'll take us close to forty-five minutes to get there from here. That'll at least give us time to figure out what the hell we're going to do when we get there."

"That'll probably depend on what we find there," he said.

I dialed Luke again.

"Anything more on Miles's cell?" I asked.

"No change, Boss. It still is showing it in the park at Great Falls."

"Thanks, Luke," I said and we rang off.

"*Rang off,*" I thought. A quaint expression going back to the days when telephone operators kept calls going with a wire plugged into a switchboard and the caller signaled the end of the call by "ringing off." When the operator heard the ring, she'd pull the plug, ending the connection and the call.

We zipped over the Rappahannock River Bridge and headed uphill into Stafford County. Great Falls Park was still a good forty-plus miles away. I wondered what—if anything—we'd find there.

"We've got this beast going eighty-seven," Darps said. "I'm going to bleed off a little speed."

We slowed down. A little. Maybe down to eighty or so. Luke called three more times to tell me that the phone hadn't moved.

Fifty-Three

We had just exited the Beltway and were heading upstream on the Old Georgetown Pike when Luke called.

"The phone still hasn't moved, Alan," he said, again.

"Okay, Luke. We're only a few minutes away from it now."

There were only two cars in the parking lot. A silver BMW Seven Series and a blue Toyota Highlander with two infant seats in the back. Sure enough, there was a young mom with two ankle biters sitting at a picnic table. She had a *Grande* Starbucks cup and was yakking on a phone. The two little guys were playing with Tonka trucks. The river was pretty high and it slammed down over the rocks with a constant roar. I don't think I'd have brought Elizabeth here when she was three years old, but Mom seemed to be keeping a keen eye on the kids who were playing happily in the dirt by the table. Darps and I walked over to the Beemer.

"That's his car," he said.

I looked in through the passenger-side window. There was a cell phone on the seat. The keys were still in the ignition. I backed away. I didn't want to touch anything.

"Let's look around. Maybe he's sunbathing naked behind some bushes," I said.

"God help us," Darps muttered.

I walked over to the picnic table where Mom was sitting. She looked at me suspiciously as folks in the D.C. area are wont to do.

"Sorry to bug you, ma'am. I was just wondering if you'd seen the driver of the BMW."

I jerked a thumb in the direction of Miles's wheels.

"The silver car? No. It was parked when we got here about fifteen minutes ago. But the kids and I are the only ones here as far as I know. I haven't seen anybody else."

"Thanks. Sorry to bother you."

"No problem."

Darps had already taken off. I grabbed my phone from the Expedition and took off in the other direction. After about twenty minutes, we were back by the parking lot. Mom was loading her two kids into the Highlander.

"He's not fucking here," Darps said in a low voice. "He's gone. Somewhere."

I was already dialing Luke.

"Hey Alan. What's up?"

"I'm at Great Falls Park. Miles's BMW is here. So's his cell phone. And his car keys. But no Miles. I'm thinking of calling nine-one-one."

"Waste of time. He's an adult. Only been off the stage for a couple of hours. Police won't touch it."

"What about you guys?"

"Nope. Even if he were still on the staff, there would be a four-hour wait and then a secretary would call the Feebs and the Park Police."

"Shit," I said. "I'm worried. Hell, the guy is eighty-two years old. These waterfalls are huge and powerful. And dangerous."

"Alan," he said, sounding patient. "You know the guy's reputation. He probably left the park with the thirty-five-year-old wife of some ambassador—in her car."

"Okay. No nine-one-one. Darps and I'll be back at the ranch in an hour or so."

I pushed a red button and pocketed the phone. There was something flickering just outside of my consciousness that was bugging me. I couldn't put my finger on it. I looked at the river, rushing by, gathering speed before it started thundering down over the rocks. It was clogged with boulders, leading up to the falls.

"Darps!" I barked. "Look at that rock!" I pointed.

"Good grief, Shipmate! There are a thousand rocks out there!"

"But look at the flat one, about four feet from shore. The one with the wet spot on it."

I pointed to a boulder that was about the size of a pool table, flat and sticking out above the rushing river about eight or ten inches. There was a pizza-sized wet spot on the rock. It hadn't rained in over a week. I stepped to the water's edge and took a jump, landing on the rock, barely keeping my balance and staying out of the water. The depth of the rushing water around the boulder appeared to be about a foot and a half. I looked around. In the water, there was a silver-colored snub-nosed revolver lying on the rocky riverbed about a foot away from the rock I was standing on.

"Oh good Christ!" I said.

"What's up, Alan?" Darps hollered over the roar of the falls.

"There's a fucking handgun on the bottom of the river right here!" I said, pointing outboard of the boulder I was standing on.

"How deep is the water there?" he asked.

"About two feet, max, I guess," I said. "Grab a stick three or four feet long and maybe I can snag it."

"No way, Shipmate," he said. "Jump back ashore. We don't want to be screwing around with a possible crime scene."

What Darps said made sense. I jumped.

"Okay. A gun in the river. No Miles. What next?" Darps asked.

"We leave. You call what's-her-name—Miles's wife. Tell her that Luke tried to call Miles, got only voicemail and used the computer to track his cell phone. The phone's GPS and the tracking software showed that it was here in the park. We came here and found his car. And phone. But no Miles. Don't say anything about the weapon in the river. And no speculation about Miles, (a) being a Chinese spy, or (b) banging some ambassador's wife," I said. "Needless to say," I added.

"Jesus," Darps said. "Are you thinking what I'm thinking?"

"That he used that pistol on himself?"

"Exactly. He could have walked through the water, sat on the edge of that rock and eaten the gun. The gunshot would have knocked him into the river and the current sent him over the falls to Christ knows where."

"What about the Chinese?" I asked. "Suppose Miles met some *Guoanbu* case officer here and things went south and the Chinese whacked him here. Got in the river that way."

"If the Chinese guy had half a brain, he wouldn't have pitched the pistol in the river here. It probably doesn't matter if Miles did it himself or if the Chinese did him. If he went into the river here—with or without the help of the gun—there ain't a snowball's chance in hell that he's alive," Darps said. "Hell, if you or I went into the river here, I doubt that we'd survive and Miles is more than four decades older than we are."

"Okay. Let's go back to the office. You call Jeanette from the truck. She can call the cops if she wants," I said. "Let's go back by way of the new place. We can stop there and spend thirty or forty minutes brainstorming for any loose ends. Even if Miles is dead, he leaves with a couple of burning issues. Being missing. And being a fucking spy."

Fifty-Four

En route to our safe hovel, Darps spied a Subway. "Let's grab some lunch," he announced. "My treat."

When we got to the safe house, I opened a couple of windows. It wasn't that hot outside, but inside, the little house was close and stuffy. Darps dragged a Subway bag and a couple of drinks into the safe house.

"Take your pick. Meatball parmigiana or cold Italian. I got us both lemonade."

"Meatball. And thanks," I said.

We unwrapped the sandwiches and took bites. While chewing, I uncapped the lemonade bottle.

"First of all," I said. "What did Jeanette say when you talked to her?"

Darps finished his first bite of the salami, ham, and provolone, dabbed at his lips with a Subway napkin, and said: "She freaked out. But I still think she was thinking more about Miles chasing some skirt rather than being in danger."

"So what did she say?"

"What she said was: 'Can you track Miles down? Get him to come home? Then I'll deal with him.' That's what she said."

"And you said?" I asked.

"You heard me. Something like, 'Let me talk to the boss and our security guys, and I'll get back to you,' is what I said. Pretty mealy-mouthed. Sorry."

"Did she say anything about calling the cops?" I asked.

209

"Nope."

"Okay, this one is for Luke and Mike as soon as we get back," I said.

Darps nodded in agreement.

"The next issue with Miles is his line of work. Dead or alive. He's a fucking Chinese spy. That means we need to call in the Feebs," I said.

"I'm not sure I agree with you, Shipmate," Darps said after taking a swig of lemonade. "If he's okay—alive and well—yeah, we definitely need to call the FBI. But it's still dicey, evidence-wise. But let's assume he's dead. Suicide or whatever. What's to be gained by bringing in the Feebs and unearthing the fact that he was spying for the PRC?"

"Talk to me," I said.

"That would cause a major shit-storm," he began. "'Top Presidential Aide Was Chinese Spy!' could be the headlines. Jeanette maybe gets screwed out of Government bennies. The Chinese get all embarrassed, not to mention pissed off. Our access to China gets cut way back. Sammy is limited to reading news items on the Internet. Christ only knows what black hole Isabel Sin disappears into. If Miles Guilfoyle commits suicide in Great Falls Park and there's no Chinese connection, there's no Chinese connection."

I finished my sandwich and thought. For several seconds.

"Okay," I said. "Let's head back to Chestertown. I think we can air this stuff with Mike and Luke. And Judy, for that matter. There may be some damage-control issues. But you're right. If the mole is dead, the mole is dead."

"But we're not one hundred percent sure of that," Darps said before swigging the dregs from his lemonade bottle.

"Roger that. Let's roll. I'll lock up."

Fifty-Five

Alexandria
April 4th
Sunday

Bohlzach's in Alexandria is, I guess, one of the funeral homes from which one is buried if one is a member of the Washington D.C. elite and lives and dies in northern Virginia. At any rate, that was where they laid out Miles Guilfoyle. In the coffin, he sported a Navy blue suit that probably cost more than my whole wardrobe. I wondered if they had to custom-build caskets for guys as big as Miles. There were cloyingly aromatic banks of enormous floral tributes arrayed tastefully on either side of the bier. I wondered if the custom of sending flowers to the bereaved had arisen from a necessity in days of yore of masking the unpleasant aroma of dead flesh. Nothing like a wake to provoke bizarre thoughts. Upright lamps cast their indirect sallow light. Purple lipstick on the corpse set off the rest of Miles's waxy, powdered features. All traces of the self-inflicted gunshot wound to the side of his head had been expunged by the mortician's magic. Also disguised were his treachery and his spying for the Peoples' Republic of China. No one outside a small *BIAS* circle— Darps, Judy, Luke, Mike, and yours truly—knew. Well, at least on our side. The Chinese knew.

A couple of fishermen in a rented boat from Fletcher's Boathouse had spotted Miles's corpse lodged in some bushes on the Potomac's Washington shore and called the cops on a cell phone. Fortunately, for the wake, he had not spent all that much time in the river. Cause of death was a thirty-two-caliber bullet that had penetrated his temple and then whipped around inside his skull like a blender blade, causing massive brain trauma. The cops found the thirty-two-caliber revolver in the Potomac at Great Falls Park. It was registered to Miles. They also, of course, found his Beemer parked there. The death was ruled a suicide even though Miles had apparently left no note.

Jeanette, his Malaysian widow, stood in a receiving line together with a couple of younger middle-aged folks who apparently were Miles's children from previous marriages. Jeanette wore a short black dress and a pair of large hoop earrings that were, to my simple mind, a little overstated for a husband's wake. Maybe that was her subtle way of expressing disapproval of Miles's skirt chasing. A number of high-powered Washington big dogs came slinking quietly in to pay their respects. Walt Whitehead came and went quickly, greeting me with a curt nod. Suzanne Racey, the Channel Fourteen anchor, came about five minutes after Whitehead left, which I thought was odd. She wore huge black sunglasses. I wondered if a blurb on the Guilfoyle wake would appear in next weekend's *Morsels and Motes*. I recognized the party-switching U.S. senator from Virginia. There were several women in black or dark gray dresses. Including Michelle Hookes, looking elegant and beautiful for all her seventy-plus years. There were also a number of younger women in dresses with brighter, more summery colors. One had to wonder about the dear, departed Miles and how many of these women represented notches on his gun, so to speak. My old classmate, President Kehoe, and his lovely wife Franny showed up as I was leaving.

"Rough stuff, Alan," he muttered as we shook hands and then he scurried inside the funeral home in the midst of his Secret Service phalanx.

Franny stopped and gave me a peck on the cheek.

"We need to get together under happier circumstances," she said.

"Amen to that," I responded, and Franny went inside amidst her Secret Service phalanx.

But no Chinese.

Darps and I had come to the wake—or "viewing" in twenty-first century parlance—together, and we left together. The sight of Miles in his coffin had knocked me for a loop, and I think it hit Darps even harder.

"Man. There's a bottle of Dewar's somewhere that's calling my name," he said as we emerged from the mortuary. "Where's the closest bar?"

"Damned if I know," I said. "You live up here. You should know."

"There's a place called The Jetty around the corner. I've never been in it. Why go to a bar when you're almost home?" he asked, rhetorically.

"Maybe because they have that bottle of Dewar's with your name on it," I said. "Let's go there."

The Jetty was dark and had a nautical theme. Nets hanging from the overhead. Polished brass port and starboard running lights at either end of the bar. Pictures of sailboats and lighthouses on the bulkheads. A number of warship models sat in lighted, glassed-in niches alongside the booths. Three Annapolis midshipmen in blues were finishing a basket of wings and a pitcher of beer at one of the half dozen tables. A couple of older guys sat at the bar, watching golf.

Darps and I sat at the bar. The bartender looked like he'd been a pirate in a previous life. *USS Bigelow-DD-942* was tattooed on the inside of his right forearm. Darps and I both ordered double Dewar's.

"Thanks, Chief," I said when he served the drinks.

I dropped a twenty and a five on the bar.

"Christ," said Darps, after taking a hefty swig. "I feel like I caused that whole fucking disaster."

"Don't beat yourself up over it, Shipmate," I said. "Miles was a big shot who was old enough to know what he was doing. He shouldn't have been selling out his country to the goddamned Chinese. They were probably paying him big bucks."

"Yeah, but if I hadn't recommended hiring him, and if I hadn't accused him of selling the family jewels, he wouldn't have gone into the Potomac with a bullet in his skull."

"You know what they say. 'If the queen had balls, she'd be the king.' Miles has probably been on the Chinese payroll for years, and we didn't have anything to do with putting him there. Someone would have caught him sooner or later."

I jerked a thumb toward the midshipmen.

"Remember when we were back there. The Honor Concept. Honor, courage, and commitment. It was like faith, hope, and charity in Christianity. 'But the greatest of these is charity,' according to Saint Paul. 'The greatest of these is honor,' according to John Paul Jones. Trouble is, you come outta there thinking that *everybody* thinks that way. But that's not true. There's always a traitor. I don't give a shit whether it's the Brigade of Midshipmen, the Roman Curia, or the highest reaches of the U.S. Government—there's always some son of a bitch who is willing to sell out. Sex, money, power, vengeance, whatever—there's always gonna be someone. Our guy was Miles. So it's just as well the bastard is lying dead in his coffin."

We drained the drinks. The bartender put two more in front of us. He picked up the twenty and left the five.

"Thanks gentlemen. The second round is on the house," he said. "Don't know what sort of crap you're dealing with, but I like to help out old shipmates."

"*Bigelow* was before my time, I'm afraid," I said, laughing.

He laughed too. He went to the register and returned with two singles, which he put on top of the five.

"*Bigelow* was my first ship. Brand spankin' new at the time. Nineteen fifty-seven. After her, I stayed in. For thirty. Saved enough to open this place. You're Navy. That makes you shipmates."

"We're both in *CivLant* now, Chief," Darps said.

"But not always. You might as well have 'USN' tattooed on your foreheads."

"Well, you've got us pegged," I said. "And thanks for the round."

"My pleasure, sir," he said, walking away.

I sipped scotch.

"I'm thinking that we should tell Sammy. About Miles," I said.

"I don't know," Darps answered, shaking his head. "Biggest problem with Miles being dead is that now we'll never know what he knew. I'm thinking specifically about Isabel."

"There is that, certainly," I said. "We'll never know what Miles knew about Chinese intel operations in the U.S. All we know is that he was a part of them. And I'm going to have to do a paper for the man. Like tomorrow. I'm just not sure what the hell to put in it."

Darps sipped his drink.

"You may want to get some face time and give him the scoop *'mano a mano.'* Orally. Don't write anything down unless he tells you to."

"Good thought," I said. I looked at my drink, drank half of what was left and put the glass down. "That's all for me," I said.

"Me too," Darps said. "Thanks again, Chief."

We left the half drinks and the seven bucks on the bar and followed the three mids out the door. They were talking about studying for a fluid mechanics test tomorrow. I wished that the biggest thing I had to worry about was a fluid mechanics test. Even though fluid mechanics could be a bitch.

We headed around the corner, back to the funeral home parking lot. Luke and Mike suddenly materialized out of nowhere.

"We figured you two would find a bar," Mike said.

"So we'll drive you both home." Luke said, nodding at me. "I'll take you back to Chestertown in the Expedition."

"And I'll take you home in the Saab," Mike said to Darps. "Your place is close enough for me to walk back here and recover my ride."

"Hey, you guys don't have to do that. It's not like we're shitfaced or anything," I protested.

"Better safe...," Luke said.

"Shit," Darps said. "If I'd known you guys were going to drive us, I'd have finished that second Scotch."

Fifty-Six

For the first time since *BIAS* opened for business, I sent off an emergency email that meant I had to see POTUS as soon as possible. I sent it to an email address that we'd set up to be used for that purpose and then only in a dire emergency. There was no message—just a "subject" line.

From: allewellyn@bias.gov

To: keys@LISound.com

Subj: Face Time

I had the reply in less than fifteen minutes. His answer had a short message.

From: keys@LISound.com

To: allewellyn@bias.gov

Subj: Face Time

Be @ MCAF Quantico @ 11 today. Wear running clothes.

Okay. I'd be at the Quantico Air Facility at eleven. Then I'd have to play it by ear. I didn't know if the message meant that Kehoe would meet me there or that I was going to be flying somewhere else to run with him.

"Judy," I said at her office door. "I'm going for a walk on campus. To think. I'll be back by ten and will be leaving by ten fifteen for Quantico."

"Bring your phones," she said, smiling.

She'd already figured out my propensity to seek a modicum of freedom by "forgetting" my phone. I patted my pocket.

216

"Got 'em," I said. "Both of 'em."

I also had a little deck of blank three-by-five cards and a pen. I found a bench in a quiet corner of the campus and jotted down a few bullets with which to brief the man. I walked back to Ripley and found Darps.

"It's *'mano a mano'* time at eleven," I said, by way of explanation when I handed him the three-by-fives.

"Looks like you've covered all the bases," he said after he read over the notes.

"Interested in joining us?" I said on a whim. My thought was that Darps had known Guilfoyle for longer than I had and had done the heavy lifting in bringing him aboard. Darps had also figured out that Miles was the mole and confronted him with that.

"Fuck. I dunno," he said. "He'll no doubt think that I'm a total imbecile for hiring Miles in the first place. And he'd be right. If I go with you, great. The President of the United States can tell me that I'm a fucking idiot to my face."

"I don't think so. *He* hired him for his last job before Miles came on with us. And if he cut him loose because he—or Whitehead—smelled a rat, then they—the White House—should have tipped us off. Remember, the only reason I'm going to talk to him is in case somebody other than *BIAS* has to clean up any messes that Miles left behind. He was only with us for a couple of weeks and wasn't much more than a bystander on the blurb we did for the man."

"Okay. I'll come. Eleven you say?"

"Yeah. We'll leave here at ten fifteen. Wear running gear."

"Sweet Jesus," he muttered, glancing at his watch. "It just keeps getting better and better." Darps runs but prefers to run alone at his own pace.

We only had a little over five minutes to change.

Luke popped into the office as I was unbuttoning my shirt.

"I understand you're running at Quantico at eleven hundred?" he said.

"As far as I know," I said. "Can you get word to them that Darps is coming with me?"

"Sure."

Five minutes later, Darps and I were heading for I-95 North in the Expedition. Thirty-five minutes later, the gate sentry at the air facility was directing us to a parking place. Five minutes after that, we were jogging with Keys and a small gaggle of Secret Service and Marines. Keys wore a Yankees cap, dark shades, and a purple Holy Cross sweatshirt.

"The guy in the lead is a Marine captain who knows the trails here like the back of his hand," the president said. "He's taking us to a trail called the 'Medal of Honor Trail.' It used to be called the 'Hill Trail.' That's kind of scary. It's not like *any* of the trails on this base are exactly flat. What's up?"

We ran past the base brig and the road surface changed from tarmac to hard-packed dirt.

"Stand by for some heavy rolls," I said. "In more ways than one."

A Marine Corps neighbor had taken me running on the Medal of Honor Trail once and it was a ball buster of epic proportions.

I dug out a plastic sandwich bag containing the three-by-five cards with my notes from a hip pocket of my shorts. The sandwich bag was for sweat protection.

"First of all, Miles Guilfoyle was a mole," I said. "A Chinese spy."

"Jesus Christ!" the president said.

We turned off the main road and then turned onto a much narrower trail leading into the woods.

"We think that's why he killed himself. Darps confronted him on it. Next thing we knew, he'd gone to Great Falls. You know the rest."

"Jesus Christ," he said, again. "Miles Guilfoyle! A Chinese mole! Are you sure?"

"Yeah. As sure as we can be without seeing him actually passing classified information to a PRC case officer."

"How did you figure it out?"

"We've known that the Chinese have known about me and *BIAS* from the git-go," I told him. "I didn't realize it at the time, but there was a *Guoanbu* spook on my ass when I came home from my first little run with Luke and Mike in Chestertown. Before you and I talked, even. There *had* to be a mole."

"Holy shit," gasped Darps as we went around a turn and faced a section of trail that was so steep we nearly had to use our hands to make it up. It wasn't all that long, but we were all sucking wind by the time we got to the top and started back down the other side. It was several seconds before I was able to talk.

"Next thing was the DiRienzo assassination. If it *was* the Chinese and if they knew you'd talked to him about replacing Girtler, there had to be a Chinese mole. Somewhere in your 'bubble.'

"Then, somebody in a van like the one seen in the vicinity of DiRienzo's murder, took a shot at Luke and me while we were running. And that was only a couple of hours after I had called Luke and Mike and requested the run. It could have been a tap on my phone, but it also could have been a mole.

"Finally there was Isabel Sin making not one, but two runs at Sammy. First one can't be tied to a mole. But the second one—in Stafford—very well could be. This time, the mole had to be inside *BIAS*. With us."

I gasped out the last few words and couldn't say anything else because we were going up another hill that was, if anything, steeper than the first one. And longer. The only sounds we could hear were our footfalls and they were almost drowned out by our breathing. I didn't say anything. I couldn't.

After about eleven or twelve more minutes that seemed like about an hour and a half, we turned right on a trail that led us down and out of the hills. A couple of minutes after jogging on ground that was more or less level, I was able to talk again.

"Who had been in your bubble and then a couple of months later was inside *BIAS*?" I asked, rhetorically. "Answer: Big Miles. Then, a little over a week ago, Miles went missing early one morning. He left his cell phone home. When he showed up a couple of hours later, he said he'd had a tennis date and forgotten his phone. Next day, Darps learned from Jeanette, his wife, that Miles hadn't brought his tennis rackets to his 'tennis date.' Jeanette was suspicious that Miles was playing around with a woman. Which we'd heard wasn't all that unusual. I was suspicious that he'd been dead-dropping info about a meeting on the PRC that we'd had the previous day. We also suspected that he'd deliberately left the phone home so he couldn't be easily tracked. And he lied through his teeth to me about that little episode.

"Finally, Darps confronted him about it. He denied everything, but the next day was when he disappeared."

"Son of a bitch," Keys said. "This trail is a killer in more ways than one."

We were barely jogging. If we'd been going any slower, we'd have been walking. Kehoe turned to my alter ego.

"Darps, did he give you any indication that your accusation was on target when you confronted him?" he asked.

"No sir. Not directly. But my immediate reaction was that 'Miles protesteth too much.' He really lost his temper. Got all red in the face and called me a 'lying fucking swine.' I've known him for quite a while and never saw him blow up like that. And then I got wind that Miles's name and *BIAS* turned up in the same Chinese telephone conversation."

"Sweet Jesus. I don't even want to know how you, quote, 'got wind of,' unquote, something like that. Not even a little bit. In the White House, we had no clue that he was talking to the Chinese," Kehoe mused. "That could be innocent, though. He must still have friends back in China. We *did* put him out to pasture—told him it would be a great time to retire—but it had nothing to do with the Chinese. He was banging that anchorwoman—Suzanne Racey. That really pissed off Whitehead. He was so pissed he couldn't see straight. As a matter of fact, when they found Miles in the river with a bullet in his head, my first thought was that Walt had plugged him. But he was at Camp David with me the whole time."

"I haven't put anything in writing—other than my little note cards here," I said, flapping the little sandwich bag. "And I'm not sure if there's any good purpose to be served by letting the world—including the Chinese—know that we know that Miles was their mole," I continued. "From a *BIAS* point of view, I think it would be just as well if the PRC remained in the dark on what we know about his extracurricular activities. But—and this is an important 'but'—I have no idea how long Miles was playing footsie with the Chinese before joining *BIAS* and what other messes he might have left behind that might need to be cleaned up."

"Christ," said the Leader of the Free World. "It's rock-and-a-hard place time. If I bring in the Intelligence Community to do a damage assessment, sure as God made little green apples, it'll leak. Miles Guilfoyle was a Chinese mole. If I don't bring them in, we'll never know the extent of the damage he did. *I* sure as shit don't know."

We ran in silence for a while.

"Sir? Mr. President?" Darps said softly. "I think there's another consideration."

"And that would be?" Kehoe asked.

"*BIAS*," he said. "If you tell the Intelligence Committee—even if it's only the Director of National Intelligence herself and no one else—and there's no leak at all, the whole *BIAS* issue could still blow up in our faces. The cat could very well jump out of the bag. If the DNI sensed you had us second-guessing her or parts of her apparatus, that could mushroom into a full-blown crisis. Over the 'relationship' thing. Between the White House and *BIAS*."

"Yeah, you're right. That settles it. I'm not going to risk a shit-storm in the Intelligence Community over *BIAS*. And if that were to happen, it'd spill over to God knows where. Plus, Alan, you implied that you weren't one hundred percent sure that Miles was on the PRC payroll. Maybe ninety-nine percent sure. But not a hundred. That's reason enough to not go public. Is there anything—*anything*—on any computer or in anybody's iPhone about this?"

"Far as I know, my pair of little three-by-five cards is the only 'record' of Miles's treachery. Other than what *Guoanbu* no doubt has. And I have no clue regarding what elements in the U.S. Intelligence Community might know. Hopefully, if someone knew or suspected anything, they'd have told you or Whitehead."

I looked over at Darps and raised my eyebrows. He gave me his "who knows?" look.

"Let's keep it that way," Kehoe said. "Run your three-by-five cards through the shredder. This conversation never took place. And remind me to never run this damned 'Medal of Honor Trail' again! Let's leave it to the nineteen-year-olds."

"If you do run it again," I said. "I'll politely decline any invitation to join you. Sir."

Fifty-Seven

Richmond
April 5th
Monday

Lieutenant Colonel Yang Zemin was seated at his desk watching television. He was surfing through various cable news channels. At nine fifty-five he called Quing Maili into his office. The forty-two-inch screen showed a clip of the façade of Bohlzach's funeral home in Alexandria. The sidewalk in front was mobbed with people and police. A convoy of black SUVs and a limo pulled up in front.

"*Mongoose's* death watch," he said. "This is a clip from yesterday evening."

"And that must be President Kehoe arriving to pay his respects," Maili observed.

"There have been numerous counterrevolutionary swine paying their respects," Yang said dryly. "Including *Mongoose's* most recent conquest, the news anchorwoman Racey."

Maili stifled a giggle.

"Is there any more information on whether Guilfoyle actually committed suicide or not? Could it have been the FBI?"

"No, Comrade Colonel. All sources are saying the news reports are accurate. That it was suicide."

"Of course, if the FBI *had* killed him, they would still claim that it was suicide."

"Comrade Colonel, I don't think the FBI would kill Guilfoyle in Great Falls Park. If they were suspicious about his relationship with the Peoples' Republic, they would have taken him to a safe house somewhere and questioned him at length. Perhaps after a month or two, when they'd finished, they'd make him disappear. But to shoot him in a public park and then let his corpse drift down the Potomac River—I can't believe they'd be so provocative and heavy-handed."

"It would probably depend on how much they knew—and how long he'd been compromised. Perhaps he'd been doubled and now outlived his usefulness. Perhaps they wanted to send a message."

"That's certainly within the realm of possibility, Comrade Colonel."

"The funeral service is tomorrow at the National Cathedral. At eleven. I want you to go. I have already instructed our embassy to make sure Isabel Sin is on the so-called 'guest list.' You will be there as an observer. I have arranged for a rental car and an embassy driver for you. The car will pick you up at your flat at nine. You needn't go out of your way to make contact with any embassy staffers."

"Yes, Comrade Colonel."

"Also, I want you to see if you can get any information regarding *Mongoose's* death from your friend Source *Lynx*. Or 'Isabel Sin's' friend. You can start at the funeral—he may be there. If not, try and bump into him at the Mexican bar in Stafford. Use the fact that Miles Guilfoyle was the former ambassador to the Peoples' Republic. Tell him 'old friends' back in China are asking how he really died or something like that."

"As you wish, Comrade Colonel."

"And if you can't contrive a 'by chance' meeting within, say, two days, call him."

"Certainly, Comrade Colonel."

Fifty-Eight

Chestertown
April 6th
Tuesday

I was reviewing and signing off on some financial paperwork that Judy had put in front of me when my cell phone serenaded me. It was Maria.

"MSNBC is going to have live coverage of the Guilfoyle funeral in a few minutes," she said. "In case you're interested. Might be interesting to see who shows up."

"Thanks for the heads-up, Love," I said. "You're right. Maybe we'll catch a glimpse of Sammy—he's planning to be there. And who knows who else?"

I picked up the remote from the desktop and surfed up to MSNBC. I had been watching *Mike and Mike in the Morning* on ESPN2, a show that it is difficult to watch at home. Maria has a highly refined loathing for the program. But then I have a highly refined loathing for the trendy, left-wing drivel that usually spews from MSNBC.

"I'll bet you were watching those morons, Mike and Mike, weren't you?" Maria asked, accusingly.

"You know me too well," I said.

"Will you be home for lunch?" she asked.

"Only if you promise not to razz me about watching *Mike and Mike*."

"That's a tough one. But I promise."

"Okay. See you about twelve fifteen," I said.

Darps showed up at my door as we rang off.

"Looks like you got the word. MSNBC is going to have some live coverage of the funeral," he said.

"Yeah. Maria just called. Grab your coffee and let's see if we can catch a glimpse of Sammy and whoever."

On screen, a newscaster with a mike in his hand and the gray stone façade of the National Cathedral behind him was holding forth about Miles, his inexplicable suicide in the Potomac, and the Washington pedigrees of the various mourners. The camera zoomed in on Michelle Hookes, clad in dark gray and a wide-brimmed straw hat, and looking regal. They zoomed in on Vice President Girtler and his wife to the extent where I could see the veep's hair transplant. At one point, I got a fleeting glimpse of someone who might have been Sammy, but there was no way to be sure. Then a familiar female figure strode up the stone steps. Tall, slender, and Asian. Well-endowed, chest-wise.

"Isabel!" I muttered. "I wonder if she's chasing Sammy."

"So that's her," Darps muttered. "You have to wonder about *her* connection with Miles."

"I'm guessing that Sammy's initial impression of her was spot on," I said. "*Guoanbu*. But who knows about her and Miles?"

"I agree with you and Sammy about her line of work. But that's as far as I go."

The camera zoomed out to show a gray-and-black hearse, followed by several limousines pulling up in front of the cathedral. The driver dismounted and opened the rear door of the hearse. Eight suited pallbearers, presumably having alighted from the limos, removed the coffin from the hearse and carried it slowly and solemnly up the church steps to the open doors where they placed it on a gurney. All eight of them were Washington heavy hitters. Then Jeanette Guilfoyle, wearing a gray suit and a black hat, followed the casket into the cathedral. The camera zapped back to the talking head with the mike. Apparently, they weren't allowing television inside the cathedral, because the guy signed off and coverage shifted to sports. I tried CNN, Headline News, and Fox, and they were all reporting other stuff. No funeral.

"Well! I can hardly wait till Sammy gets back," Darps said. "You don't think Isabel has the chutzpah to make a pass at him in church during a funeral, do you?"

"Christ, Shipmate. I don't know what to think. I'm just a poor high school math teacher who's in over his head," I said. "But like you, I can hardly wait till Sammy gets back here."

I finished off the paperwork at eleven fifty-five. My guess was that the funeral would be ending right about now. Sammy had told me that he planned on coming back to Ripley Hall, probably stopping en route to grab a sandwich. I reckoned that would put him back in Chestertown around one thirty. I put the last of the papers in my outbox and headed out for my lunch date with Maria.

The day was sunny but blustery and chilly, yet the walk to fifteen-oh-six Prince Henry Street was not unpleasant. Maria gave me a nice, juicy kiss as I walked through the door. We sat at the kitchen table. She had fixed chicken salad sandwiches and a fresh pot of coffee. There was a bottle of San Pellegrino mineral water on the kitchen table in addition to the sandwiches and coffee.

"Did you see the funeral coverage on MSNBC?" she asked.

"Of course. And thanks again for calling with the heads-up. See anyone you recognized?"

We each took a bite of chicken salad sandwich. She chewed for a few seconds before answering.

"Well, of course I recognized the vice president and his wife," she said.

"How about Michelle Hookes?" I asked.

"I think so. Petite, older woman with a straw hat?"

"Yup. She may be the next vice president," I said. "And rumor has it that the dear departed Miles had a dalliance with her a few years ago."

"Good Lord," she said.

"Recognize anybody else?" I asked.

She finished another bite of her sandwich and took a sip of San Pellegrino.

"I'm pretty sure that Channel Fourteen anchorwoman, Suzanne Racey, went into the cathedral," she said.

"You're right," I said. "Rumor also has it that old Miles was boffing her too."

She put her sandwich down.

"Do you mean to tell me that you hired that—that snake, knowing he was screwing half the women in Washington?"

"Well he did have a reputation," I said, lamely. "I only heard about 'Racey Suzanne' a couple of days ago, though."

"What is it about Washington that turns men into animals like that?"

"Well, in Miles's case, it takes—or took—two animals to tango, so to speak. Actually more than two. One male and Lord knows how many females."

Maria shook her head and sighed.

"I guess you're right. It's not just the men."

She sighed again.

"I guess all we can do is keep ourselves and our baby girl on the straight and narrow," she said. "Who did *you* see in the video of the funeral?" she asked, changing the subject.

"I *think* I saw Sammy," I said. "But I couldn't be sure. I *am* pretty sure I saw Isabel Sin and couldn't help but wonder if she was shadowing Sammy. It'll be interesting to hear what he has to say when he gets back to the office."

We nibbled Pepperidge Farm Milano cookies with the last of our coffee.

"Thanks for lunch, Sweetie," I said, giving her a little smooch on the nose.

She smooched me back. On the mouth.

"When do you have to be back?" she asked.

"One thirty," I moaned as she undid the top button of my shirt. "Lemme lock the door."

The breeze had died down and the air was milder for the walk back. I could be wrong, but I think there was a new spring in my step as well as a new hint of spring in the air. Even if I was a few minutes late.

Fifty-Nine

Quing Maili dressed as and carried the identification of Isabel Sin. She instructed Lin, her driver, to park at the National Zoo and told her that she, Lin, was free to visit and enjoy the zoo until one thirty. Both women had mobile phones, so if there were any unexpected developments, they could contact each other. Maili cautioned, however, that once she entered the National Cathedral, she would not answer her phone, which would be set to vibrate rather than ringing aloud. Then she set off on foot in the blustery April sunshine for the cathedral and the funeral of Agent *Mongoose*—Miles Guilfoyle. She had never been to a Western funeral and was somewhat apprehensive. Yang had told her that the cathedral was large and the number of guests would also be large, so she could remain inconspicuous, which is exactly what she intended to do.

She showed her passport and an engraved card that Yang had given her to an usher who led her to a pew on the far left side and fairly close to the front of the enormous cathedral. There was a sprinkling of uniformed military officers of various nationalities—probably military and naval attaches from different legations. She thought she recognized two Chinese Embassy staffers two rows in front of her. She doubted that she'd be able to spot *Lynx* in a crowd like this. And it certainly wouldn't do to draw attention to herself by craning her neck, turning around, and peering at the other funeral guests. She was relieved that, when the service began and they wheeled the highly polished coffin down the aisle, it was closed. The ceremony lasted just under an hour. When it was over, the coffin was wheeled to the rear of the cathedral and through the doors. Guilfoyle relatives, including his widow, followed. She saw Vice President and Mrs. Girtler leave with their Secret Service escort via a side door. Maili—Isabel—joined those guests nearby as they headed for a couple of different

228

exits. Back in the sunlight outside, she blinked as her eyes adjusted and looked around. She saw mostly backs of heads as people headed away from the cathedral. There was absolutely no chance of running into *Lynx* here. She decided to visit the Mexican bar-cum-restaurant in Stafford in the evening and see if he was there. If not, she'd call him on his mobile tomorrow. Turning left on Garfield Street, she began her walk back to the zoo.

She was waiting for the light on Connecticut Avenue when she saw him across the street. *Lynx!* He appeared to be heading for the Metro station. She braved a possible jaywalking ticket and darted between traffic against the light.

"Mr. Chen! Sammy!"

He looked up, surprised.

"Isabel! Hi! What are you doing here?"

"I just went to a funeral. Now I'm going to meet my roommate. At the zoo."

"A funeral? Guilfoyle's?"

"Yes. He used to be the American Ambassador to the Peoples' Republic."

"I know who Miles Guilfoyle is. I was at the same funeral. Are you forgetting that I travel frequently to China?"

"No, of course not. I first met you in China. So you know him? Er, knew him?"

"Yes. I knew him. Pretty well, actually. I don't normally attend funerals of people I don't know. But I'm flabbergasted! To see you here! First, the bar at the Mayflower, then Carlos O'Kelly's in Stafford, now here at the Woodley Park Metro Station. That's a lot of coincidences. And now, you're off to the zoo?"

"My roommate has a car. She drove me. She wasn't asked to attend the funeral. So she parked at the zoo—it's convenient to the National Cathedral. While waiting for me, I'm sure she looked at the animals. Especially the pandas."

She smiled thinly.

"Did you know Miles Guilfoyle?" Sammy asked.

"No, no I did not. Our embassy called me and asked if I would volunteer to be a member of the Chinese contingent at the funeral. So here I am! Miles Guilfoyle was a very popular ambassador in China."

She smiled and glanced at her watch.

"Um, would you like to have lunch? My treat. I have some questions about Western funeral customs."

"What about your roommate?"

"I told her I'd meet her in the zoo at one thirty. It's just five after twelve now. I didn't know how long the funeral would last."

"Well, I was going to grab some lunch at Union Station before catching a train back to Chestertown. But we could get a sandwich right here in the zoo. And you don't need to treat. Dutch would be fine."

"'Dutch'? What does that mean?"

Sammy laughed.

"It's short for 'Dutch treat.' That means you pay for your lunch and I pay for mine."

"Okay," she said. "Let's do Dutch for lunch in the zoo."

They both got semi-stale ham sandwiches and bottled water and found a table that was relatively clean.

"At the funeral—or memorial service—what's the difference, by the way?" she asked as she unscrewed the cap on her water bottle.

"I think at a funeral there's supposed to be a corpse. The funeral is generally held before the body is taken off to a cemetery and buried. And I think a memorial service can be held after the body is buried. Or without the body being present. But now, with cremation becoming so popular, I'm not really sure what the distinction is."

Sammy took a bite of his sandwich and followed it up with a sip of water.

"What about the music?" Isabel asked. "It didn't sound like all dirges."

"That's quite a word. 'Dirges.' And you're right. It used to be that way. Funeral music was, well, funereal. Dirges. But nowadays, people look at funerals differently. So the music is more along the lines of a celebration of the dead person's life."

"Even if that life ended by suicide?"

"Yeah. I think so."

"What do you think about Ambassador Guilfoyle? Did he really commit suicide? A lot of his old friends in China are wondering. Probably some of the Chinese people you know are wondering, too."

Sammy took another swig from his water bottle.

"What do you think, Isabel?" he asked.

"Me? I have no idea!"

"You must have some idea. You wouldn't be asking me what I think if you didn't."

"Really, I don't. But if you go to *Facebook* and *Twitter*, you'll see that there are a lot of people—people in China—who think that somebody murdered Miles Guilfoyle and the U.S. Government is covering that up."

"There are always rumors like that when somebody commits suicide. Especially when they're government big shots and leave no note."

"Well, Mr. Chen. What rumors are you hearing?"

He stood up.

"I've got to run. Train to catch."

He leaned over the table, his face close to hers, and whispered. Then he straightened up.

"Bye," he said.

Sixty

Chestertown
April 6th
Tuesday

"Sammy just got off the train," Darps said, leaning into my office. "He should be here in fifteen or twenty minutes. Said he'd like to shoot the breeze with us as soon as we can."

"Right after he walks through the door works for me," I said.

Right after Sammy walked through the door, the three of us walked back out the door. With a jerk of his head, Sammy had indicated that he preferred to talk outdoors.

"I just walked through Town Centre Park on my way here from the station. There's nobody there. Plenty of empty chairs."

The park was a little patch of grass and concrete that had a bandstand where they had free concerts in summer. There was a fountain and about a dozen or so metal tables with chairs. The fountain had been turned off for the winter in November. It had been turned on a week ago. We reached the park in less than five minutes.

"Let's sit by the fountain," Sammy said. "The white noise is good."

We took chairs at a table alongside the fountain.

"Isabel. Again," he said for starters.

"I'm not surprised. We saw her on MSNBC. At the cathedral," I said.

"It gets better. Not only was she at the funeral—and I didn't see her there, by the way. I was headed for the Woodley Park Metro station afterward, and she chased me down. Literally. She said she'd just come from the Guilfoyle funeral as part of a PRC Embassy contingent that attended because he was a well-liked ambassador to China. We ended up having sandwiches at the cafeteria at the zoo. Desperately shameless or shamelessly desperate—I don't know which describes her best. She really pumped me about Miles's death and whether it was really suicide. It was like some superior told her, 'Get your ass to Guilfoyle's funeral and find someone who'll tell you whether he killed himself or somebody else did it.' She wasn't subtle at all."

"So what did you tell her?" I asked.

"I stonewalled her for a bit, but she kept pushing. Finally, I whispered to her that I was hearing rumors that it was either a jealous wife or a jealous husband."

"Sammy—you sly dog," Darps said, grinning.

"No. I'm serious. That's literally what I whispered in her ear."

"How did she react?" I asked.

"I don't know. Soon as I told her, I left."

"Well, it'll be interesting to see if anything comes of that. What you told her is certainly credible. The Chinese doubtless know of Miles's reputation as an ass man," I said.

"Shit. For all we know, what you told her might be true, regardless of what the cops say," Darps said. "On the other hand, we can eliminate the most likely suspects. Jeanette was home the whole time. I was talking to her on the phone. A landline. So it couldn't have been her. Henry Hookes has been dead for lo, these many years. So it couldn't be him. Whitehead has the rock-solid Camp David alibi. And I have no idea who else old Miles might have been banging."

"Nor do I," I said. "But if he spurned Suzanne Racey, maybe she could have done it. By herself or with the help of a hit man. Even though she wasn't a jealous wife or husband."

Then I changed the subject.

"In the course of your conversation with Isabel, did you find out anything more about her?" I asked. "Like where she works? Or lives?"

"No. She did mention a roommate. Said the roommate has a car and drove her to the zoo because it was convenient parking for the cathedral. According to Isabel, her roommate wasn't on the guest list for the funeral, so she was planning on checking out the animals. That was about it. They were supposed to reconnect at one thirty."

I stood up.

"Do me a favor, Sammy," I said. "Write me up a detailed summary of today's little run-in with Isabel. It won't really be for me, as I'm going to pass it right on to Luke and Mike and see if they can smoke out a little more information on her."

We walked back to campus and Ripley Hall. I figured I had logged a good four miles of walking in Chestertown today, and I still had the mile from Ripley to fifteen-oh-six Prince Henry when I went home this evening.

Sixty-One

Chestertown
April 6th
Tuesday

Tuesday is Maria's day to volunteer at the hospital. She spends the whole day scampering around the building, taking patients from rooms to labs, and vice versa. Walks God knows how many miles. When she gets home, she's whupped. Back when I was a teacher and had the summers off, I volunteered to do dinner on Tuesdays during the summer. When I went back to school in the fall, I'd thought it would be churlish of me to opt out. Maria, the sly fox, didn't see the need to re-assert her kitchen mastery on Tuesdays, so a life-long custom was born. Today I'd forgotten all about it until I stepped out the door of Ripley Hall. Fortunately, Chestertown has a decent German deli—Maxl's—and I stopped there on my way home. I got some pickled herring for Maria and me. Elizabeth tried it once and I thought we were going to have a projectile vomiting episode. But Elizabeth does like grilled *bratwurst* and hot German potato salad. She'll even put a few strands of *sauerkraut* on her sausage. I splurged and bought a six-pack of dark Bavarian beer with which to wash down the herring, wurst, potato salad, and sauerkraut that Max wrapped up for me. Then I splurged again and purchased a half Black Forest chocolate cake. One should never shop for food when one is starving.

When I arrived at fifteen-oh-six with my drool-inducing aromatic deli packages, the local chapter of the Chestertown Oprah Women's Society was meeting in my living room. Oprah was doing a feature on cheesecake. Waiters and waitresses were wheeling out carts of it for the studio audience to the sound of hoots and squeals. From the looks of things, Oprah herself had developed a fondness for the dessert in recent months. Tala and Esmé had joined Maria and Elizabeth. There was a little bit of snickering and giggling going on amongst the younger three; Maria appeared to be multitasking with one eye on Oprah and the other on a P.D.

James novel. I reflected that it was a good thing I'd had the sense to make my stop at Maxl's.

In the kitchen, I poured myself a beer, held the glass up to the window and admired the beer's rich molasses hue. Then I poured Maria a sherry, which I took to her before retreating to the family room for a look at the day's mail, snail and electronic. I was damned if I was going to watch Oprah and her girlfriends lean into the cheesecake. Maria left the chicklettes to their snickering and giggling and followed me into the family room.

"I stopped at Maxl's on the way home. Brats, rolls, et cetera. I think there's enough for T and E if you want to ask them to stay for supper," I said. "And I also got some herring, not to be wasted on the pimple set. Want some?"

"Why don't you ask the girls if they want to stay for dinner and bring the herring in here on your way back?"

I set my beer down and went back to the Oprah room.

"We're having a German supper—bratwurst and German potato salad—and you guys are welcome to join us if it's okay with your folks," I announced.

The girls exchanged looks, the meaning of which was lost on me but seemed clear to them. Out came the cell phones. I returned to the kitchen, spread herring bits and a handful of Ritz crackers on a plate, and went back into the family room. Maria was looking at her email, so I glanced at the snail mail.

"They're both staying. For dinner," Elizabeth announced from the doorway. "Their folks said it would be okay." She said "Eww," when she saw the herring.

"Any funeral news?" Maria said.

"Oh yes!" I said. "And how!" And then I told her about Sammy's encounter with Isabel. That got her up on her Miles-was-such-a-swine horse.

"I can't believe that you and Darps could have hired someone with barnyard morals like his," she said.

I took a sip of the excellent German beer.

"We hired him because he was a lawyer with a lot of China experience. And all the stuff about his sex life is rumors," I said, a bit lamely.

"China experience!" she snorted. "He was probably screwing that Isabel Sin creature as well!"

"Hmm. Isabel. I never even thought of that," I said. "Time to par boil the brats and fire up the grill. And I'll see if I can sweet-talk the Lorelei maidens into setting the table."

The *Abendessen* was good. That's the good news. The bad news was that the pre-teens ate like starving dogs in a smokehouse. No leftovers. Not a crumb.

At nine thirty, Elizabeth and I walked her two chums home. That probably got me another half mile of Chestertown pavement pounding for the day.

The two girls—always polite to a fault—thanked me effusively before they said goodnight.

"Mr. El, any time you need help in unloading German food, we're available," Tala said.

"I'm stuffed, Mr. El," Esmé said. "That chocolate cake will probably give me bizarre dreams. But it sure was good! Thanks for a great supper!"

On the way back to Prince Henry Street, I said, "You have excellent taste in friends."

"They do, too," Elizabeth said with a chuckle.

I chuckled as well. And I draped my daughter's shoulders with my right arm and hugged her to my side.

"I also have great taste in daughters," I said.

Sixty-Two

Maili had her *Isabel Sin—Lynx* contact report finished before Lieutenant Colonel Yang Zemin returned to the Richmond office from lunch. She had placed the printed report on his desk. When the colonel came in, he hung up his Burberry trench coat and raised his eyebrows questioningly.

"My report on the discussions with Source *Lynx* is on your desk, Comrade Colonel. I suggest you peruse it and then, of course, I'll be available to discuss the report with you."

MOST SECRET

6 April

Per your instructions, I attended the funeral of the former U.S. ambassador to the Peoples' Republic of China, Miles Guilfoyle, at the National Cathedral in Washington D.C. An usher looked at my passport and guest card and seated me in a section that I believe was reserved for the *Corps Diplomatique*. Aside from the American Vice President, his wife, Guilfoyle's widow, and a number of staff members from our embassy in Washington, I recognized no one. Source Lynx claims to have been there, but I did not see him until later. (See below.)

I left the funeral after the rites concluded. Again, I recognized no one. I started back to the National Zoo where driver Lin had parked. I was preparing to phone her and advise that I would return early when I spotted Source Lynx approaching the Zoo-Woodley Park Metro Station. I accosted him. He recognized me at once. He remarked about our 'coincidental' meetings at the Mayflower Hotel bar in Washington, then at the Mexican place in Stafford, and finally here at the Metro Station in northwest Washington. His tone was dripping with sarcasm about the "coincidences."

Feeling compromised but having my eyes on mission accomplishment at all costs, I pushed on. We arranged to have lunch. In the zoo's cafeteria. Disgusting. After exchanging small talk about western funeral customs, I pushed Source Lynx about the circumstances of Guilfoyle's death. He "stonewalled" me, as the Americans say, and then, as he prepared to leave, he leaned over me and stealthily told me that rumor has it that Guilfoyle had been murdered by "a jealous wife or a jealous husband." By that, I'm sure he meant either Guilfoyle's wife Jeanette or the husband of some Washington socialite whom Guilfoyle had bedded.

I am sure I am compromised. Source Lynx commented snidely on the "coincidental'\" nature of our repeated encounters. I was relentless and not at all nuanced in trying to extract information—however tenuous—about insider talk regarding Guilfoyle's demise. Lynx is an enigma. He's not Chinese, but not totally American either. I believe he may have a twisted sense of humor and uses that perniciously to create bogus impressions. Then, he delights in sitting back and observing the disarray created by his deliberately false impressions.

It is my strongest recommendation that I—or Isabel Sin—have no contact with Source Lynx in the foreseeable future.

Quing, Maili

MOST SECRET

Lieutenant Colonel Zemin picked up the porcelain bell and rang it.

Maili took that as a sign that the colonel was upset. Normally, he would have called her quietly. She and Li hurried into his office.

"Sit, Maili. Li, bring cognac and cigarettes."

Li appeared relieved as he left to fetch the cognac, cigarettes, and utensils. Yang sat silently at his desk, drumming two fingers of his left hand on the manila folder that contained Maili's report. Li returned with a lacquer ware tray, a bottle of Martell, two glasses, a pack of Marlboro reds, and an ashtray. He poured an inch of cognac into each of the glasses and left silently.

Yang was also silent. He opened the cigarette pack, stood up, and offered a cigarette to Maili, which she silently accepted. Then he took one himself and lit both of them before sitting back down. He picked up one of the glasses.

"Let us drink to those fucking imbeciles in Beijing who forced us into destroying—*destroying*—a potentially brilliant espionage operation!" he snarled. Then he tossed off all the cognac in his glass.

Maili took a sip of cognac and followed it up with a strong puff on her cigarette. She was confused. Not by what she had included in her report, but by the colonel's reaction to it.

"I'm sorry, Comrade Colonel. I just don't think— " she started to say.

"No, no. Do *not* apologize. Those fools in the Politburo pushed you— and me—into an untenable position! I no more believe what Source *Lynx* told you about *Mongoose* and his death than I believe *Mongoose* wasn't blown. He was killed—either by his own hand or by others—because his connection to us became known. And, because those idiots in Beijing can't find their asses with both hands and a pack of running dogs, any chance of us exploiting *Lynx* has been flushed down the toilet as well!"

Yang sloshed another inch and a half of cognac into his glass and puffed furiously on his cigarette.

"The burning question is 'what now?' And the buffoons in Beijing are choosing to remain silent."

He took another hefty slug of Martell. Maili couldn't remember having seen him so agitated. She sipped cognac and inhaled tobacco smoke.

Sixty-Three

I got up a few minutes before seven. Maria and Elizabeth weren't stirring, so I was careful not to slam any doors or rattle any kitchen utensils when I retrieved the newspapers and started the coffee. It was a perfect Virginia spring morning; warm enough to run in the t-shirt and shorts I'd slept in. I sneaked back into our bedroom, grabbed a ten-dollar bill, plus a pair of running shoes and socks, and sneaked back out. My run took me down to the river and, by design, past Einstein Brothers' Bagels where I made a brief stop. Cinnamon and raisin bagels with plain cream cheese for all three Llewellyns this morning. When I got back to fifteen-oh-six Prince Henry Street, it was a few minutes till eight and the beautiful women were still abed. I figured I'd give them fifteen more minutes of z-time before holding reveille for nine-thirty Mass at Saint Katherine's. I had settled down with my bagel, coffee, and the *New York Times* when my cell chimed on the counter. It was a text. From Darps.

√ *out M & M's in today's Mirror.*

I guessed he meant the *Morsels and Motes* column, which runs on Sundays. Trouble is I don't subscribe to the Mirror. But I did walk into the family room, fired up the laptop, and found the online edition. And sure enough, *Morsels and Motes* was posted therein. There was a blurb on the Guilfoyle funeral:

Guilfoyle Funeral Rites & Rumors. *Elder statesman* **Ambassador Miles Guilfoyle** *was laid to rest in Congressional Cemetery on Tuesday following a funeral*

Mass at the National Cathedral celebrated by **Episcopal Bishop Leonard Hall. Jeanette Guilfoyle,** *the ambassador's surviving spouse, accompanied by several immediate and extended family members, was present.* **Vice President and Mrs. Girtler** *were in attendance along with a large number of members of the Washington Diplomatic Corps.* **Mrs. Henry Hookes,** *widow of the late millionaire and a former ambassador herself, attended. Rumors persist that Vice President Girtler will be stepping down soon for health reasons and Mrs. Hookes may be his interim replacement. Whether she'll be running on the ticket with* **President Kehoe** *in the next general election is anybody's guess at this point.*

"Jesus Christ," I muttered.

"Dad!" said Elizabeth, startling me. I hadn't heard her come down the stairs. She disapproves mightily of me gratuitously taking the Lord's name in vain. "We're going to be in church in a little over an hour!" she added sternly.

"Sorry, Kiddo. My bad."

I thought of the *Morsels and Motes* item and wondered who let *that* cat out of the bag, if it was true. Even if it wasn't true, the fact that the rumor was being floated didn't bode well for Mrs. Hookes's safety. I dialed up the special number I had for Luke and Mike. Mike answered right away.

"Seen today's *Mirror*?" I asked.

"First of all, I just got up. Second of all, even if I'd been up since zero-five, I wouldn't have spoiled my Sunday morning by reading that rag."

"Well, you might climb down from your high, moral horse and check out the online version. Run your eyeballs over the *Morsels and Motes* column," I said.

"Jesus. The gossip column. That's the worst part of a very scummy newspaper. But I'll check it out."

"I think you should. There's a 'morsel' in there that relates to a conversation you and I had two or three weeks ago."

"Hold on," he said.

I could hear keys clacking. Then I heard Mike's voice in the background.

"Jesus H. Christ," he said, off in the distance. I was glad he wasn't on speaker and Elizabeth couldn't hear. Mike came back on the line.

"Thanks for the heads up, Alan," he said. "I'll tip off the duty officer. I'm not sure where this is going to go. Keep your phone on."

"Actually, I'm going to turn it off from nine thirty till about ten thirty while I'm at Mass."

"Leave it on and set it to vibrate. If it goes off, check it out as soon as you get out of church, just in case we have to get together," he said.

Maria had come downstairs while I was on the phone with Mike. She and Elizabeth had found the bagels and were noshing away. Maria had a cup of coffee and Elizabeth had a glass of orange juice. Maria looked at me as I hung up and raised her eyebrows, questioningly.

In response, I picked up the laptop and put it in front of her, exposing her to *Morsels and Motes*.

"Yikes!" she said.

"'Yikes, indeed," I said. "This could be a huge problem for Madam Michelle."

"Yeah," Maria said. "But I guess the good news is that she probably doesn't jog on the mall like Congressman DiRienzo."

"That plus the fact that I just handed off the ball to the Secret Service," I said.

Privately, I wondered if this was grounds for sending another emergency email to Cheetah. Then I considered the source of my anxiety—a tawdry gossip column in a low-rent newspaper—and decided against it. I glanced at my watch. Time to shower and dress for church. I decided to pray for a little help in figuring out what to do.

Just before the Offertory, my mobile trembled in my pocket. I exercised a fair amount of self-control and let it go on trembling until it presumably switched over to voice mail. Thirty minutes later, we stepped out into the April sunlight and I pulled out the phone and shaded it with my cupped hand. There was indeed a new voice mail message and I dialed it up. No surprise—it was Mike.

"By the time you get out of church and listen to this, I should be at Ripley Hall. Any chance you can swing by on your way home? We need to shoot the shit a little."

"Um, I'm going to walk over to the office, ladies. Something has come up—I'm sure you can guess what it is," I said. "It shouldn't take long. I'll just walk home from there."

Mike and Luke were both there. Nobody else. About thirty seconds after I let myself in and bid them "good morning," the front door opened and in strolled Judy.

"I followed you, Alan," she said with a grin. "I was at Mass and saw you split off from Maria and Elizabeth after you came out of church. Then you started heading this way and I figured maybe something was going down that I should know about. Tell me I'm wrong and I'll go back to my original plan, head for home and fix myself a Bloody Mary and a ham-and-cheese omelet."

"Maybe we can wrap up this business in ten minutes, go to your place, and you can fix all of us Bloody Maries and omelets," Luke said, smiling.

I poured myself a mug of coffee and Judy did likewise.

"Let's sit around the table and see what we've got," I said.

We sat. I looked at Mike and raised my eyebrows.

"We got a problem," he said. "Or Michelle Hookes has a problem."

"Michelle Hookes? The rich woman? Ambassador? Somebody want to enlighten me as to what's going on?" Judy asked, a tiny note of exasperation in her voice.

Luke opened a leather folder and took out a newspaper. He handed it to Judy. Some of the lines of print were highlighted.

"Today's *Mirror. Morsels and Motes.* The gossip column."

"Thanks, Luke," she said and began reading. After about fifteen seconds she looked up.

"Mother of God," she whispered. "DiRienzo all over again. Who leaked *that?"*

"Nobody," Mike said. "There's nothing to leak. And the boss is really pissed. He says he never discussed Hookes becoming vice with anybody—

including her. And has no plans to do so. They're putting together a press release at the White House that'll go out in an hour or so and which will try and put some distance between the president and the Hookes-veep rumor. And I'm guessing it'll be pretty emphatic. He's got a call into her now—she's at Mass—asking her to issue a denial as well. He expects she will—they're actually pretty good friends. But, regardless of the fact that it's all bullshit, there's still a problem."

"No Secret Service protection," I guessed.

Both Luke and Mike nodded.

"Exactly," Luke said.

"I don't think there *is* a problem," I said. "Nothing personal, but can't you guys just notify the D.C. Metropolitan Police of the threat?"

"Already have. And they're 'increasing their presence' around her home, as they say."

"She probably doesn't jog on the Mall. And she's a millionaire many times over. She can easily hire private security," I added.

"Actually, she walks every day. In Rock Creek Park. That's worse than jogging on the Mall from a security standpoint. We have talked to MPD and the Park Police about that. And, when he talks to her, the boss is going to suggest—strongly suggest—that she hire someone to provide protection," Luke said.

"There's only one thing that bothers me," I said.

"What's that?" Mike asked.

"Remember a couple of weeks ago when Miles was here and you and I talked in the head about getting the paper we were working on up the road to the White House?"

"I know what you're thinking. I told you about a rumor about Hookes possibly replacing Girtler. And I asked you if Cheetah had mentioned it on your morning run," Mike said.

"Any idea where that rumor started?"

"Negative. And I asked around this morning. Seems it was just a shithouse rumor."

"Be interesting to know who started it," I said thinking of the erstwhile Whitehead-Racey connection, and stood up. "I think we're done for today. See everybody tomorrow."

Sixty-Four

Richmond
Sunday
April 11th

The email was maximum priority and Lieutenant Colonel Yang Zemin was advised of it by a coded cell phone message at four forty a.m. He retrieved the message from the computer and then had to drive to the office in order to decode it. The message was terse.

From: KowloonStar@gwailow.com

To: HainanStrip@gwailow.com

Subj: Quing, Maili

Terminate Quing soonest. She has outlived her utility and compromised a most sensitive operation. Replacement will be in Richmond within forty-eight hours.

Yang unlocked the safe and retrieved a Type 77 seven-point-six-two-millimeter pistol in a shoulder holster and a loaded magazine. The Type 77 handgun was a mainstay weapon in the Peoples' Liberation Army. Yang stumbled into the darkened outer office and retrieved a packet of Marlboro cigarettes from Li's desk. He sat quietly in his office and smoked two cigarettes in the dark. Then he slipped the magazine into the butt of the pistol, racked the slide to chamber a round, and clicked the safety on. He put the holster's strap over his left shoulder and shoved the Type 77 into the holster before donning a leather jacket. He took out his keys, returned the nearly empty Marlboro pack to Li's desk, and left the office.

Quing Maili awoke at her usual time of between six-oh-five and six ten. She padded into her small kitchen and turned the front burner of the stove on under the teakettle that she had filled the night before after

246

watching NCIS. She then stepped back into her bedroom, removed her pajamas, and dropped them on the floor. Naked, she stepped into her bathroom, relieved herself, and started the shower. While the shower water warmed, she retrieved deodorant, makeup, and a hair dryer from a drawer in the bathroom vanity and placed them beside the sink. She slid open the glass door to the shower and felt the strong jets with her right hand. The water temperature was perfect. She stepped in and savored the hot water jets beating down on her head and body. Picking up a plastic bottle of Pert shampoo from the shower caddy, she poured about a tablespoonful of the viscous green liquid into her palm, set the bottle down, and began to massage the shampoo into her hair. Between the noise of the shower and her eyes being tightly shut, she neither heard nor saw the bathroom door open.

She did hear the echoing slam of the seven-point-six-two-millimeter pistol but only for a split second before collapsing under the twin showers of hot water and shattered glass. Two more rounds thudded into her body, pushing her torso back against the tile wall of the shower. The mixture of blood and hot water swirled down the shower drain.

Lieutenant Colonel Yang Zemin replaced the Type 77 in the shoulder holster under his jacket, which he zipped up. Still wearing pigskin leather gloves, he picked up and pocketed three ejected brass shell casings from the tile floor of the bathroom. He paused and looked down at the wet, bloody corpse in the shower. Shaking his head, he clucked his tongue twice.

"What a pity, what a loss," he muttered.

In the kitchen, the kettle began its high-pitched whistle. Yang left the bathroom without turning off the water. He went into the kitchen and turned off the burner under the steaming kettle. The whistle slowly died. Yang let himself out of the apartment's front door and walked unhurriedly down the stairs.

"What a pity," he muttered again. He shivered with a sudden chill.

Sixty-Five

I got a short run in before breakfast—just about four miles in a little under a half-hour. The weather looked and felt ominous—heavy, dark clouds and skittish little wind gusts moving the humidity around. Maria and Elizabeth were at the kitchen table eating boiled eggs and toast when I came down after showering. I turned on the burner under a saucepan with water and an egg and put a couple of slices of bread in the toaster. Then I poured orange juice and coffee and sat down. As I was picking up a section of the newspaper, I noticed Maria and Elizabeth exchanging a look. Maria gave a little nod. Suddenly I was very nervous.

"Hey, Dad," Elizabeth said.

"What, Sweetie?" I asked, my heart racing and palms sweaty.

"Did you have a dog when you were a kid?"

I sighed in relief.

"Yes, Kiddo. I sure did. A collie. Named Donna."

"Well, I was thinking," she said. "It'd be nice if we had one. Tala's and Esmé's families both have dogs and they're really nice. And fun."

I got up to start my toast—the egg water was boiling.

"Let me talk to your mother about it," I said.

"We—Mom and I—already talked about it," she said. "She likes the idea, too."

More and more, as Elizabeth gets older, she and her mother seem to be developing a tendency to scheme, conspire, and gang up on the old man. They seem to have some sort of intuition for forecasting any objections I might raise on whatever issue. Then they engineer end runs around them

248

before I even know what they are. The shaky delusions I may have held once upon a time about paternal infallibility were rapidly eroding.

"Well, let's think about it and talk some more," I said lamely.

Maria's nose was buried in the newspaper.

"Esmé's parents know guys who breed Labrador retrievers," Elizabeth said. "That's where they got Reilly. He's a great dog."

I could sense the construction of the set up. I knew I didn't stand a chance. And I know Reilly and he *is* a great dog.

"Let's talk about it some more this evening," I said, cracking my egg.

Maria looked up from the paper and winked at me. All three of us knew I was only delaying the inevitable. I buttered my toast.

An hour and a half later, I was sitting in Ripley Hall checking my email when Sammy popped in with Darps in tow.

"Check this out," he said. "This morning's *Jeffersonian*. From Richmond," he explained, holding out a piece of copier paper.

Chinese Woman Shot to Death in Fan. Identity in Doubt

Victim's Passport Found. No Entry to U.S. Recorded.

By Karen Vesey *Richmond Jeffersonian Staff Writer*

Sergeant Richard Glynn, Richmond Police spokesman, reported that a Chinese woman was found murdered in the shower of her Monument Avenue apartment Sunday.

"It was a particularly vicious attack. She was shot several times," Sgt. Glynn said. He stated that the woman's Chinese passport found in the apartment was in the name of Quing Maili and had a U.S. visa. Immigration officials told police that there was no record of anyone by that name entering the country, putting her identification in doubt. The passport has been sent to a laboratory for testing, Glynn said.

A small color portrait that could have been a passport photo accompanied the article.

"Isabel," Sammy said, tapping the paper with his forefinger. "Isabel Sin. Without a doubt."

"I disagree," Darps said. "There's plenty of doubt. If this chick has more than one name, she could well have more than two."

"Right. All I'm saying is that this woman is the same one who introduced herself to me as Isabel Sin. And gave me a business card with the name of Isabel Sin engraved thereon."

"Brainstorming time," I said. I glanced at my watch. "Let's convene in the small conference room with Judy, Mike, and Luke in fifteen minutes."

I thought of Miles. The dear departed. His insight and experience would have been tremendously useful in a situation like this. On the other hand, his treachery probably could have caused us a boatload of damage as well. We'd have to start looking for another lawyer—soon.

Our meeting was an exercise in frustration because of so much we didn't know. We didn't know who Isabel Sin—or Quing Maili—really was. We didn't know a damned thing about the American-Chinese Cultural Exchange Association in Richmond. And—God knows where else. And because of our—BIAS's—isolation, we couldn't query the Intelligence Community about them. Strangely enough, Sammy's Internet search yielded absolutely nothing. We had no idea if the woman's death was in any way tied in with Guilfoyle's. All we knew was that Isabel wouldn't be pestering Sammy any more. Sammy and I both voiced our curiosity about whether or not someone else would show up to take her place. Luke reminded us that Sammy's write-up of his meeting with Isabel at the zoo was being laundered through the Secret Service in hopes of some additional information. Very slim hopes. That was where we left it. Like I said, it was a frustrating meeting. Thin gruel.

At a few minutes before five, Maria called.

"Wanna ride?" she asked. "It's pouring—in case you haven't noticed. I can pick you up any time."

I looked out the window and she was right.

"Sure, Sweetie. Any time you're ready," I said, gratefully. I had a short windbreaker, no hat, no umbrella. I'd be drenched if I walked a mile through the soaking rain. I'd walked in this morning, and I didn't like to use the GI Expedition for commuting.

Five minutes later, I saw her Jetta pull up in front of Ripley Hall. I'd already shut down my computer. Darps and Mike were still aboard.

"See you guys tomorrow," I hollered as I went out the door.

As I darted through the cold rain, I saw that Elizabeth was sitting in the shotgun seat up front and recalled the probing attack at the breakfast table this morning and feared the worst. I yanked open the back door and jumped into the back seat.

"Good evening, Ladies," I said. "Thanks for coming to my rescue," I added with the merest trace of irony.

Smiles radiated from the front seat and we were off, off campus, heading south on Route One.

"Dad, remember I told you that Esmé's parents have friends who breed Labradors?" Elizabeth asked sweetly.

Good Christ, I thought. *She's not even going to wait till we get home!*

"Yes, Kiddo," I said. "Vaguely," I added, crossing my fingers.

"Well, they had a new litter of puppies three weeks ago. Two black, two yellow, and one chocolate."

Maria fooled with the windshield wiper control, feigning disinterest. This indeed was the final assault.

"Have you seen the puppies," I asked.

"No, but I got directions. We could go look now."

"It's out towards Culpeper. A farm fronting Route Three," Maria added.

I noted that she was in the right lane. To go west on Route Three, one needed to be in the right lane. To go home to Prince Henry Street, one would need to be in the left. Mentally, I felt the locks of the set-up clicking into place.

"Sure—why not?" I said. I knew when it was time to hold 'em and when to fold 'em, as the song says.

The rain made the Route Three traffic even worse than usual, and I gleaned a tiny morsel of satisfaction from the fact that Maria, Elizabeth's co-conspirator, was in the pilot's seat dealing with the traffic instead of me. Not far from the *BIAS* safe house, there was a white sign by the side of the road. *Wilderness Retriever Kennels,* it said. *Labradors and Goldens. Ken and Marcia Sachs.* Maria turned on to the muddy road by the sign.

"We're right on time," she said. "They should be in the barn on the left."

I swallowed my sarcastic reaction about my superficiality in this process. They had called ahead to tell Ken and Marcia we were coming. Hell, they probably already had the dog named.

"Corazon," Elizabeth said. "It means 'heart' in Spanish. We'll call her 'Cory.'"

The chocolate puppy was a female and Elizabeth decided immediately that she was the dog for us. Actually, I wouldn't be surprised if she hadn't made the decision several days ago and was just now easing Dear Old Dad into things. I wrote out a deposit check to Wilderness Retriever Kennels for a hundred bucks, and we agreed to pick Cory up on May second—three weeks from yesterday. Ken and Marcia Sachs were a nice, surprisingly young couple, and I mentally wished them well as we headed back down their muddy farm road. When we finally got home, I deliberately shorted myself on ice and poured an extra dram of scotch into the glass. Between the demise of Isabel Sin and a puppy named Cory, it had been one bastard of a day.

Sixty-Six

Richmond
Wednesday-Thursday
April 12th & 13th

Lieutenant Colonel Yang returned to his office and sent a short, coded email.

From: HainanStrip@gwailow.com

To: Kowloonstar@gwailow.com

Subj: Quing

Subject terminated.

After sending the email, he locked himself in the restroom and vomited violently, even though he'd had nothing to eat. He rinsed his face with cold water and returned to his desk. Spending almost an hour on the task, he cleaned the handgun he'd used earlier that morning. Then he stepped into the restroom and vomited again.

He splashed more cold water on his face and rinsed his mouth. Returning to his desk, he had Li bring him cognac and cigarettes. He spent the day drinking and smoking. Shortly before one o'clock, Li brought him a portion of pork-fried rice from a nearby restaurant. He took a few bites, threw the rest in the garbage, and then went back to the cognac and cigarettes. Leaving the office early, he took an unopened bottle of cognac with him, returned to his apartment, and drank until he passed out.

Thursday morning, Yang had an excruciatingly fierce headache, the result of a monstrous hangover. At the office, he savored a cup of tea and cleaned the seven-six-two handgun again. He felt a momentary wave of nausea, but it passed. He had some more tea. His staff was now down nearly to nil. Li was useful as a general factotum here in the office, but he'd had no training as a field officer. Yang had sent the idiot Kwan back to China and the four female agents who had watched Llewellyn's house in Chestertown to the whorehouse in Nevada. Now, on Politburo orders, he'd "disposed of" Quing. It wasn't the first time he'd had to terminate a field officer, and he knew it wouldn't be the last. But Maili was more than just a field agent. He thought about dulling the pain in his head as well as the pain in his gut with cognac and decided on a steam bath and a massage instead.

"Li, I'm going to the gym and will go to lunch after that. I'll return by one."

The temperature in the so-called "wet sauna" at the gym was over one hundred forty degrees Fahrenheit. Sixty Celsius! The sweat fairly popped from Yang's pores. He wondered about Maili's replacement. Male or female? Young or old? Experienced or ignorant? Competent or useless? He needed replacements for Kwan and the female agents soon, but he needed Maili's replacement immediately.

After about twenty minutes, Yang left the steam room, a towel wrapped around his waist. A young woman beckoned him into a large shower room and gestured for him to sit on a built-in bench. Retrieving a large sponge from a bucket of sudsy water, she scrubbed Yang, dumped the bucket over his shoulders, gestured for him to stand and left him, turning on a valve on her way out. Hot water shot out from over two hundred jets in the walls and ceiling and rinsed him almost instantly, but he still lingered, adjusted the temperature of the water upwards. The headache was nearly gone and he could feel a small pang of hunger.

"Massage?" the woman asked as he wrapped a towel around his waist.

He nodded. She picked up two, large white towels and draped them over a massage table and motioned for him to lie down on his stomach. He was always surprised by the power of her hands.

When he left the gym, the sky had cleared and the air felt like the temperature had jumped ten or fifteen degrees. He walked to the Lions of Cathay restaurant where he had Beijing noodles with minced pork and bean sauce, washed down with a bottle of Tsingtao beer. By the time he paid his check, he was feeling close to normal.

Li stood when Yang entered the office at precisely one o'clock.

"A woman is here to see you, Comrade Colonel. Her name is Yiyun Jin. She is waiting in the library. Shall I send her to you?"

Yang glanced at his wristwatch.

"Wait fifteen minutes. Then send her to me," he said.

He skimmed through his email and was exiting from his mailbox when there was a knock on his door.

"Come in!" he said.

Li opened the door and stood aside, allowing a woman to enter into the room.

God damn it! Yang thought. *Another tall Mongolian!*

The woman bore an uncanny resemblance to Maili. Same height. Same impressive figure. Her outfit was more formal than what Quing customarily wore. She wore a dark brown suit over a pale blue blouse. Either she had been briefed or it was a coincidence, but her dark brown shoes were flats. Yang half-rose and reached across his desk to shake her hand.

"Comrade Yiyun. Welcome. Please have a seat," he said, returning to his chair and gesturing toward the seats next to his desk. He nodded to Li at the door for tea.

As soon as Li had closed the door, the woman unzipped a slim leather folder.

"I have instructions from the Ministry," she said softly, taking out a piece of paper. "The revisionist bitch Hookes is scheduled to give a speech in Stafford, Virginia, Monday evening. I have the details. Our instructions are to take her down. Permanently."

Yang almost choked.

"Mao's teeth!" he growled. "I have no staff! Other than you and Li, who is nothing more that an office boy."

Li chose that moment to come into the office with the tea tray. He remained impassive and Yang really didn't care whether he had heard him or not. When he left and closed the door, Yiyun spoke up.

"Comrade Colonel, the team is the two of us—you and I. I will drive. The embassy driver took me to the site on the way here. Our casing was thorough. I am advised that you have a rifle and ammunition. I can take you to inspect the site now, if you like."

Sixty-Seven

Chestertown – Stafford
Monday
April 17th

The "emergency" ring tone on my cell phone startled me as I walked the last few meters to number fifteen-oh-six. It was the *Kyrie eleison* from Mozart's Mass in D. It could only be Kehoe or Darps. I glanced at the screen. Darps.

"What's up, Shipmate?"

"Hate to blab this over the phone. I'll probably go to jail. But it's a *huge* fucking emergency!"

"Well quit bullshitting and talk to me, man."

"Remember my old girlfriend?"

He must have meant the one who fingered Miles as a Chinese mole.

"Yeah. I think so."

"She called. 'Meet me at Gravelly Point,' she says. 'Thirty minutes.' I went by bike. Hold on."

All of a sudden the whiny roar of jet exhaust thundered from the phone and almost blew the earwax into my brain. Gravelly Point was the park right off the northern end of the main runway at Reagan National Airport.

"Pedaled my ass off. She said they picked up some chitchat to an address for a Chinese national in Richmond. The chitchat mentioned Michelle Aitch. Seemed to mean 'Take her down. Tonight. In Stafford.' That's all."

"Chitchat" no doubt meant, "chatter." "Michelle Aitch" had to mean, Michelle Hookes. Which any idiot listening to our conversation would figure out in a heartbeat.

"She just left. The old girlfriend. Maybe she and I will end up in the same jail. Maybe we'll end up in the same divorce court if she keeps calling me at home."

"Jesus Christ," I said. "I think we just landed in the fucking red zone, Shipmate. Anything else?"

"Isn't that enough?" he asked. Another jet roared over his phone.

"More than enough," I said after the sound of the jet blast faded. "Thanks. Now let me see what I can do about it."

I rang off and dialed the Mike-and-Luke emergency number while trying to figure out what I was going to say when one of them answered. It was Luke who picked up after the first ring.

"Yo, Alan. What's up?"

"I don't know. Do you know anything about Michelle's whereabouts? Like right now?"

"Funny you should ask. Yes and no. She left her apartment a half hour ago. The MPD cop stepped into the head to take a leak. When he came out, her Mercedes was gone. He rang her doorbell. No answer. Called her on her landline and her mobile and got dumped to voice mail both times."

"What about her 'private' security?"

"She has none. She never hired anyone."

"Jesus H. Christ! Isn't there anyone who knows where she went?"

"The D.C. cop said she mentioned something about going to Quantico, but he wasn't sure she meant tonight."

"Has anyone called the Virginia State Police?"

"Yeah. The MPD called them. They also called Maryland. BOLO with her and her car's description and tag number."

"Okay, thanks. If you hear anything, call me on the mobile."

"Alan—don't do anything crazy."

"Luke, at this point I don't have a clue as to what to do—crazy or otherwise."

"Roger. I hear you."

I called the Quantico Public Affairs Office and got voice mail. Then I called the Chestertown *Courant* and got one of their sports writers. Whom I knew from my coaching days.

"Beth, it's Alan Llewellyn, formerly from Augustine Washington track. I need a *huge* favor."

She laughed.

"I don't know if I can do 'huge,' Alan, but try me."

"Could you check with your news desk and see if they know anything about anything that Michelle Hookes might be involved with at Quantico this evening."

"For you, Alan, I'll be happy to do that. Lemme call you back."

Three minutes later, she did.

"There is a dinner. Retired Marines and FBI agents. At the Globe and Laurel in Stafford. Cocktails started ten minutes ago. One of our guys heard a rumor that Michelle Hookes was the speaker. We have a reporter and a photographer there covering it."

"God bless you, Beth. I owe you."

I looked at my watch. Five forty-one. If Michelle had skipped out of her apartment on P Street thirty or thirty-five minutes ago, I calculated it would probably be twenty-five or thirty minutes before she got to the Globe and Laurel. I turned and started running back towards Ripley Hall. I needed the Expedition. And the forty-five. And a break with the lights in town as well as the state troopers on I-95.

I got all three and pulled into the lot at the restaurant at six twenty-nine. The colt was in the shoulder holster, a magazine with six rounds was in the butt, and one round was in the chamber. Safety was on. I circled the lot and found a parking space at the southern end. I jumped out and headed for the entrance when I noticed two things—a blue Mercedes with D.C. plates pulling into the lot and a familiar-looking silver-gray Honda Odyssey van parked about six cars from where I'd parked the truck. I pulled the Colt out of the holster and thumbed off the safety and things unfolded in my brain. Michelle Hookes parked at the far end of the lot opposite where the Odyssey and I were parked. She alighted from the Mercedes—she was wearing a navy blue suit and a red hat. I started to jog towards her and glanced over my right shoulder where I saw the back doors of the van open slightly and a rifle muzzle emerge.

"Madam Ambassador! Get down!" I yelled and fired, just as I saw and heard the report of the rifle. I had aimed for the opening between the van's two back doors. I missed but the slug slammed into the right-hand door, and I fired again, hitting the left-hand door this time. The van backed up with a squeal of rubber, and I shot again, hitting the right-hand back door down low. The driver of the van slammed on the brakes, turned and started speeding forward toward the parking lot's exit, and I fired two more times, shattering the driver's side window, and the van crashed into a parked car and stalled.

I turned. Michelle had not hit the deck. She was standing beside her Mercedes with a peeved expression on her face. I looked back at the van and saw no signs of life, although the rifle muzzle still protruded from between the doors, pointed downward.

"Ms. Hookes! The guy has a gun! He's trying to shoot you! Get behind a car!"

A wave of middle-aged guys with short haircuts started pouring out of the restaurant. A couple of them pulled handguns. One was drawing a bead on me. I dropped the forty-five like it was radioactive.

"The guy in the van has a rifle!" I yelled. I had one hand up and with the other I jerked a thumb towards the Honda. "He just tried to shoot Ms. Hookes!"

I was sure I was going to be arrested if I were lucky. If not, I could be dead soon. The parking lot started filling up with police cars from various jurisdictions.

"Hands on your fuckin' head!" somebody screamed at me. I complied.

A couple of ambulances and a fire engine joined the party. Lights were flashing and static and radio traffic filled the spring air. Cops with flak jackets and Kevlar helmets approached and opened the van. After a few minutes, they stepped back and talked to the EMTs who unloaded two people onto gurneys. One was completely covered; the other one was sitting halfway up. I think it was a woman, but I wasn't sure. It looked like they were administering oxygen and some fluid in an IV. Some guy talked to Michelle for a few minutes and then came over to me. I still had my hands on my head.

"You can put your hands down. Who the fuck are you?" he asked. He had a badge on his belt and a Glock in his right hand. It was pointed at the ground.

Michelle had followed and was right behind him.

"Watch your mouth, young man!" she snapped. "I demand to be treated with respect. At a minimum, that means not having to listen to foul-mouthed hooligans hurl obscenities at a man who just saved my life!"

The cop rolled his eyes, reminding me of Elizabeth. Just then, a black Expedition screeched to a halt at the side of Route One. There was no room left in the parking lot. To my immense relief, Mike and Luke jumped out.

"Madam Ambassador, why don't you have a seat in the Expedition over there," I said, pointing at my truck. "There should be an unopened bottle of water right in front. Help yourself."

"Thank you. I will. Right now, I'd prefer scotch, but I understand."

"U.S. Secret Service," Luke said while the two of them held up their IDs. "Alan here works for us. Contractor. Assigned to protect Ambassador Hookes here."

The cop studied their IDs and then looked at mine for a while.

"What company?" he asked.

"Classified," Mike said. "It's a clandestine contract. If you'll get me a list of the jurisdictions involved, I can ensure that you get whatever paper you need to clear things up."

"Hell, man! I've got one stiff and one wounded on my hands here! And you're talking about 'clearing things up' with a piece of paper. Are you crazy?"

"You can do whatever the hell you want with the stiff. Same for the other casualty. They're probably undocumented Chinese. My guess is that you'll never ID either one of them. My guess also is that the State Department and FBI will be here in a few minutes. Turn everything over to them and all your problems go away."

A uniformed state trooper came over.

"They're transporting the female and the body to Martha Washington Hospital," he said.

The ambulance turned on the lights and gave a little squeak with the siren and headed out of the parking lot.

Luke glanced at his watch and jotted something down in a little notebook. Two sedans with D.C. tags pulled up.

"This is probably State and FBI now," Mike said. Then he turned to speak to me.

"Why don't you keep Ms. Hookes company in the truck?" he said.

He didn't have to tell me twice. But I picked up the Colt first.

Forty-five minutes later, I drove the Expedition into the driveway at fifteen-oh-six Prince Henry. I was too beat to park it on campus and walk home. Mike and Luke were escorting Michelle Hookes back home—one in the car with her, the other following in their Expedition. I was glad that she had gone home rather than coming here. No way would there have been enough scotch for both of us.

Epilogue

Chestertown – Wilderness
Tuesday
May 2nd

The cover-up of the antics outside the Globe and Laurel was quite a contrivance, but it worked. Luke and Mike were instrumental and the local cops were only too happy to have State and the FBI take a real mess off their hands. The only problem was my buddy Beth at the Chestertown *Courant*.

She called me the following evening right as I walked in the door.

"Remember me, Alan?" she asked, sweetly. "Beth Garrison who did you a 'huge' favor yesterday?"

I tried to be noncommittal.

"Sure, Beth. And I'm grateful. You were a big help. Thanks."

"And I'm looking at a photo of former track coach Alan Llewellyn standing in the parking lot of the Globe and Laurel with a gun in his hand. And it's not a starting pistol. And I'm thinking that one good turn deserves another. What gives, Alan? What the hell were you doing in the middle of that mess yesterday?"

"Look, Beth. I can't talk about it on the phone. But you're right about one good turn, etcetera. I'll buy you lunch someplace nice and maybe we can discuss things a little."

"News gets old quickly, Alan. How about dinner? This evening? And how nice is 'nice'?"

"Teacher Man?"

Teacher Man was an upscale, quiet pub that had opened a couple of years ago in Chestertown. It was a little pricy, but the atmosphere was nice and the food was excellent. We made a date for an hour later and my palms were sweaty when I got off the phone. Maria was shooting me some spooky looks. I called the Luke-and-Mike emergency number. Again. I explained my problem.

"I'll take care of everything," Mike said. "What does she look like?"

I told him and gave him the address of the pub.

"I'll buy her a nice dinner and an excellent bottle of wine, plus I'll pile on some Secret Service B.S. and tell her you weren't available today," he said.

I was relieved. Beth might be pissed when I didn't show, but probably not as pissed as Maria would be if I had to drop a bunch of money buying dinner for an attractive, young female reporter. Next day, Mike told me he even walked her back to the *Courant* building and got her to hand over the photos that included me.

Cheetah came down to Quantico a few days later to run, and I joined him at his invitation. We ran the Rifle Range loop at a relaxed pace.

"The docs did an angioplasty on Syd. They say he's good to go and he says he'll stay on for the rest of the term if I want. I want, so the VP resignation issue is moot for now," he said.

"Similarly, the PRC-*BIAS* issue is moot for now," I said. "The fuckers are all dead or out of town. But Sammy says they'll be back."

"I'm sure they will," he said. "But I think the next big thing for you guys is going to be a big paper that a new interagency working group is finishing up. It's pretty broad brush. Western Europe and the Arabs."

"Sounds interesting," I said.

"It's pretty meaty," he said. "And you're going to have to move fast."

At the White House, Walt Whitehead resigned as chief of staff, ostensibly to manage the campaign of a New Yorker who wanted to be DiRienzo's replacement. And Cheetah, the rat-bastard, tried to hire Darps away from *BIAS* to replace him. Darps, God bless him, told him not in a thousand years. Kehoe finally hired some hack from the RNC. He also hired Michelle Hookes for a similar assignment to the White House advisor slot held by the dear departed Miles Guilfoyle before he retired and came to us for the end game. She wasn't a lawyer, but she did have extensive Middle East experience and knew a hell of a lot of D.C. Big Dogs.

Back at Ripley Hall, it was nice to get out of the crisis mode and into the mode of getting smart. Analysts were traveling, we were putting out papers, and Darps and I gave a lecture to the Martha Washington University Foreign Affairs Conference. Judy and the geeks were building up our virtual library. Sammy was getting ready to move his wife and girls up to Chestertown from Jupiter.

At fifteen-oh-six Prince Henry Street, spring was exploding all around us and excitement mounted as the end of school approached. May second was a beautiful day, and I left the office a couple of hours early. Time to pick up the new dog. If you had seen my MasterCard statement of late, you'd think I was purchasing a racehorse. With her newly sharpened flair for melodrama, Elizabeth declared: "Oh my gosh, I'm *soo* nervous! Can Tala and Esmé come with us?"

"Of course, Sweetheart."

The five of us piled in after I loaded the "small" dog crate in the back of the old Explorer and headed out Route 3 to Wilderness Retriever Kennels. If you'd seen the check I wrote after we got there, you'd still have thought that I was purchasing a racehorse. And when I looked at "little" Corazon, the equine analogies continued to play out as it occurred to me that she must be eating like a horse. She had doubled in size. After twenty or thirty minutes of billing and cooing, the six of us piled into the Explorer and headed back to Chestertown. I glanced at the safe house as we whizzed past it and thought about Darps and I meeting there, Miles the Mole, Isabel Sin, and Chinese spies watching our house. Then I glanced in the rearview mirror at forty-five pounds of chocolate-colored, fur-covered, tail-wagging, and squirming canine and knew that my life had just become a hell of lot more complicated.

The End

ACKNOWLEDGEMENTS

To John, Colonel Bob, Admiral Bill, Colonel Jim, Robert, Commander Chuck, Lieutenant Colonel Pete, Major Nick, Master Sergeant Tom, and a whole host of others who taught me "the game."

To Karen, my dear and eagle-eyed editor. And especially Betty, for her quiet good sense. She kept me in "the game" without being consumed by it.